ALSO BY ZACH FORTIER

Non-Ficton
CurbChek
Street Creds
CurbChek Reload
The CurbChek Collection
Hero to Zero
Landed on Black

Biography
I Am Raymond Washington

Fiction
Baroota: The Hunting Ground
Cachibaché
Izadi
Chakana

Science Fiction
Volk: Book One in the Overseer Series

Scan the QR Code to the left to
purchase Zach's other books.

ABOUT THE AUTHOR

Zach Fortier was a police officer for over thirty years specializing in K-9, SWAT, gangs, domestic violence, and sex crimes as an investigator.

He has written five books about his life in police work. CurbChek won the bronze medal for True Crime in the 2013 Readers' Favorite International Book Awards. Street Creds and Curbchek Reload won a gold and silver medal respectively for True Crime in the 2014 Readers' Favorite International Book Awards.

His other works are Hero To Zero, which details the incredibly talented cops that he worked with that ended up going down in flames, some ended up in prison and one on the FBI's ten most wanted list. Landed on Black described the toxic culture of the police department and streets, ultimately leading to the realization that Zach has been afflicted with PTSD. I am Raymond Washington is the only authorized biography of the original founder of the Crips and has been awarded bronze medals in 2015 by both IPPY and Readers Favorite International book awards. Baroota: The Hunting Ground is Zach's first fictional work, and is the start of this series.

If you are looking for gritty, true crime stories, be sure to check out all of Zach Fortier's novels. Zach currently lives in the mountains of Colorado, with his wife Christina.

CACHIBACHÉ

BOOK TWO OF THE DIRECTOR SERIES

BY ZACH FORTIER

CACHIBACHÉ
Copyright © 2017 Zach Fortier

Published by

steeleshark
press

ISBN-13: 978-0692878804
ISBN-10: 0692878807

Visit the author at:
Website: *www.zachfortier.com*
Goodreads: *www.goodreads.com/author/show/5164780.Zach_Fortier*
Blog: *www.authorzachfortier.blogspot.com*
Facebook: *www.facebook.com/authorzach.fortier*
Twitter: *www.twitter.com/zachfortier1*
Instagram: *http://www.imgrum.org/user/zachfortier/505378433*

CONTENTS

Cachibaché:

"piece of junk, a gadget, worthless to one;
priceless to another."

"Sometimes it's the princess who kills the dragon and saves the prince."
~ *Samuel E. Lowe*

FORWARD

The journey back to Moses Lake had begun nearly immediately after they'd left Green River, Utah. Initially, Nick had been concerned about reappearing in the area too quickly. They waited a little over a week, talking over plans, discussing who they had met and who they needed to avoid. Surprisingly, the list was very short. They realized Jay had kept them contained very well for his own reasons; those reasons now worked in their favor. It had nearly been a month since they first arrived in the small town, so the chances of them being remembered were slim. For Nõn, the chances were nearly zero. She had barely left her room, except for a trip to the post office and a meal with Jay. She had purchased beer for Nick, but that too had been a very quick contact, and she had left the clerk very little reason to remember her. Nick's only real encounter had been at the restaurant while eating with Jay. He was pretty sure the waitress would remember him and Jay by association. It was the woman's job to remember minor details about her customers, so he would have to be careful there. Just to be safe, they had decided to return to Moses Lake a week apart; Nick first, then Nõn would arrive a week or so later. That way, anyone who had seen them would not remember seeing them together. They had to be careful; if they were recognized, their plan would never work. In spite of all their preparations, there was one person they hadn't paid attention to, hiding in plain sight, and they were both unaware of his presence. It would be a reality check when he finally came forward and announced himself.

CHAPTER ONE

Waiting at the bus stop in Spokane, Nick was irritated. The bus was late, 10 minutes so far, and no one in the station had an answer to explain to the irritated, edgy man. "Why?" Nick mumbled under his breath, swearing random curses at the bus driver and the world in general. He was in a bad mood, and the bus being late, really anything or anyone being late was a trigger for the darker side of his surly personality. Late was inexcusable in Nick's world. His anxiousness and irritation were compounded by his future fellow passengers on the bus. To Nick, the entire bus looked like it would be filled with large, overweight people who had spent their entire lives waiting at the drive thru lane of their local fast food dispensary. Ordering way more food than they should've and then following their now long dead grandparents' advice to clean everything off their plates, because "you know there were people less fortunate in the world who had nothing to eat." These passengers had evidently taken that advice and run with it, to a ridiculous extreme. Nick had lost 15 pounds during the two weeks in Panama, and in Camp Baroota. Mentally, physically leaner and angry, Nick wanted to get on with hunting The Director. Nick vented his frustration by angrily pacing outside the bus station, like a big cat in a cage in the zoo. He had one purpose: to bring The Director to his knees, and do it with violence and prejudice. Nick stopped pacing abruptly. He fortunately realized everyone in the station was watching him and assessing his angry mental state. He had brought unnecessary attention to himself and his quest, and he had to be more careful. Nick sighed, stopped and leaned against the brick wall of the exterior of the building. Sliding down to a squatting position, Nick brought his excess physical and emotional energy under control. The dark clouds of anger that filled his eyes slowly started to dissipate. The hunt of The Director would more likely than not be a marathon, not a sprint. Nick reminded himself that he had to remember that.

When the bus finally did arrive, it pulled up slowly, lumbering into the parking lot like an ancient dinosaur; tired and overworked, it leaned side to side before stopping. The Driver engaged the airbrakes, and the bus belched a loud hiss. The Driver then opened the door of the bus as he announced they were at the Spokane bus station and the passengers now had ten to fifteen minutes to get a drink or hit the restroom before they would begin loading for Moses Lake. He then exited the bus whistling, farted loudly and then quickly walked into the newly remodeled station.

The Spokane Greyhound bus station had been at this location for several years. Initially, it had been in an area that allowed easy access to the services Greyhound provided from both the I-5 and I-90. That had been the plan some seventy years ago when the original station was built; now, however, the area had slid into poverty, and even the new two story building, complete with police substation, could not restore the now drug dealing, crime infested neighborhood to its former glory. Nick felt at home in the neighborhood. This was an area that felt familiar. He had worked an area similar to this one for more years than he could remember, but that was another time, and another life. Actually, several lives ago, before he met Joann, and before Camp Baroota. Life, it seemed, was like that; like chapters in a book, you turned the page and moved on. The story continued, and there was no way to rewrite it and keep your favorite characters. What mattered now was what happened next. Keep moving, that was the lifelong lesson for survival that Nick had learned early on. Keep moving or die.

Nick watched as a Spokane cop parked his car in the no parking zone outside the front of the building and got out. He was obviously a "day cop"; Nick knew this instinctively. The cop made no eye contact with anyone walking around outside the building. He made no visual check of the people around him, looking for weapons, watching hands and watching behaviors that might give some clue or hint of an impending attack. Soft hands reached out and opened the glass door to the building, the police radio blaring loudly, too loudly, announcing a police officer was approaching. Nick rolled his eyes, thinking Forrest Gump said it best, "Stupid is as stupid does." This guy was a poster child for every police academy class of what not to allow yourself to become as a cop. Self-important, soft and unaware of his environment. Nick smiled to himself – a dark, evil smile – and thought, *Wonder how deep and loud this guy would shit himself if he found himself in the jungles of Panama, facing Jay and Camp Baroota.* Nick giggled, adding to the already disturbing range of emotions he'd displayed while waiting for the bus. Whether he realized it or not, Nick was coming apart. Baroota had changed him, and even though he continued to deny it, the brutal reality of his experiences at the camp had impacted him. He had already been damaged, severely so, before the faux mission to rescue victims of human trafficking had begun. Now Nick's metal stability had redlined. Deep inside his compromised mind, steam was venting and ancient barriers were cracking. It would not be long now, and everything Nick had tried to contain for so long would erupt and be set free. Nick knew he had to find The Director quickly to appease the coming storm. If he didn't? Well, he didn't want to think about the consequences. Meltdowns had happened before, but he had always been able reign in the darkness. Long now it had slept. No doubt Jay had no idea what he had bargained for when he brought Nick onto the team. Jay had used the term "wild card" when he referred to Nick. Jay had no idea what that meant, not really. The darkness was stirring, and Nick knew he had very little time left to bring it back under his tenuous control.

Nick had been vaguely aware of a man watching him as he sat by himself pushed against the wall. The man had been sizing him up, making quick judgments about his ability to thwart an attack. The robber smoked his cigarette and made his decision. Nick would be an easy mark; he was alone and obviously unaware of his surroundings. He had separated himself from the proverbial herd and was now easy prey. The would-be robber took one last deep drag on his low-end cheap ass cigarette and dropped it to the ground. Grinding it out under the heel of his well-worn boot, he zipped up his olive drab green field jacket and motioned with his head in Nick's direction. "Hey buddy, can you spare a smoke?" The ploy had worked over and over; whether the victim had a smoke or not, asking for one opened lines of communication. Most people were threatened by a stranger's request for a cigarette, uncomfortable their space had been invaded. They fell back on well-entrenched behaviors established in grade school when the class bully asked for a piece of candy, or a quarter for lunch. They folded like a lawn chair, and that was when the thief struck. The thief had already started his confident walk towards Nick, sure his tactic would once again be fruitful. Soon he would be several blocks away, the "mark's" wallet emptied and dumped in a garbage can. If the "mark" refused to surrender the wallet immediately, he discovered how easily it was to be stabbed in front of the police substation, right under the cops' noses, and they had no idea it was about to happen. It took a wolf to catch a wolf, and the "day cops" weren't wolves.

Nick was aware the man's hands were in his jacket pockets immediately after he'd thrown the cigarette to the ground. The question was a ruse; Nick knew what was coming and looked darkly into the man's eyes.

The "mark" looked directly at him and began to speak. The tables were suddenly turned, the thief confused. He heard, "No, I don't smoke, and if you want to keep smoking, you'd best think twice about taking another step." Nick stood abruptly, all his pent-up energy unleashed in one explosive move that put him instantly into an upright defensive stance. The movement was rapid, smooth and totally unexpected by the thief. He stopped in mid-stride, hands raised out of his pockets, held up at shoulder level, and he began to back up.

"It's cool, cool. No harm, no foul. I'll just be moving along now. Peace, brother."

Nick didn't respond. He watched the man's hands and body posture. The transformation was instantaneous. The thief would move on to an easier target. Nick's message had been clear.

Anyone who saw the brief confrontation between the two men outside the bus station would've thought nothing of it. Or at least that was what Nick hoped as he entered the building and headed to the restroom, preparing to board the aged bus and make the trip back to Moses Lake.

Twenty minutes later, the passengers began to line up at the bus door. The Driver was checking tickets and stacking their luggage and knapsacks near large steel doors of the center cargo hold of the bus. Nick unhappily noted "ten to fifteen minutes" had grown to twenty.

"Hello, Mr. Hansen, welcome aboard Greyhound." And then, "Thanks for choosing Greyhound." The practiced and worn out greetings flowed out of The Driver as he conducted his daily routine loading. Over and over Nick heard a different and yet obviously practiced greeting as The Driver verified the passenger's tickets allowed them a seat on his bus. Nick was in the middle of the group on purpose. Better not to be first or last in the group. Hide in plain sight somewhere in the middle of the group and remain anonymous. "Welcome back to Moses Lake, sir, hope you enjoy your trip," The Driver said nonchalantly. Nick boarded the bus and walked down the well-worn center aisle, looking for a seat hopefully next to the least offensive person he could find. He was pleasantly surprised to find a seat empty, near the window and at the middle of the bus. He sat down and looked out the window, lost in his own thoughts. What would be his next move? Where to start looking for hints of The Director? He had no idea; he was flying blind, looking for anything that might give him a hint of what to do or where to go. The Driver boarded the bus and closed the bi-fold door. The dull sway of the vehicle let the passengers know they were underway. Soon most of the occupants would fall asleep, lulled into slumber by the bus' gentle sway. Nick couldn't sleep; he watched out the window, dissecting the events of the day. Analyzing conversations and the context they were spoken in, replaying every moment, looking for anything amiss. Finally, it hit him. "Welcome back to Moses Lake, sir." That had been the bus driver's comment to him as he checked his ticket. Nick thought about each and every comment The Driver had made to the passengers; not one had been "Welcome back to Moses Lake." Nick continued to stare out the window. If The Driver was one of The Director's men, he'd made a serious error. Nick was now aware of him. And if he wasn't one of The Director's men, who was he? Why did he remember Nick, or did he? Nick was thinner, tanned and sporting a ragged ten-day old salt and pepper goatee. He took out the dark lensed Wiley Rage sunglasses he'd worn the past ten years or so and put them on. Nick faced the window, but his eyes, now concealed by the dark shades, were focused on The Driver.

For the first fifteen minutes, there was nothing, no careful look in the rearview mirror, no furtive glances in Nick's direction. Then like an eagle looking for prey, The Driver looked directly at Nick. His eyes did not waver; they each stared at each other, watching and assessing. Nick's eyes hidden behind the lenses could watch The Driver's every action while he was unaware he was being counter surveilled. *Welcome back to Moses Lake, sir,* Nick thought to himself, smiling. *Well, that was quick. Now I have something to do and someone to watch.*

An hour and a half later, The Driver pulled the bus to a stop and announced, "We've arrived at Moses Lake. Enjoy your stay, and thank you for choosing Greyhound." He exited the bus and began to unload the luggage stowed away in the baggage compartment. As The Driver handed items to each passenger as they claimed them, Nick observed his every move from his window, waiting for the remaining passengers to exit the bus. He then got up, sure that no one was left on the bus, and looked at The Driver's identification on the sun visor above his torn and tattered Captain's chair. Nick noted his name and date of birth, probably false if he was one of The Director's men, but at least a place to start. He also memorized quickly the driver's license number. It was a Washington State commercial driver's license. The form was legit; the name most likely was not. Either way, a place to start. Nick smiled an evil smile as he left the bus. Walking past The Driver, he said, "Michael, thanks for the ride," and walked away. Nick felt sure they would be meeting soon under very different circumstances.

CHAPTER TWO

A week later, Nõn too was on her way back to "The Hole", as Nick liked to call Moses Lake. He'd told her about the bus driver and asked her to keep her eyes open for anything they might need to be aware of. Nick had a busy week; he had a job at the billeting office they'd stayed in, and an apartment. He'd found an older Toyota pickup for sale and contacted the owner of the truck, who said he just wanted to get rid of it. It had nearly 200,000 miles and had just stopped starting one day. It was rusted and ugly, and he felt no one in their right mind would buy it. He wanted 300 bucks for the truck, the amount he'd recover from salvage. Checking out the motor, going through the motor system by system, Nick found there was no spark coming from the electronic coil to the plugs, a common stoppage and easy to fix. Nick bought the rusted-out truck and had it fixed and running with a used coil from eBay.

Nõn had a much different experience than Nick on the Greyhound. There was no testosterone contest with the local thieves and robbers, although she was ready for anything, her trusted knife sharpened and easily accessible. Nothing threatening happened. Zip. Nada. She didn't see the Greyhound station the way Nick had described it. The cops he described an inept and soft, seemed professional and courteous to her. The other passengers weren't nearly as offensive as he'd described, and the bus driver wasn't aware of her at all, no threat whatsoever. Nõn stared out the window as the bus' motor droned on, the huge tires making occasional clacking noises as they crossed cracks in the roadway. To her, it sounded like a keyboard on a laptop computer as its owner busily typed away. It reminded her of how much she missed her writing. She thought about Nick's paranoid description of the trip he'd taken to Moses Lake. She was worried about his sanity – and to be honest, having second thoughts about this whole endeavor. Why push their luck with The Director? The whole experience seemed surreal now, and she wondered if it wouldn't be a much smarter idea just to lay low and live their lives, or at least what was left of them. His insight had saved them in the time of crisis, but his edgy demeanor was wearing on her. His constant juvenile jokes, the smart-ass comments, it all grew tiresome.

The bus driver announced they'd be arriving in Moses Lake shortly and to look around their seats and make sure they had all their belongings. Nõn texted Nick and told him she was close. They'd decided not to meet in public, but that didn't prevent Nick from watching her from a distance. He wanted to make sure they missed nothing this time.

When they finally did talk, Nick asked about the bus driver, what had he said exactly? He wanted verbatim the conversation the bus driver had had with Nõn and the other passengers. Nõn found this very tedious and told him exactly that. She couldn't remember every comment word for word, and she told Nick over and over there was nothing threatening about the bus's driver. Nick was already getting on her nerves, and she'd been in Moses Lake less than a day. He was more and more demanding, impatient and edgy. Finally, after they hung up, Nõn showered and went to sleep. She'd rented a room at The Sage N Sand hotel and needed to get started on finding a job and an apartment as soon as possible if they were to begin their plan.

Nick hung up with Nõn, frustrated beyond belief. The bus driver had obviously remembered him, an average middle aged white guy in an ocean of average middle aged white guys, and still he'd made the comment "Welcome back." Nõn was a redheaded black woman, fit as hell, and stood out in this ocean of old white dudes. How had The Driver missed her? Perhaps Nick thought The Driver was just being careful. Playing his hand close to the vest, making sure he didn't alert them to his presence any more than he already had. Nick thought for a while and finally decided that must be it. The Driver was trying to do damage control. He'd already been careless; no need to be foolish. Nick smiled and thought to himself, *Too late, I'm already on to you, man; way too late to be careful.*

The following day was tedious at best. Nõn applied for a job at a local diner, as was their plan. This would enable her to be hidden in plain sight as much as was possible given her appearance, while exposing her to a large percentage of the population of Moses Lake. The idea was for her to be aware of new patrons, out-of-towners who could possibly lead them to The Director. Meanwhile, Nick was working as a janitor/cleaner at the billeting office. Dumping garbage, cleaning toilets. And the whole time, he too would be watching for anything out of the ordinary. The plan seemed sound, they'd talked it over and it made sense. Made the most of the resources they had available, and if need be, working these low status jobs, they could disappear in a heartbeat and no one would notice.

After a week of dumping garbage and scrubbing shit stains, Nick decided enough time had passed to start working on the bus driver. Hoping he would have settled back into his routine, Nick sat outside the Moses Lake Greyhound bus station and watched from the seat of the rusted-out Toyota 4x4 he'd purchased in town. He'd checked the bus schedule and knew when the bus from Spokane was due to arrive. He arrived 15 minutes earlier, just to be sure. The bus arrived 25 minutes later. Nick sighed and muttered to himself, "Late as usual, asshole" as the bus pulled up and leaned side to side, crossing from the roadway into the parking lot. A moment later, the bus driver stepped out. Nick whispered to himself, "What the hell happened to you, man? Gain a few pounds, fall off the Weight Watchers wagon? Jenny Craig membership expire? Richard Simmons lose your number?" As the short, rotund man waddled to the bus station door, Nick started the Toyota and pulled across the street to get a closer look at the bus driver. "Shit," Nick blurted out; this was a different driver. He sat and watched the man, as he thought maybe this is why Nõn saw nothing weird, because there was nothing weird. Nick pulled away from the curb and pointed the 'Yota towards his new home, already a plan forming to locate The Driver using other tactics.

Once he arrived home, he called Nõn and asked her what the bus driver of the Greyhound bus she had arrived in looked like. She described the fat, dumpy driver Nick had watched earlier. "That explains why you saw nothing unusual on your trip; this is a completely different driver," Nick said. "Now I get it, I thought you'd just missed it." Nõn was silent, still not convinced Nick had really seen anything. Finally, she told him she was starting at the diner in the morning in a voice that left no doubt she wasn't looking forward to it. Nick was oblivious to her disdain for the job. He exclaimed, "Good, so we get started tomorrow throwing out our nets to see what dark things swim in Moses Lake." Nõn rolled her eyes and sighed. She was doing the best she could to stay motivated and focused on the plan they'd formed, but she longed for her life, the life she had before Baroota. Nick, on the other hand, had no life to return to; his wife was dead, career over, kids grown with lives of their own. The Director was his single point of focus. His sole reason for going on.

Nick watched the bus station for several days, hoping to catch the mystery driver. He assumed The Driver had taken a couple of days off or perhaps switched routes, but his surveillance of the bus station proved to be a bust. No sighting of the mystery driver. He'd just vanished. Nick had to take a different tack. How to find The Driver, yet do it in a way that's overt and covert at the same time. Nick watched as another bus pulled in and noticed on the right rear corner a message for anyone on the road: "Our drivers are courteous and professional, call this number to report any incident of discourteous driving." Nick smiled; that was his in. He quickly wrote down the number and called.

"Hello, this is the Greyhound complaint center, may I have the bus number you're reporting?"

"Hi, my name is Will, and I don't have a complaint about a bus. I've been trying to find a way to report a great experience I had with your company a couple of weeks ago. I was a passenger on the route from Spokane to Moses Lake, and the bus driver was just amazing. I wanted to thank him personally, so I've been trying to catch him at the bus station here in Moses Lake. However, it appears he may be assigned to a different route now, and I was wondering if you could help me?"

"Well. sir, that's what we at Greyhound love to hear! Do you know the bus driver's name?"

"I do, his name was Michael Spacy."

"Let me see if I can find his next scheduled day to drive. Can you please hold on, sir?"

"Yes, I can." Nick smiled, thinking this was too easy. A few moments later, the woman's voice returned to the line.

"Sir?"

"Yes."

"I'm afraid Mr. Spacy is no longer working for us. He quit suddenly and left no forwarding information. It was very odd; he's been a regular driver for us for many years and had an excellent record. But about a week or so ago, he just quit. I'm sorry."

"That's quite all right. Thank you for your help anyway."

Nick ended the call on his smart phone. Staring out the window, he sat for several minutes, thinking, *What's next?* Finally, he started the truck and started rolling through the gears of the standard 4 speed transmission. He needed to drive. Driving always cleared his head.

CHAPTER THREE

Two months had passed. For Nõn, it had been a very long two months of waiting tables, taking orders, and barely tolerating the juvenile attempts at flirting the local men thought were clever pickup lines sure to make the new waitress at the diner drop her panties. This was Nõn's version of hell. She was miserable. She missed writing, and the intellectual stimulation of the travel and interviews. There had been nothing in the conversations she'd had with the patrons of the diner to lend any hint of The Director or any of his people being in Moses Lake. She'd been paying attention; there just was no hint, not a sign, whisper or anything to give her hope that this plan would bear fruit.

Meanwhile, Nick was as focused as ever. He'd joined Snap Fitness, a local gym, and had been working out feverishly when he wasn't at work. Hard, heavy lifting, pushing himself to failure nearly every day seemed to be the only thing that burned off the excess energy. He was angry, and the more he thought about Jay, Joanna and the whole setup they'd planned, the angrier he became. The betrayal cut deep. He thought he and Joanna had worked through their problems. He'd stayed through her affairs, and lies. The reality was, he couldn't leave her. She was the first woman in a long time he'd felt a connection to. She was flawed – deeply flawed, he knew that – and yet he felt they'd connected. He had; she hadn't. She'd played him, played her part well, and his need to be with her had nearly gotten him killed. The gym was his hideout, a place to blow off steam. His biggest problem was, he was older now, his body battered, and his psyche wounded. Muscles and tendons that had been carrying him for over fifty years of fights and training were no longer able to benefit from the hormones of youth. Mentally, he was spent as well. The rage that had fueled his workouts in the past was now just an empty, dark hole that burned as brightly and hot as it ever had. His body, however, was running on fumes.

The intensity of his workouts had caught the attention of the manager of the gym. She'd nodded to him occasionally as he entered and went to his favorite bench to begin his routine. Finally, after watching him frustrated with the lack of progress in his lifting routine, she approached him and tried to strike up a conversation.

"You trying to cash in on a life insurance policy?" she said in a gravelly, deep voice.

"What?"

"I said, are you trying to kill yourself for a reason, or you just hell bent on wearing out my weights personally?"

Nick glared at her, sweat running down his face and arms. "Can't kill what's already been dead."

"What's that mean?"

"Nothing."

"You're the manager, right?"

"Yes, I manage and own the gym. You've been coming here for a month and apparently are hell bent on injury, the way you work out."

"Ya, so? What's your point? I pay to come here to lift. I'm not interested in spin classes, if that's your end goal."

She rolled her eyes. "Jesus, relax. I'm just making an observation. I know a thing or two about pushing yourself too hard. I used to be ranked third in the U.S. in women's bench press in my weight class, then one day it all fell apart. I literally pulled my wrist joints apart doing clean and jerks. Now I manage this place. So maybe you might want to listen when I say you're pushing too hard – or maybe not, and you can go screw yourself." She turned and walked back to the counter.

Nick watched as she walked away. Third in the U.S. in bench? Easy to look up. He grabbed his smart phone and Googled her name. A quick search pulled up her name and records. She was legit. She definitely had the gym demeanor down. She wasn't here to walk around in pink silk shorts that were two sizes too small, showing off the family jewels. She took no shit off anyone. Nick included.

He finished lifting, wiping the excess sweat off the equipment and replacing the weights on the racks; gym etiquette, and a mandatory requirement in her gym. She'd made it clear at the beginning: clean up after your lifts, or you'll be banned from the gym. She meant it. Nick liked her take no prisoners attitude.

He walked to the counter. He stopped and looked at her; she glared back.

"What? You need something?"

"Sorry, I didn't mean to come off so abrupt. I'm just tired."

"Ya? Maybe you need to not push so hard."

"That's not an option. I have to train for a…job."

Nick stuck out his hand and said, "My name is Nick."

"I'm Ali, Nick, and I can't shake your hand, remember? My wrists are destroyed." She held up both arms, scarred from repeated surgeries.

"Damn, that must have been rough!"

Nick looked at her wrists and noticed even though she was obviously seriously injured, she was still fit. Her arms were toned, cut and still had some muscular size.

"So what's your secret? I see you're injured, but still look fit."

Ali looked warily at him and replied, "Good genes, I guess."

"OK, if you say so," Nick said suspiciously. And then, "See you and your good genes tomorrow, Ali third in the U.S."

She waited until he left the gym, then pulled his records. He'd paid with cash on a monthly membership. Looking at the photocopied driver's license in his file, she muttered to herself, "Nick, huh?" The name on the license was William Brady.

Nick and Ali didn't talk again for several days. She watched him from the counter as he continued trying to prepare for what he hoped would be a final and violent encounter with The Director and his people.

Finally, one day as he entered, she said, "Hi, Will." Nick paid no attention to her greeting. He didn't even flinch, and continued to his favored bench. Ali thought to herself, *William, my ass; you don't even flinch when I say your name. Who does that?*

When Nick finished, she watched him with a critical gaze. Everything about him felt wrong. The way he walked, the workouts, and now *Call me "Nick", but my name is William.*

Ali called out, "Hey, Nick!"

Immediately, Nick turned and looked in her direction. "What?"

Ali shook her head; yep, something is wrong here. Dealing with people day in and day out, she'd developed what she called her "GayDar"; she knew immediately who was straight and who was gay in the small town. "GayDar" also let her know when something was wrong or off. Ali's "Gay-Dar" was fired up, and rainbow colored searchlights were going off somewhere in her mind. She didn't like this guy, whoever the hell he was.

"When you're done, come over here."

"OK, when I'm done."

Nick finally finished, cleaned up and walked to the counter. Ali pushed the copy of his driver's license across the counter. "Says your name is William Brady, but you don't answer to William, Will or Bill. I know, because I've called out to you and you didn't even flinch. But I call out Nick, and you immediately respond. What's up?"

"Oh ya, well, I'm not used to William yet. I've been Nick for a lot longer."

Ali looked at him suspiciously. "What the hell does that mean? Are you undercover? Are you a cop?"

"I was in another life, before I died."

"What the hell are you talking about? Are you running an investigation in my gym?"

"You wouldn't believe me if I told you."

"Try me, Nick or William or whoever the hell you are."

"How about this: I tell you what's up, you listen till the end, and then you answer my questions?"

"Do I need an attorney, Nick? Shouldn't you advise me of my rights first?"

Nick laughed. "Relax! When I'm done, you won't believe a word I've said – but trust me, it's all true. How about you close and lock the door. This is gonna take a few minutes, and I don't want the whole damn world hearing this."

Ali raised her eyebrows. "Lock the door, huh? Really? Do I look stupid? I may be injured, but I can still kick your ass if you get stupid. You got that?"

"I do. I get it. Here, take my cell and dial 911. You can hold it. So you'll have my name and my phone if I get stupid. All you have to do is press send. Boom, 5-oh will be on the way. Deal? Lock the door. Listen, and you decide. Then it's my turn, OK?"

Twenty-five minutes later, Nick finished. "That's the deal. Sounds like bullshit, huh?"

Ali hadn't moved; she watched everything Nick did while he told his story, recalling Baroota and the team and finally seeing Jay with Joanna. Her "GayDar" was silent. No rainbow warning searchlights had gone off. She sat silent watching. Finally, she spoke in that deep, husky voice, "And your question for me?"

"Ya, that. Well, I'm guessing you might have a connection I could benefit from, judging from your muscle mass post-injury surgeries."

"Meaning what exactly?"

"You've seen my workouts; I need to improve faster than my body will allow at this age. I need an assist. I was hoping maybe you could hook me up with some of your 'good genes'."

The room was silent. She stared at Nick. "Seriously? You're a cop, and you are asking me this?"

"I was a cop – *was* a cop, past tense. Now I'm on a mission to find this guy. I must up my skill set to defeat him. I need your help. It's just you and me here, no one else is listening."

Ali unlocked the door and told Nick to leave. She handed him his phone and said nothing. After he walked out, she opened up the company laptop and began her own search.

The next day when Nick arrived at the gym, she watched him walk in. Halfway through his workout, she walked over and sat down.

"I looked up some of your bullshit story on the Web. I found enough to verify some of what you said. So, your plan is to kill this guy when you find him?"

"Yep, slowly."

"Just like that?"

"Just like that."

"And to be clear, you want help achieving your physical goals. Not killing him?"

"Yes, and I'm more than willing to pay. The killing part? That's mine and mine alone."

"Oh, you'll pay. This kind of help isn't cheap and will require you to obtain some of your own supplies. I can only supply product; the rest is on you."

"How much can I get at a time?"

"Six months' supply at a time."

"Awesome. Thanks. When do I pay you?"

"Tomorrow before I order it. I need cash up front, and you'll never know where I get it, so don't ask."

"How much?"

"$200 a vial, so $1200 cash tomorrow. In an envelope, leave it on the counter after your workout, wrapped in the towel you clean up the equipment with. I don't want the whole damn world knowing about this."

"$1200 cash tomorrow. Done. And thanks."

The next day, Nick showed up with the required cash. Ali handed him a list of other pharmacological assists she thought might help.

"I suggest you look into these as well. You won't need my help to obtain them, and they're safe and effective. Being a cop, I'm sure you know the workarounds for saline and syringes?"

"I do, thanks again."

"Don't thank me. You'll probably drop dead in my gym if you don't back off on the workouts. But I can see that isn't an option. "

"No, it isn't."

Ali turned and walked away, no nonsense as ever; when she was done speaking, the conversation was over. Nick smiled and went back to his deadlifts.

Nick's workouts and routine hadn't gone unnoticed. Twenty minutes before he came to the gym, a 1993 Honda Civic had pulled into the parking lot across the street from the gym. The Driver sat and waited, making notes and watching for patterns in the traffic and people who frequented the area. Surveillance, real surveillance, was a craft, an art form. Observing someone in plain sight, not hiding, but out in the open and yet covert took a skill set few possessed. The car had to be common, unremarkable, and the observer had to set up in a location that not only didn't draw the attention of the person they watched, but every single person in the area needed to be blind to their presence. The Driver had been hiding in plain sight for so long, it was now his normal. Used cars, plain clothing. Making sure nothing you did made you memorable. From the shoes you wore to the food you ordered. Nothing could draw attention to you. The Driver had prided himself on this skill set and had become accustomed to being unknown. Then "William Brady" had pulled that little stunt on the bus. Checked his company identification, called him by name. He couldn't take the risk of being located, so he'd quit the job that had enabled him to hide in plain sight for so long. Whoever "William" really was, The Driver had no idea; not yet. But he knew on a gut level something was wrong with "William". So, he watched and waited, waited for William to slip up and give away his real agenda.

Nick left the gym and as usual walked to his aged, rusted Toyota. As skilled as The Driver was, he was no match for a paranoid street cop. Nick always checked the area, looking for people watching him. Looking for cars that were consistently present. Thirty-plus years of surviving in the inner city and the police department's dog-eat-dog world had instilled in him a level of "awareness" that was honestly clinically diagnosable. Nick liked to say, "Paranoia is only an issue if you aren't being watched and hunted. If you have no reason to be paranoid." But Nick had plenty of reasons. He noticed the Honda and two other cars, a 1999 ford Taurus SHO and a 1998 Chevy Impala, that were both occupied. He made a mental note to keep an eye out for them. If they were watching him, he'd know soon enough. He sat in the truck for a moment and made notes of the license plates of the three cars, just in case the plates were switched or rotated. Finally, he pulled out of the parking lot and went to his one room apartment. No one followed.

CHAPTER FOUR

While Nick was working the local black market, Nõn had reached her breaking point. She was quickly becoming more and more disgusted with Moses Lake and its citizens. If one more redneck asked for a "little brown sugar" with his coffee, she swore she would take out her knife and gut the bastard right there in the diner for all to see. The idea made her smile. That would be a sight: tables of uneducated self-important diner patrons shitting themselves while she sliced and diced one of their comrades. This wasn't healthy. She was angry every day. She hadn't survived all the demon's abuse and then Baroota to live life as a waitress. Sure, the other girls seemed to be OK with the constant inappropriate attention and incredibly painful and awkward attempts at flirting. A couple of them admitted they actually liked the attention. Nõn didn't. Her commitment to the hunt of The Director was waning quickly. Finally, one day the cold flame of her commitment to The Director's demise ended. It was over, simple as that. She didn't survive all life had mercilessly thrown at her to live in this hell on Earth. What was the point of surviving Baroota, to then go on living as a prisoner in your own self-imposed exile? No more.

Nõn was at her apartment, staring out the window at her drab, dreary existence. Even the sight of the cloud-filled sky seemed dark and oppressive. Nothing brought her happiness any more. She made up her mind that she was done. Period. Nick had lived this life of hunting and plotting for so long, he no longer realized any other existence was possible. His whole reason for joining the mission that ended up being Baroota was a last vengeful off-the-books slaughter. Their only real bond had been they'd survived the camp and Jay's hunt. Even her prophetic dreams had stopped. There was no more guidance, no more follow-the-wolf-through-smoke-filled-battle-grounds-at-all-costs. To her, it was clear: she was off her life path, and that needed to change immediately. But how? By the time her morning Tai Chi routine was completed, she had a plan. Her spirits were immediately lifted with a plan of her own that promised hope.

Nõn went to work that day smiling for the first time in many weeks. She greeted the regular customers smiling. Poured coffee for the old men, who arrived as part of their daily ritual. Every diner has them, the older crew of men who have retired and adopt the diner as their escape from nagging, annoying wives. It is their version of their wives' "girls party". They made their usual barely disguised sexual comments to her, trying to elicit some kind of reaction. Today, though, she smiled and brushed them off; no angry glares, just a smile and a nod. One guy commented too loudly, "Looks like someone got laid last night. About damn time, too. Jesus you're a surly one!" The group erupted with laughter. Nõn didn't react to the comment and just continued on with her day. Earlier this morning, she'd left a message on the voicemail of an old friend. It seemed like years since they'd talked, but it had only been a few weeks. Since arriving in the Hole, time had changed for Nõn. Hours seemed like days, weeks like years. Her life had become tedious, miserable and barely tolerable. She needed to get her life back on track, and with any luck there would be a return call with good news.

A regular patron came into the diner and sat in Nõn's area. She walked over to the table where he sat and asked if he would like a cup of coffee.

"Yes, one coffee black. Make it decaf." No smart-ass comments, no stupid "I like my coffee like I like my women, strong and black." Nõn smiled and replied, "One decaffeinated coffee coming up. Anything else?" Usually this was answered with another barely veiled sexual comment. Sometimes it was "What's on the menu that's sticky sweet?" or "What I'm looking for isn't on the diner's menu, sweetie"; the variations on the theme were endless and barely creative. This time the patron replied, "BLT, please, and fries." Nõn smiled; at least there was one guy in this miserable shit hole of a town that wasn't an ass. "BLT with fries, coming right up."

The Driver watched as the waitress walked away. She was familiar. He knew at once he'd seen her before. The memory was vague and distant, but she was remarkable; a black woman with red hair in a small Washington state town. Also, she had a slight accent. He made a note to check his tapes. The crazy old guy in the gym, and now this; there had to be some connection. His life of hiding in plain sight had taught him many things. First and foremost, there are no coincidences. None, ever. It's just a matter of connecting the dots. Most people are barely aware of the world around them. Grazing like cattle in a pasture, blissful, barely aware of the rancher's predatory eye. Unprepared for the horror of the slaughterhouse until it's too late. The Driver understood this. He'd spent his life surviving by recognizing the barely noticeable changes in the proverbial wind, reading the writing on the wall and being out the door and down the street, gone into the night when the men in black Tahoes arrived.

The Driver ate his BLT and drank his coffee and headed back to the ancient farmhouse that served as his "Bat Cave", as he called it. The Bat Cave was ground zero for his life's mission. There, he felt safe, surrounded by computers and servers, top tier monitors and computer equipment. It was the only place that made sense to him. He hid in plain sight on the Web, using information others posted on social media, sold to whomever paid the highest price. He loaded the surveillance videos he'd hacked and stolen and began to piece the mystery of the aged gym rat and redheaded waitress together.

CHAPTER FIVE

The return call Nõn had been hoping would come that day or maybe the next didn't. She was deeply depressed; no message, and no return call she'd missed. Time that previously had been so compressed now seemed like a prison sentence. To do an eight-hour shift at the diner was now time at a standstill. She looked at the clock repeatedly. Life was unbearable. After her shift at the diner, she went home and turned on the water in the shower. When it was hot enough, she stepped into the shower, then slid slowly down the wall. There were no tears; she hadn't been able to cry since she was a child. She'd survived too much to cry, but that didn't stop her from feeling deeply depressed. The shower droned on, pounding on her head. The white noise of the water's relentless impact was comforting. Then briefly a noise; she almost missed it, she was in such a deep depression. There it was again. She shot out of the shower like a fighter pilot ejecting from the broken shell of his jet. The shower curtain was in her way, and she ripped it down to get free from what now felt like a malevolent spirit's attempts to stop her. Her phone was ringing! Loud and clear now, it rang again. Amazing she thought how that sound now cleared the darkest of clouds that had haunted her. She picked up the phone and answered it.

"Hello?"

"Nõn?"

"Yes, how are you? Did you receive my message?"

"I did. Sorry I didn't call you back right away. I have to admit, I was surprised it took this long for you to reach out to me. I didn't call you back because I wanted to have a definite answer to your request."

Nõn closed her eyes, a barely audible reply escaping her dry mouth. "And do you have a job for me?"

"Yes, I do, but it's a rather difficult one, actually. We've heard of a tribe of women in Ukraine. They believe themselves to be Amazons, the Amazon women warriors reborn. We need a woman of exceptional skills to do a piece on them. Originally, we sent a male reporter. That ended badly; trust me, you don't want to know. The details…they're grim. This definitely requires a special touch. I think possibly a woman who the Amazons could respect might be the best option. I thought of you initially. That was a couple of weeks ago; however, the powers that be here at NPR decided to send the male reporter instead. Nõn, before you say yes, realize what you're saying yes to. There are 150-plus Asgarda; that's what they call themselves.

They're as mean as any group of soldiers you've ever encountered, maybe much worse. Think it over before you say yes or no. I'm sure there will be other opportunities."

Nõn didn't hesitate. "Yes, I'll do it. When would I leave?"

"Are you sure? I mean, it requires travel to Ukraine. These women chewed up our male reporter and sent him home a beaten, bloody mess. You'll have no protection. If they turn on you, you'll be on your own. They have no respect for anyone who can't hold their own in combat. To be honest, I think they're completely insane, but our human interest division wants the story."

"Just tell me when to be ready, and I'll be ready."

"OK, I'll let you know. It may take a few days to get everything lined up. Take the time on your end to get ready as well. Glad to have you back! Honestly, I've missed our late-night talks. No one listens like you do!"

They said their goodbyes and hung up. Nõn felt relieved. Finally, she had hope. Then almost immediately, there was anxiety. She'd have to tell Nick their alliance was over. He would have to locate The Director himself.

The heat was oppressive as Nick stepped out of the rear door of the billeting office. The air hung heavy, formidable, and ominous. Nick stopped and took off the ball cap he was wearing and wiped the sweat from his forehead. Looking up at the mid-day sun, he squinted. Finally putting his hat back on, he picked up the handle of the Rubbermaid tote he'd been pushing and continued towards the large beaten and scarred dumpster at the rear of the parking lot. The distance seemed longer today than normal. It wasn't far to walk, really, but the air around him seemed to slow his progress; it felt like walking underwater, every step was an effort. Smiling to himself, he knew it wasn't real, the air wasn't really a malicious force pushing against him. He was fatigued from his workout the night before. The assistance Ali had promised hadn't yet arrived, but he at least now had hope. At fifty-four, his body didn't recover from the stress he put it through in preparation of the days to come. The confrontation with his enemy was coming. He could feel it. It wasn't a thing you could describe to someone who had never experienced it. Somewhere in all we are and know, there's a sense or perhaps an awareness of things outside our current knowledge of the human mind. He'd tried to explain it to Nõn once, and he saw she heard the words he'd spoken and had some understanding of what he was trying to say. After all, she had her guardian, the priestess she felt watched over her and protected her. Like a Stone Age man watching a smart phone in action, most of us are equally unaware of this part of our existence. We stumble through life with no learned sensitivity to it. Nick, however, had learned to trust this feeling. He called it a gut feeling when pressed, but the reality was it was more than that. It was like someone or something was there in his thoughts, in the shadows of his mind, watching, listening and occasionally whispering. Occasionally when he was alone, he actually spoke out loud to the feeling, taunting it, daring it to be more specific, come forward and speak louder. Nothing had ever come forward.

As the awareness had grown, he could feel something was coming, and he'd better be prepared. His workouts had increased in intensity, the firearms training as well. He pushed hard to be ready, but without a deadline to meet, the future seemed endless. When would the time arrive? No idea; could be a week, could be a year.

Arriving at the dumpster, he separated the trash he'd removed from the billeting office from the rest of the tote's contents. The plastic bags were easy to identify because he'd tied them off differently; those that came from the office had a single knot, the rest were tied with two. A subtle but important identifier that enabled him to hide his ongoing covert plan in plain sight. Double knots removed and thrown into the dumpster, he turned to make sure no one was watching, then put the single knot bags into the back of his aging Toyota pickup. This had been his routine for some time now. Work, train, prepare, wait and sift through the garbage, looking for clues to see if The Director was near. So far, nothing.

As Nick made his way back to the building, he stopped and pretended to tie his shoes. Looking up, head down, he saw it again. The Honda Civic no doubt it was the same one, rusted with green paint. Rusted rims as well, but the tires, brand new, performance tires, probably speed rated as well. The car didn't appear to be occupied, but it was more likely The Driver was slumped down and hiding. Or perhaps watching from another vantage point. Nick made a note of the license plate and was nearly positive it matched the one from the gym. Best to be positive. He walked back into the building, went immediately to the top floor, and watched as he stood back far enough in the window not to be visible. Just as he thought, he saw movement across the parking lot adjacent to the billeting office; there was a lone man standing near a group of trees that had grown wild at the back of the lot. Nick watched while the man watched the building. *Your ass is mine! And then after you've told me all your dirty little secrets, I'll drop what's left of your broken body on The Director's doorstep, bitch.*

The lethal game of the two predators, each hunting the other, had begun. Nick felt he had the advantage already. He could play stupid and strike when the time was right. Lull his enemy into complacency. The trick was to plan to strike before your enemy struck, or you were screwed. The mongoose and the cobra locked in a death match; make a mistake, and it's over.

That night, Nick called Nõn to tell her the good news – good news to him, at least – that he was being watched by one of The Director's men. He was pretty excited that his plan was in fact viable and working.

"Nõn, hey, it's Nick. I have some good news."

"Hello, Nick, I too have some news. Please, you may go first."

"Sure, OK. Well, it's a long, detailed story to describe, but the nuts and bolts of it: I've been watched now for some time. I finally was able to verify it for sure. I noticed a pattern of three cars present at the gym I've been working out at. The same three have been there day after day. The cars move around the lot, but always the same three. Anyway, today at work I saw one of those three cars, an older green Honda in the parking lot. I watched from a window on the top floor of the building, and there was a guy watching, standing near a group of trees. Can you believe our luck? It's only been a few months, and already we're knee deep in The Director's ass! He doesn't know it yet, but his perfect little world is about to come unraveled."

Nõn rolled her eyes as she listened. Seriously, Nick was becoming unhinged. Moses Lake was a small town; cars only had so many places to park. She was sure there was a perfectly good explanation for the car appearing in two places in the same town. Had Nick noticed the car in 4 or 5 places, she would have been less skeptical; however, she said nothing negative. Better to be upbeat and positive to lessen the impact of her news. She was leaving, and in her mind the sooner, the better.

"That is good news! Are you sure?"

"Yes, I'm sure. I have the plates from the car, and now that I know he's there, I just have to backtrack him to find out where he's staying. Then it'll be time for a short, yet satisfying chat before sending him on a short trip to meet his maker." Nick was giddy, frighteningly so, as he talked about killing The Driver.

Nõn grew impatient with his ridiculous metaphors. Always a veiled disguise to cover up the reality of the violence and horror of the things he'd done, and would do again.

She said, "Nick, I have to talk to you. I need you to listen."

Nick was silent; the tone in her voice made him stop and take a breath. He already knew what she'd say. The good news had come too late. She didn't have the mindset to hunt The Director, to do what it took to catch an animal like this. Nick did; it was a skill set developed and honed to the sharpest of edges. He quietly said, "Don't go."

Nõn was silent. The loneliness in his voice cut deep. She ignored his request. "I have a job offer. It's writing again, under another name, another identity, but I would be doing what I love again. I will be leaving in a few days, Nick. I have to go. I cannot go on like this."

Nick said nothing for some time. Finally, he said quietly, "When are you leaving?"

She replied, "I do not know yet, but soon. The details need to be worked out, but it could be tomorrow, or in a week. Listen, I tried to do this, but it is not me. Try to see it from my point of view. How well would you function if we had gone into my world and you had to be a journalist? How happy would you be? You are still in your world, hunting, tracking, pursuing. This is no different for you than our false mission with Jay. You just switched targets from the human traffickers to The Director. You must see that? It is all the same!"

There was silence on the line for many minutes. Nick could see it clearly through her eyes, and it was painful. He had no other choice, and neither did she. They were bound by their survival only. The shared experience of surviving Baroota had forged a bond neither could deny; however, it hadn't changed who they were.

Finally, he said, "I agree. I see you're right. This is your path. However, I need you to promise one thing. Please. Make this promise and keep it."

She closed her eyes; she didn't want to make any promise or swear any oaths. She was finished with this vendetta. She wanted to be free of this sick world they had entered. Finally, she responded, "I will make no promise; I will not be bound by this any longer. I will consider whatever you ask, but I will not promise anything."

Nick felt the bond they shared unraveling; like a steel cable breaking from the strain of the weight of its load, it was unraveling. It was strange to feel so suddenly alone. The call had started out with him giddy with the good news he wanted to share. Now it felt meaningless.

He said, "When I call – and I will call – please then consider coming back."

She thought for a moment...what could it hurt? Finally, she replied, "When you call, I will consider it. That is all I can promise." She hung up.

Nick listened to the quiet nothingness of the phone. Had this been a landline, there would have been a dial tone now. Interesting, he thought, that he'd never noticed how empty the cellular phone hang up sounded. One moment you're listening to life; the next, darkness, silence and death, death of the connection. His eyes hardened. Nõn was right: she had her life, there was still hope there for her. His life, Joanna, the mountain home, it was all gone. The silence he now listened to was real. This was it, this is what was left for him. His connection to the world, to anything good in the world – if there was anything good left – was over. He had one purpose, one end. He vowed to make it terrifyingly spectacular.

Deep inside Nick's dark, twisted mind, an animal-like consciousness stirred. Darkly satisfied by the emptiness that surrounded him, it bathed in the hopelessness he felt, like a teenage girl lying in the hot sun surrounded by hormonal boys. Finally, its time was coming. Had it been a big cat and felt this, it would have purred loudly, stretching, yawning as it bared formidable teeth. But it wasn't a big cat. Finally, its time was at hand. Nick was isolated, disconnected from the world, his sanity beginning to deteriorate. Nick's lifelong control over it was weakening.

CHAPTER SIX

The Director sat back in his chair, reading from the list of potential candidates for the facilitator of Camp Cachibaché. The loss of Camp Baroota had been financially difficult for him. The patrons of Baroota had paid handsomely to hunt their prey. The experience had been most satisfying for them, and in turn they'd paid his fees with no complaints. He needed someone with exceptional and rare skills to make Cachibaché equally profitable. After reading a few files and resumes collected by his research staff, he decided to interview one candidate. One specifically he felt matched his requirements. It was remarkable how well she fit. It was as if his need for an exceptionally broken and twisted mind had reached out into the universe, and the universe had delivered. He liked that idea. He liked it a lot. As if it was his destiny to provide this service to the right people, and the universe agreed. The Director pressed the line on his desktop telephone and intercom and spoke. "Arthur, would you step in for a moment." It wasn't a request. They both understood this. Arthur had been his secretary for many years. He complied immediately with every request The Director had made, from day one of his employment. He was completely and unquestionably loyal; The Director owned him.

Arthur knocked at the door and waited.

"Come in, Arthur."

"Yes, sir, how may I be of assistance?"

"I would like this woman contacted and brought in for an interview. She holds promise, real promise. Also, I'd like to see all of her files, everything. I want to know her most intimate secrets before she arrives for the interview. I have a very good feeling about this one, Arthur!"

"Yes, sir. Right away sir."

Arthur left the office and closed the left door of the double doors that allowed access to the office.

The Director walked across the office to the walnut doors of his liquor cabinet and opened it. On one side, his favorite bottle of scotch sat with corresponding glasses. He reached for the bottle and removed it from the shelves. Removing one of the crystal whiskey glasses, he smiled. He liked the feel of the glass in his hand. It was made of the finest crystal by the good people at Cash Crystal. He had them specially made; the glass had to be held with a cloth, because at his request the people at Cash Crystal hadn't been polished or dulled the glass' decorative edges. Cash Crystal had demanded a waiver and release of any responsibility and liability should someone be injured by the crystal. He immediately complied. They were razor sharp. The contrast of the lethal sharp-edged crystal and the smooth warmth of the Macallan Single malt Scottish whiskey made him smile. He picked up the glass with one of the dried blood red cloth napkins at the bar and walked across the hardwood floor of his office to his chair. After his meeting with that disgusting pilot Pat, he'd found he'd been so mentally scarred, he could no longer enjoy his beloved "Laphroaig." The mere smell of it reminded him of the foul stench she'd gleefully unleashed on his office. Additionally, she'd forever made his favorite classical cello piece a thing of the past. One note of Bach's Cello Suites, and he was drawn back into the dark memories of Pat and the stain of her toxic personality. The past was the past. Pat had received her due. She'd been properly disciplined in the Gulf of Mexico. The detailed report the captain of the boat had sent him of her demise had so warmed his heart, he'd paid the man double his usual fees. It was hard to find good help, and when he did, he'd shown his appreciation of them. The Director dimmed the office lights and queued the overhead surround sound system. Mozart's Piano Sonata 2 in C major K-279-II, performed by Bernd Krueger, filled the room. The piece was elegant and refined. The Director sat in his chair and thought about the upcoming interview with this latest nightmare of a human being. He hoped for her sake she would be more re-fined than Pat had been.

At that exact moment on the other side of the North American con-tinent, in direct contrast to The Director's posh office, Nick was arriving at the gym; the pharmaceutical assist Ali had promised had arrived. The first of many injections had been painful. Nick embraced the pain; it felt real. According to a Google search, the needle length required was 2 inches. The product had to be delivered directly into a large muscle mass, and deeply. Syringes had been easy to come by; given Nick's street background, he understood the healthy workarounds for safe subcutaneous injections, and they were simply acquired. The reaction of his body was nearly instanta-neous. Not only did he sleep better, he felt better. His appetite improved, his mood as well, in spite of Nŏn's pending absence. As The Director was sitting down to enjoy his Scotch and Mozart, Nick was drinking a Smart Water and pressing play on his iPod touch. Lying back on the bench, he closed his eyes as the musical piece began. When the piece finally reached its full fury, drums and electric guitars driving home the emotion, accom-panied by M. Shadows' intense vocals, Nick unracked the weights and be-gan the bench repetitions to the beat of Avenged Sevenfold's, "This Means War". The contrast of the two men couldn't have been more clearly defined than at that moment. Thirty reps later, Nick re-racked the bar. Thirty reps at

225 pounds; finally, improvement. Nick was feeling progress at last. Mud Vayne's "World So Cold" began a few minutes later as Nick returned to the bench and unracked the bar and began again. The song's lyrics would be prophetic.

Across the gym, Ali watched and shook her head. The reflection of the look in his eyes in the gym's mirrored walls spoke volumes. God help whoever had pissed this old man off.

The Director had no idea of the blind fury coming his way. A collision course was set. Neither was really aware of the other, not yet; however, their destiny was set in stone. When it finally did happen, it would be under the direction of a woman more lethal and more intelligent than either understood was humanly possible. She would calmly dismantle both of their worlds.

Two days later, Nõn was ready to go. She'd cheerfully quit her job and made arrangements to get to the airport in Spokane. The thought occurred to her to ask Nick to drive her there, but then she changed her mind. She decided it would be best to make a clean break, say goodbye and go. Simple as that. There was no reason to pretend there was a reason to stay. She had noticed nothing in the diner. That idea had been a bust, in her opinion. Perhaps Nick was right and he had found a link to The Director. It didn't matter to her; this wasn't her fight any longer.

"Hello?"

"Nick, it is Nõn. I am calling to let you know I am packed and leaving. I will be headed to Spokane, and from there to Los Angeles."

It was quiet for a moment, then finally Nick spoke. "Good luck. I hope it works out for you. If I need to reach you? I mean, can I reach out to you if something comes up?"

"Yes, you may. I will keep the same phone number when I switch to an international phone. Send a text or an email. I will get back to you when I can."

"Sounds good. Thanks."

The line went dead. Nick thought again how weird it was he'd never noticed before how there was no sign of anything after another person hung up. Now it seemed ominous.

Nõn was in the wind; where she'd gone, she hadn't said. Nick didn't ask. He just knew she had an assignment and she was going to be writing again.

Nick looked at the now silent smart phone. A grim smile crossed his face...time to get serious about finding his secret man crush.

CHAPTER SEVEN

A couple days had gone by, and Nick felt the absence of Nõn more than he thought he would. Driving around Moses Lake, he found himself thinking, *What if she changed her mind and came back and was really still at the diner? No way,* he thought, *but then what if?* He turned the 'Yota around and headed to the diner on what he understood was a foolish, hopeless and pitiful endeavor. She was gone; he just needed to see it. The phone call hadn't seemed real...to see that she was really gone...he needed to see it, know it and feel it. Nick pulled into the diner and rolled slowly through the parking lot, looking for a parking place. He stopped suddenly. "Motherfucker," erupted from his mouth. The green Honda was parked in the parking lot. He looked around to see if there was anyone watching. There was no one. The son of a bitch had been at the diner, probably the entire time watching Nõn, and she had no idea. At first he was furious at her. How could she be so naïve? He'd told her the car's description, and she'd ignored him. Then the more he thought about it, it made sense. Just like she'd said, this wasn't her fight. She didn't want to be here. She wanted to move on. He couldn't. He sighed and backed the truck up. He had to find a good place to watch the Honda and not be seen. Nõn leaving had provided him the opportunity he needed. No way was he going to let this chance go.

Nick quickly assessed the parking lot: there were two entrances/exits, and he had to find a point where he could see both, and quickly. He left the parking lot using the opposite entrance he'd entered. In a few short minutes, he'd found a place to observe the two entrances/exits from a block away. Parked under a tree, he sat and waited, mumbling to himself, "Your ass is mine. It's on, man crush. You may have gotten away with fronting her, but it'll cost you." The more he thought about this piece of shit watching Nõn, so close he could hear her conversations, watch her walk, the more angry he became. He realized he'd put her in danger, asking her to walk in his world. His breathing became slowly more urgent.

Shit! What the hell was I thinking? Fuck! She was a civilian and had no idea of this world. Yeah, she'd survived a lot, but she never, ever set foot in the streets as a combatant. This was an entirely different world. Sharks silently patrolled the concrete streets in police-package Crown Vics, looking for anything amiss. Wolves ran in packs, hunting the sheep. Nõn was neither. Strangely, Nick identified with both, shark and wolf, and the occasional psychopath. One foot in all worlds, that was Nick.

Nick waited for 10 minutes before he saw the green Honda exit the diner's parking lot. He started his trusty 'Yota and slowly pulled away from the curb, following from a considerable distance. A dark smile crossed his face. He muttered, "Just a matter of time now; your life is gonna take a nasty turn, my friend. You should've left me alone. Watching Nõn? You really shouldn't have, huge mistake! Now you *will* pay." The death match of Mongoose and Cobra began in earnest now.

CHAPTER EIGHT

The Driver entered the diner on the same day of the week he had before, expecting to see the redheaded black waitress. She wasn't immediately visible. He went to a table in what had been her assigned area and waited to be served. When the waitress finally did arrive, he was disturbed to see it wasn't Nõn. He ordered his usual BLT and fries and decaf coffee. He looked around to see if perhaps she was in a different area. No, she just wasn't here. He suddenly felt very uncomfortable, fearful. What had he missed? He scanned the restaurant, looking for something wrong; there was nothing. Still, the shivers of fear wouldn't leave him. Had he been a bit more aware of his surroundings, he would've realized somewhere deep down, his subconscious was aware of a rusted Toyota truck slowly moving in the parking lot. The movement of the vehicle similar to a Great White shark on cruise control in the depths of the ocean, hunting, always moving, and hunting. The driver of that truck had eyes as lifeless as a shark searching for its next victim.

The fear he felt was very real, and he could find no reason for it. He tried to shrug it off, but he couldn't. Finally, when his waitress arrived with his food, he asked about the black waitress. Was she here? He'd forgotten to leave a tip last week and now felt bad about it and wanted to make amends.

His current waitress told him, "No, she quit suddenly and left town." His appetite was curiously gone. He looked around the diner again. The feeling of impending doom was unshakable. He kept shivering, twitching, looking over his shoulder here and there. He should've listened to his intuition.

The Driver left the diner after giving up on finishing his BLT and fries. The coffee tasted strange, and everything suddenly felt wrong. He needed to get out of the diner. He paid and walked out into the parking lot and stopped, looking around for any sign of something wrong. Living on the edge for so long had sharpened his awareness. He knew something was wrong, but what?

The Driver pulled out of the parking lot and headed straight home. He felt a strong need to be in the safety and familiarity of "the bat cave." Surrounded by his computers and monitors. Comforted by the hum of the fans keeping his Cisco servers cooled. The set up in the bat cave was impressive and necessary for his covert ops. He felt relieved to be leaving the diner and quickly headed directly home. Normally, he would have checked his rearview mirror. Normally, he would have doubled back to make sure he wasn't being followed. Today, though, he was so rattled by the feeling of impending doom at the diner, he did nothing he would've normally done. It would cost him dearly.

The Toyota pulled off the roadway about a mile back as the Honda pulled into a driveway several miles outside of town. The driveway led to an old farm house surrounded by acres and acres of wheat grass fields. Nick watched with a pair of aged Pentax binoculars. He'd used a similar pair on the streets, but they'd been destroyed in the drone strike on his home. He found another pair in a pawn shop in town and picked them up for pennies compared to what he'd originally paid. They felt vaguely comfortable and familiar. They were small and compact, 16x24 power lenses reached out and made the farm house come to life. Nick could see cameras on every corner. *Probably has sensors, too*, Nick thought. *Ground zero.* Nick laughed. *Cameras! As if they stopped anyone.* He started making a mental list of the things he would need to infiltrate the farm house.

Nick turned the truck around and headed back to town. Time to hit the gym, then home and Google Earth. He would have topographical and satellite maps of the area around the farm in incredible detail before the night was over.

Later that day at the gym, Nick was climbing the world's tallest building on a Versa Climber. The goal had been to achieve the peak in 20 minutes. He hadn't made it yet, but he felt invigorated by the breakthrough today in locating the Honda at the diner and following its owner to his lair. At 19 minutes and 58 seconds, he reached and then passed the virtual peak of the Burj Khalifa, the tallest building in the world. Ronnie James Dio screamed on his iPod they were the Last in Line. The cadence needed to reach the peak in 20 minutes was quite insane; anything less than 140 feet a minute, and it would be fruitless. He was dripping with sweat, his legs felt like rubber, and his arms ached from the lactic acid. The fatigue felt good for once.

Ali walked past as he finished and muttered, "Make sure you wipe off my equipment; it looks like shit when you're done sweating all over it."

He smiled and said, "Always do!" He understood this was her way of favorably acknowledging his hard work. The closest thing to a compliment she'd ever give anyone. Outside, the green Honda had just pulled up across the street. Like clockwork, this gym rat; he shows up, sweats a lot, then leaves. Observing him without him knowing was way too easy. The Driver smiled. The fear he'd felt earlier had disappeared. He felt back in control, on track. Soon enough, he'd figure out who the old gym rat really was, then begin the process of dismantling his world, one keystroke at a time. Typical muscle head, probably barely graduated high school and lived life lifting boxes, doing labor, and rarely did a synapse fire simultaneously with any other synapse between those empty ears. The Driver knew the type, the guy that got the girls, drove fast cars, and then once high school was finished, their lives went to shit. The real world hit, and they had to accept the life of the pond scum they were. Meanwhile, guys like him rose to the top of their respective fields. It would definitely be most satisfying to take this gym rat's life apart.

Meanwhile, arriving at LAX, Nõn was greeted by Carrie, her contact at NPR. The two women hugged, then walked to Carrie's grey Dodge Durango. Nõn had only a carry on, so they didn't have to wait for luggage. Nõn was excited to be back in the field, and she was looking forward to the challenge. Carrie explained as she navigated the difficult L.A. traffic that Nõn would be leaving on a flight in the morning, and she handed Nõn the tickets as she drove. Nõn saw they'd booked a seat on Virgin America Flight 232. It was an economy seat. She would change flights in Chicago, then travel on to Warsaw, Poland, where she'd board Polish Airlines Flight #769 and travel on to Odessa, Ukraine. The entire flight, with layovers and flight time, would take just over 20 hours. It was real! She was back in the field, doing the work she loved. In less than 48 hours, she would be among the Asgarda.

Carrie explained as she drove that she'd love to catch up, but things were hectic at NPR. She might have time for dinner with Nõn, and that was a maybe. The two women continued their small talk. Nõn had missed this, the urgency of the deadlines, the rush of traveling to different places and dealing with difficult people, then extracting a story and obtaining details most would have missed. This is what she had trained to do. She had been an incredible talent, and it felt good to be back in the mix.

The next day, Nõn arrived at LAX. Carrie had been unable to make the dinner date. It had been a short and sweet meeting with her friend, and the trip was about to begin. Nõn had learned some things about the Asgarda from videos and articles, but there wasn't much available. *All the better,* she thought, *good to be the first one to bring them into the light.* Some of the information was contradictory. In one article, there were over 150 members of the Asgarda; however, in a more recent video it appeared there were less than a dozen, and then those were mostly young girls, soft and frail and hardly warriors. Nõn watched that video repeatedly. There was something missing here. This video made the Asgarda look more like glorified Girl Scouts, definitely not formidable. If this was true, who had beaten the reporter NPR sent to do the story on them to a bloody pulp? A lot of unanswered questions; there was much here for her to learn, that was obvious.

32

Nõn began to outline the questions she had and the potential directions the piece she would be crafting could take. It was part of her tried and true process of understanding a subject from as many different angles as possible, then pursuing the angle that held the most truth and interest for the reader. Nõn had learned in her travels each piece had many truths, and perspectives. It was her job to bring to light the truth that best defined the subject she had been assigned to write about, but being open to the possibilities of that truth was the difficult part. Many times, she had arrived at a completely different perspective than she had expected. Had he been with her, Nick would have called this "seeing the world with new eyes." Additionally, he'd point out she needed to be open to the painful reality of the story instead of shaping it to fit into a zone of comfort for the reader. Nõn continued making her notes. Fortunately, the flight was long, for she had much preparation to do.

By the time Nõn landed in Odessa, Ukraine, she had a list of questions that needed answers. The more she watched the videos and read the articles about the Asgarda, she realized there must be more to the story. They were hiding something, but what and why?

Nõn was to meet with the founder of the Asgarda, Katerina Tarnouska. She founded the Asgarda in 2002. Nõn had to travel to the mountains of western Ukraine to the city of Skole, in the area of Lviv Oblast. From her research, she'd learned the area had been subject to many changes in culture, and national identity. At one time or another, the area had been annexed into Austria, Germany, Poland, and eventually Soviet Russia. The reason for the many countries' interest in the region was it was part of an important travel route from Kiev Ukraine to Hungary. The total population of Skole was approximately six thousand plus in 2013, a curiously small population center to house the reborn Amazons...perhaps that was the reason Katrina chose it? A lot of questions to be answered. Nõn was surprised to learn the only way to reach the Asgarda camp was by foot. An hour-long walk following foot paths that meandered here and there through heavily wooded mountains. Nõn finally arrived at the camp with the assistance of a guide sent by Katerina. She was shown to a tent and told their interview would begin in the morning. Nõn slept deeply that night. The trip had been long, and she was tired after the several miles' hike through the mountains.

The following morning, she was woken up by a young woman and told they'd be starting their morning run soon. Would she like to accompany them? Nõn asked if Katerina would be running with them? The girl said, "No." Nõn then declined. She was here to do the interview, and she asked the girl to show her where she could clean up, and maybe have a hot shower. The girl smiled and said, "Follow me," then took Nõn to a nearby mountain stream. There would be no hot shower. There was no running hot water in the remote area of the Carpathian Mountains. The girl smirked as she left Nõn to wash up. The passive message had been sent and received: she was no longer in the civilized area of Ukraine.

After Nõn had washed in the freezing cold mountain stream, she returned to her tent, where she noticed slight changes: someone had been in her tent and gone through her things, then put them back; almost perfectly, but not quite. She'd expected some level of suspicion from the Asgarda, especially since the information on the Web was just so inconsistent. Every interview and article contradicted the others.

About an hour later, the girls returned from their run. They were exactly what the video had shown: young girls, hardly formidable. They washed and laughed in the cold water, screaming and giggling like teenage girls anywhere would. Nõn watched and thought, *What if this is it? This is the Asgarda?* The girls finished, then prepared for breakfast.

Nõn finally met Katerina and was given the standard well-rehearsed tour and speeches about the founding of the Asgarda and the purpose of giving the women of Ukraine a better sense of self. Katerina explained the Amazons were historically occupants of what had become Ukraine, according to the Greek historian Herodotus. Other historians placed the Amazons in modern Iran and Syria, but Katerina chose to believe Herodotus' account. Nõn was politely attentive and made notes and asked appropriate questions. She received appropriate answers. The entire interview was very canned and rehearsed. Nõn waited until she felt Katerina was sufficiently comfortable her questions had been answered, then began the real interview.

"I appreciate that you have allowed me to be your guest here, but I do have a few questions, if you would be so inclined?"

"Of course. Please ask me your questions."

"OK. First, the Amazons are considered historically to be fierce warriors, capable of defeating any man on the planet in hand-to-hand combat, and that was in a time of very intense warfare in this region. The girls I have been witness to here at the camp this very morning are just that: girls, giggling and laughing; not formidable warriors worthy of the Amazon legacy.

"Second, according to the Web references I have read, there were 150 members of the Asgarda in 2009. Today, I counted 10 total present in the camp, and that includes you and the alleged trainers of the giggling, happy girls you call your Asgarda. What has happened to the Asgarda since 2009? Did the rest of the women leave? Did you have a falling out among the members?"

The questions continued on. Nõn pointed out in one video, there was an interview with a man who was reported to be Katerina's trainer in kickboxing and martial arts. He claimed women fought more emotionally than men, and men had learned to control their emotions in battle, while women had not. He also said it was a woman's first duty to give birth to children.

Nõn continued. "Is that an official view of the Asgarda? Women are bound by duty to give birth to children, and that is their first duty? Seriously? No disrespect to you or your Asgarda, but from what I have seen so far, the girls here in your camp are barely a step up from the girls I saw walking the streets in Odessa, in far too short skirts to send any message other than sexual availability. Additionally, I think those women would be more formidable in a fight than any of the girls in your camp."

Katerina was obviously displeased with Nõn's tone and the content of her questions. Her face had hardened, and her eyes, previously bright and playful, were now hard and cold.

"The reports of our numbers in the article you refer to were greatly exaggerated. That was a Russian media ploy to tie our organization to politics. We made the mistake of supporting a popular woman politician and wore shirts showing our support of her. The media then referred to us as her Amazon army."

Nõn replied, "Am I to understand, then, that this entire Asgarda society, your 'Amazons reborn', is a small group of virginal high school age girls who can barely defend themselves? Seriously? Katerina, you do remember the male reporter we sent to do this piece a short while ago? He was sent home badly beaten. Are you asking me to believe he was beaten up in a teenage pillow fight with these girls?"

Katerina stood and glared at Nõn. "Our interview is over. You have been very discourteous and will be escorted from the camp in the morning. Good day."

Nõn hoped her challenge had been heard by whomever actually ran the Asgarda. This group was hopefully a front; if not, she had come a long way for nothing. She could have spoken to more formidable female warriors in Moses Lake.

Nõn returned to her tent and prepared for either the trip home or a visit from the actual leadership of the Asgarda.

Dinner that night at the camp was very uncomfortable. The girls were extremely quiet. No one looked at or spoke to Nõn. The meal was served on a crude wood table similar to an American picnic table, and the food was simple and basic. Nõn noticed there were forks, spoons and knives – and remarkably – paper napkins at each place setting. Really? Modern Amazons used paper napkins at their meals? The meal was over with quickly, then Nõn went back to her tent and lay down.

CHAPTER NINE

Nõn must have eventually fallen asleep, because she was woken up by the sound of footsteps approaching her tent. It was pitch black outside; there was no moon to light the meadow in which her tent had been pitched. She had no idea of what to expect, but she prepared for a fight. Nõn immediately and quietly stood, prepared for an attack. She listened and heard nothing. The night had become eerily silent. Several moments passed, and still she heard nothing. Had she been dreaming? The attack came quickly and quietly. She fought back but was quickly overwhelmed and subdued by several assailants. Her hands were secured behind her back and a hood made of crude fabric of some kind placed over her head. She was dragged out into the night and the primordial forest. Not one of her captors had spoken a single word during her abduction; to her, that implied extreme discipline. Under the hood, Nõn smiled, despite being tied and bound in the middle of the night. This was an improvement over the mindless tasks she'd carried out at the diner less than a week earlier. She was afraid, no doubt, but she also felt alive for the first time in months.

Nõn was dragged for some time; the actual distance she had no idea of, but it was somewhere far from the camp. She listened to the footsteps of her captors and counted 5 distinct patterns. Most had the same approximate gait; one, however, had legs apparently much longer than the rest. That gait was much slower, and the footfalls more substantial. After who knows how long, they stopped and Nõn was dropped abruptly to the ground. Still not a word had been spoken by her captors. There was nothing but silence.

Nõn waited. She heard what sounded like a large fire, the wood occasionally popping as the tree sap exploded. She listened and heard some milling around, but nothing else. Then finally, a set of footsteps approached. Her hood was removed and her bonds cut. She rubbed her wrists as she looked around her at a large circle of formidable women, all glaring at her disapprovingly.

"You are the Asgarda, I assume?"

No reply came. Just hardened glares. Stone faces showing no emotion. Finally, one of the women spoke.

"We are who you have come to see. We will see if you deserve to be in our presence. To earn our respect, you must face the warrior of your choosing. Pick one of us to do battle with. Should you at least hold your own against her, we will consider your request to speak with us. Do you agree?"

Nõn replied, "I assume I have no choice, since none was given in being brought here. Yes, I agree."

Again the woman spoke, "Choose your opponent, then, Nõnkos Zia."

Nõn got up and brushed her clothing off, then replied, "Anyone will do, I suppose. Why don't one of you step into the circle? I assume we fight within the circle."

The request was answered immediately. A stocky woman, heavily muscled, stepped into the circle and began to disrobe from the waist up.

"It is our custom to do battle naked from the waist up. Hopefully, you have some training in the martial arts, Nõnkos Zia. Your male predecessor had none and was quickly dispatched."

As the Asgarda opponent disrobed, the women started to speak words of encouragement to her; the group started to liven up as the thought of their friend in battle with Nõn excited them. The woman handed her clothing to someone in the crowd surrounding them and turned to face Nõn, Nõn saw she was extremely fit. She thought regretfully, *Perhaps I should have picked someone after all, someone smaller, less formidable. Too late now.*

Nõn said, "I prefer to fight with my clothes on, thank you."

The voice said, "No, that is not our custom. Do not dishonor our customs as your predecessor did. That would not be wise."

Nõn sighed deeply, then slowly began to unbutton her shirt. When she'd finally removed her shirt and dropped it to the ground, she turned and faced her opponent.

There was silence for a very long time as the story of her scarred body was absorbed by the now stunned and quiet group of women. No one moved. No one spoke. For Nõn, it was an experience she'd had over and over again. The horror of her scarring spoke for itself. There were no tears among the Asgarda, but their collective feeling of animosity towards her had diminished.

Nõn's opponent turned and spoke in the local dialect to someone in the group. There was a response Nõn couldn't understand, then her opponent faced her again.

"We will speak in English for your benefit, agreed?"

Nõn replied, "Yes, agreed."

"Our leader would like to know where and when your scars originated."

Nõn replied, "My scars originated in my childhood. I received them in my homeland of Africa." Her accent began to thicken.

Silence again.

A voice came from the group; Nõn couldn't tell from who. The voice spoke for several minutes in the native dialect. No one moved.

Finally, Nõn's opponent spoke in English. "Our contest will have to be on a day other than this. Our leader has decided we shall accept that you have shown already by the scars your body bears that you are deserving of our respect. Do you agree to these terms?"

At once, Nõn felt both ashamed and relieved. She didn't wish to be pitied for her scars and the abuse she'd endured. She also had no desire to fight this woman for no reason other than to prove herself.

Nõn replied, "I do not accept these terms as you have stated them. Ask whomever is making this choice, is our fight postponed out of pity? And if that so, then no, I do not accept, nor will I ever accept these terms. Period." Her accent was now thick and heavy. The change in her speech was noted immediately.

The group was silent. The opponent was silent. Finally, the group split and a woman walked into the circle, her footsteps heavy and the gait long and slow. She was very tall and heavily muscled. Her gaze was intense and confident. She left absolutely no doubt in Nõn's mind that she was the single most formidable woman she'd ever seen. Heavily muscled shoulders, arms, legs and back. Raven black hair fell carelessly around her shoulders. She walked directly towards Nõn with a purposeful stride. Nõn noticed a heavy sword sheathed at her waist. She stood in front of Nõn and looked directly into her eyes; Nõn returned the gaze defiantly, her neck craned upwards. No words were spoken for several minutes, the two women assessing each other's character.

The tall woman finally broke her gaze and quickly reached for Nõn's shirt, picking it up and handing it to her. "We have no pity here, Nõnkos Zia. We do, however, have respect for women warriors, which I see you are. Please join us as a guest."

Nõn accepted her shirt and began to dress. The mood of the group of women transformed instantly. The previously oppressively tense air suddenly changed to a peaceful camaraderie. The Asgarda leader walked back into the group and disappeared, then another woman approached and spoke. "I have been assigned as your liaison. I will answer your questions and facilitate your interviews. I am pleased to meet you." Nõn asked her name. "My name is Katrena Rebrova."

Nõn asked, "And her name? What is her name?" Nõn nodded as the tall woman disappeared into the night.

"She prefers Westerners like yourself call her Bexx. Her first name in our language sounds like 'Taco'. When she was in America, she said, she learned that name had a slang meaning she did not care for. So, she adopted Bexx. Only her closest allies are allowed to call her by her real name."

"And her last name?"

"No one here knows. We do not ask. She is intensely private about her name and her past. Everyone here has a past, some darker than others. I think, judging from your scars, you do as well."

Nõn nodded. "Yes, we all do."

Katerna said, "Come, meet the rest of the Asgarda."

CHAPTER TEN

The latest files on the potential candidate for the facilitator of Camp Cachibaché were delivered to The Director. The files were thick and contained the most intimate details about the candidate's personal and professional life. Arthur felt sure The Director would be pleased with the depth of the investigation. The Director had received the files in their entirety this morning, and he'd asked not to be disturbed while he perused the information. Several hours later, The Director activated the interoffice communication network and asked Arthur to step in. Arthur knocked at the door and waited.

"Come in, Arthur."

"Yes, sir, how may I help you?"

"Yes, Arthur. First off, are there any messages pending I need to address?"

"No, sir, your morning schedule is still clear."

"Excellent. Arthur, these files are superb! Please extend my congratulations and appreciation to our investigative unit."

"I will, sir! Glad you're pleased with their work."

"I am exceedingly! Please reach out to this woman and set up an appointment for an interview as soon as possible. Make it clear we will pay for her travel expenses. I see she was recently fired from her last position, and we want to be able to take advantage of those circumstances. Let's make this a priority. I want an interview date and time secured today. Get on this right away before she secures some other employment."

"Yes, sir."

Arthur left the office in a rush. He understood when The Director was this enthusiastic about a candidate, it was unique and the timing was critical. He began making the necessary phone calls, and once the appointment was set, he arranged for travel and lodging. Arthur returned to The Director's office door and knocked.

"Yes, Arthur, come in."

"Sir, the arrangements have been made. The interview is scheduled for tomorrow afternoon. The candidate will be staying at our usual lodging facilities. As with our previous candidates, I've made the arrangements for video and audio surveillance to be prepared and installed in her room."

"Excellent, Arthur. Good work."

"Thank you, sir."

Arthur understood immediately from The Director's body language he'd been dismissed, then left the office.

The following day, the candidate arrived at The Director's office. The live feeds from the surveillance of her room had been made available to The Director all morning. He watched carefully and smiled; she was exactly as he'd hoped: well educated, polite, refined, and a psychopath – all excellent traits for the position of facilitator.

Ten minutes before the interview had been set to begin, Arthur notified The Director the candidate had arrived. The Director smiled; she was punctual as well.

"Arthur, please send her in."

The woman entered The Director's office and smiled happily.

"Hello, I'm Doctor Lennie Warsaw," she said as she extended her hand to shake The Director's.

"Doctor Warsaw, welcome. Please sit down. May I offer you a drink?"

"Please, yes. What do you have?"

"What would you like? I have Macallan, fifty-year-old single malt scotch, if you would like a glass."

"Oh no, no, I don't drink alcohol ever. I'd like a glass of water, or perhaps a Diet Coke if that would be available."

The Director poured the smoky dark liquid into his beautifully cut Cash Crystal whiskey glasses and picked it up with a cloth napkin. He walked back to his desk and picked up the phone.

"Arthur, please secure a Diet Coke and a glass with ice for our guest while I begin the interview."

"Yes, sir, right away."

"Doctor Warsaw, I hope your flight was comfortable?"

"Yes, sir, thank you."

"And the room, it is to your liking?"

"Yes, again very nice. Thank you, for asking."

The Director smiled and nodded. "Please, call me Oelsen." The Director smiled as he started to outline the parameters of the interview. "Doctor Warsaw, just so we're clear: I'm looking for a particular skill set, which I'm hopeful you possess. For me to be able to determine if you do in fact possess these skills, I'm going to ask you a series of questions you wouldn't normally be comfortable answering. This will not be a typical interview. It will require your utmost honesty."

"Well, of course, Oelsen. I'd be happy to answer any and all questions you ask. And please call me Lennie."

"Fine, Lennie. First of all, can you tell me about the circumstances in which you found yourself seeking employment?"

Lennie smiled uncomfortably and began to detail a long, drawn out explanation which described her vacating her last job; it left out the details about her being fired for misappropriating funds and failing to make deadlines. She'd been granted a position as a department head at an international university and had been found most lacking in the position.

The Director made notes. The files he'd been given on Lennie disclosed she was a diagnosed psychopath, and he expected her to lie about the circumstances surrounding her dismissal; it was a promising sign.

The Director nodded. "Uh huh." He made a few notes. He made the silence extend uncomfortably for several minutes, just staring at her, saying nothing, noting there was a peculiar odor in the room of barely masked body odor and perfume. He made an additional note to check on her personal hygiene habits in the files. Then as he looked up he noticed her teeth. They were perfect, too perfect. He made another note in the files.

Lennie smiled and smiled. Five minutes had passed, and she felt incredibly uncomfortable. She stood suddenly and walked to the liquor cabinet, commenting on the contents.

"I see you have 6 wine bottles here, as well as the scotch. Do you drink wine, Oelsen?"

"Occasionally I do, yes. I like the way they round out my cabinet."

Lennie reached for a glass while The Director watched in anticipation. He smiled at the inevitable conclusion of her picking up a glass.

Lennie picked up the glass and immediately cried out. Blood began to flow through the intricate designs on the deadly crystal glass.

The Director handed her a cloth and told her to keep the hand elevated. He didn't end the interview, but instead just continued as he explained, "I hope you appreciate the elegance of my crystal glasses while also recognizing they're at the same time lethal. I had them specially made."

The formerly uncomfortable, insane smile that had been on Lennie's face was now replaced with a very strained, tense attempt at a smile. It waxed and waned as she wondered what to expect next.

The Director finally dove into the files he had on Lennie. He asked about her history of mental illness and asked for verification that she'd gone into psychology in her academic studies in an attempt to understand her own issues. She nodded yes.

"And I see here in your daughter's medical records you made a request that during her own therapy, that a post-hypnotic suggestion be made to enable you to control her?"

Lennie uncomfortably said, "Um, yes, I did."

"And is it still effective?"

"At times, yes."

He went on to describe how a friend of hers had been interviewed and detailed a disturbing account Lennie had told of her and her husband using a cocktail of prescription drugs on that same daughter to induce an incident of sleepwalking, which they then documented with a video camera and used to write a paper for an Abnormal Psychology class. "You both received an A on the paper, I see."

The smile that had been slightly present on Lennie's face was now gone. She replied in an irritated voice, "Well, the way you frame it sounds so, um, heartless and diabolical. I mean, we did make sure she was safe, and we only used pharmaceutical grade prescriptions. It wasn't like we used street drugs."

"But you did experiment, an unethical experiment, on your own daughter, correct?"

"Yes, I suppose, if you choose to frame it that way."

The Director nodded. "I do. That is exactly how I choose to frame it." He looked over the top of the papers he held in his hand with a stern look. "This bit of information in particular interests me. I see that during your daughter's initial therapy, she disclosed in a session that she confronted you about the sexual abuse she experienced at the hands of your father. She told her therapist that when she confronted you about it, you acknowledged that you knew he was abusing her and did nothing about it. Why? I'm curious why you did nothing to protect her, knowing your father was sexually abusing her? Did he abuse you?"

Lennie, now stripped of all her social façade, began, "Yes, I knew he'd abused her. And I told her at the time she confronted me that no matter what he'd done to her, he'd done much worse to me. She was very angry and couldn't understand that I was looking out for her best interests."

"Perhaps you could explain how you were looking out for her interests while abandoning her at five years old with a man you knew would sexually, physically and emotionally abuse her. By the way, it says here you were enrolled in school at the time and had fought for custody of her, then left her with your father and returned only occasionally to check in. Is that accurate?"

Lennie said nothing to explain her actions, but she did say, "Yes, that is correct."

The Director replied, "I see."

The Director continued to detail one event after another, most criminal in scope and at the very least indicating a mind seriously compromised and flawed.

Finally, he said, "Have you ever been diagnosed as possessing any psychological disorders during your own therapy?"

Lennie, stern faced, replied, "I would guess you already have that answer in your paperwork."

The Director nodded. "Yes, I do, but I would like to hear it from your own mouth."

Lennie hesitated. This wasn't the interview she'd hoped for. The Director knew her most intimate secrets, and she was a little bit worried what else he might know about her. "I was diagnosed as having Obsessive Compulsive Disorder and was treated with electroshock therapy."

"And the treatment? It was successful?"

Lennie nodded affirmatively but said nothing.

"Any other diagnosis you would like to share?"

"No."

"I see here you were diagnosed as a first facet or Factor 1 Psychopath. Is that correct?"

Lennie responded abruptly, "What the hell does it matter?"

The Director cringed and slowly put down his paperwork. He glared at her darkly and said, "Excuse me?" The tension in the room was unbearable; The Director hated vulgarity. Up until this point, Lennie had performed perfectly. She was everything he'd hoped she'd be. But then she'd slipped up and shown him her more vulgar side.

"Lennie, I am looking for a person of peculiar skills and abilities to run a rather delicate psychological...shall we say experiment. I do expect you to maintain professionalism at all times. I have reviewed hundreds of potential candidates, and you are at the top of that list at the moment; however, I will not tolerate such language. If this is an indication of who you are, then I must know now. Is it?"

"I apologize, Oelsen. I misspoke. It was unprofessional of me and should not have occurred. Please forgive me. And to answer your question, yes, I was given that diagnosis." She smiled and straightened the wrinkles of her pant suit with her uninjured hand.

"Excellent. Arthur, you may bring in Dr. Warsaw's drink now."

"Actually, Oelsen, if I may, I think I'd actually like a small glass of Macallan, if the offer still stands." Lennie smiled as she felt a droplet of sweat slowly sliding down the skin of the small of her lower back.

The Director smiled. "Why, of course." He got up from behind his desk, went to the bar, and poured her a drink much larger than she'd requested. He handed it to her carefully wrapped in a cloth and smiled. "Now, you know to be careful with my beautiful glasses; they tend to bite if you aren't mindful of their dark side."

Lennie smiled and began to sip at the caramel colored Macallan. An hour later, she was considerably more comfortable and relaxed.

The Director continued. "I have one final question. I see here you enrolled your daughter in a modeling agency. She was to participate in a photo shoot with a photographer that had, shall we say, questionable motives. The report says she was 14 and expected to model in a bikini. Correct?"

"Yes, it is," Lennie said cheerfully, then took a larger swallow of the Macallan.

"My report indicates you knew this particular photographer liked to recruit young girls for movies of a sexual nature and your daughter was being actively recruited. You knew this?"

"Yes. She was a very attractive young woman, and we felt she may have a promising future in that industry. So, my husband and I sought out the photographer and enrolled her in his agency. We felt given her sexual history, this may provide her with a more acceptable outlet for her interests."

The Director replied, "By her sexual history, you mean her promiscuity? Primarily a result of your own father's abuse?"

"Yes, exactly."

The Director put down his papers and queued the interoffice communications. "Arthur, please bring in the contract for Doctor Warsaw to review."

As they waited, Lennie spoke, "What exactly is the position I'm interviewing for?"

The Director detailed the direction in which he wanted Camp Cachibaché to go. It was to be located remotely. The clients were brought to the camp under the guise of receiving therapy for a variety of phobias. Their treatment was supposed to be a new and revolutionary version of systematic desensitizing therapy which would "cure" them of their phobias; in reality, the sessions were designed to do the opposite and create a state of panic and terror, the idea being to produce the greatest amount of terror imaginable in each client. The sessions were to be filmed and the unedited copies of those sessions sold to the highest bidder.

When The Director finished explaining the finer details of Cachibaché's real agenda, he asked Lennie, "Would you be interested in being the psychological director of this camp?"

Lennie responded exuberantly, "Yes, most definitely."

Arthur brought in the contract and handed it to Lennie.

"I am sure you will find our offer most lucrative. If there is any question, let me know."

"I do have one small request. As an academic, publishing is extremely important for my status in the field. Would I perhaps be able to publish any results of these tests? I understand most tests are going to result in an outcome the academic community would view in a less than favorable manner; however, it would be an absolute treasure of abnormal psychological data."

The Director smiled and responded, "Of course we can discuss that. I am sure we can come to some sort of agreement."

Lennie was openly surprised at the salary and benefits she'd been offered, and she felt remarkably comfortable after the interview. Finally, someone appreciated the gifts she brought to the table. She stood and said, "Oelsen, I'm sure I'll give you the results you're looking for in your camp."

"I believe you will, Doctor Warsaw." The Director smiled as she walked out of the office.

Later that night, The Director watched the live feed from Lennie's room. She had disrobed and was washing her underwear in the bathroom sink. Afterwards, she sat down on the couch and began to chew on her fingernails; *Nothing too peculiar there,* he thought. He was then horrified as she pulled up her left foot to her mouth and began to chew on her toenails. A disgusted look crossed his face.

"Arthur, come in here."

Arthur came into the room. "Yes, sir?"

"Come and look at this. Tell me, am I seeing this correctly?"

Arthur walked around the desk and looked at the live feed as Lennie began chewing enthusiastically on the next toenail. The two men were silent and horrified. Arthur softly whispered, "Good Lord, sir, that is quite alarming."

"Yes, it is."

Just when they thought it could not get any more disgusting, she stopped and pulled out her dentures and examined them. A toenail had become lodged in-between the teeth, and she attempted to remove it.

"Auugh!" the two men blurted out in unison as they each turned away from the screen in disgust. The Director thought to himself, *Well, that answers the question I had about her teeth. They aren't hers.*

"I have seen enough, Arthur. Thank you for verifying that I was not mistaken."

"No, sir, you were not. It is alarming, but she does have the necessary skill set you require for the camp."

"True, she does lack any empathy, and that will be critical for the test's success."

46

CHAPTER ELEVEN

Nearly 10 days had passed since Nŏn had arrived in the Asgarda Camp. Nick, meanwhile, had been busy in his off time planning his incursion into The Driver's "bat cave." He waited for the first day of the new moon and made his move. The Driver had no idea of the human nightmare that was heading his way.

Nick had located several static surveillance cameras, and using Google Earth he'd determined the best direction to approach the farm house. There was a slight fold in the field to the west and rear of the house. He planned to approach the house using that fold, then take out the camera that provided eyes on that approach. Nick had purchased a Crossman pump pellet gun and an ATN X sight day/night scope. It took some adaptation to make the two compatible, but it had been a workable solution for his needs. He'd planned on approaching the house just before dawn and shooting out the camera lens, making it shatter, but not making the camera electronically stop working; the idea was that The Driver would run remote diagnostics on the camera and see that it checked out, but he would be unable to see Nick's approach until it was too late.

Nick approached at night, as he had planned, after hiding his truck in a heavily wooded field approximately a mile away. He approached wearing all black 511 tactical gear and a Balaclava. His hands were also covered with black leather gloves. Anyone who happened to have a bad case of insomnia that night would have been unable to detect his movement on the moonless night.

Turning on the scope and targeting the camera, Nick took his first shot and missed.

The focus on the scope was off, and not for the first time, or the last. Nick cursed under his breath; age had taken a toll on his formerly 20/15 vision as well. Another shot, and another miss. Nick laughed and whispered, frustrated with himself as he pumped up the air pressure on the pellet gun. "It's the little things you miss as you get older. Old age blows!"
The next shot hit the lens and shattered it. Nick let loose a small celebratory "Yeah! About damn time."

Nick hunkered down and waited as the sun slowly started to rise.

Inside the "bat cave", The Driver was waking. He'd planned on a quick check of the cameras, then he would head to town and watch the greying old man go through his gym rat routine. He had to admit, he admired the old goat's tenacity. He kept at it on a consistent basis. The Driver discovered one of the cameras had a dead screen. He conducted a system check and discovered the camera was electronically functioning, but the picture had been lost at 0300 hours, according to the video feed. One second it was crystal clear, the next it was distorted. This kind of malfunction had happened before; a moth had landed on the camera lens. Another time, a perfectly timed bird dropping had christened the lens on one of his cameras. These things happened. It was part of having 24/7/365 coverage. The Driver checked the perimeter alarms and saw nothing had been triggered. No worries, he would head out to the parking lot and take his final notes on Nick's routine, then head back to the bat cave to begin his attack. When he was done with the old man, he would have no financial backing or credit cards, and his driver's license would show revoked. Outstanding warrants for assault on a police officer would appear on the national databases, and cops took a special interest in offenders who harmed one of their own. The old man would never know what had hit him till it all came crashing down around him. The Driver smiled at the thought. This would teach the old man for daring to think he could catch The Driver.

Nick watched from the field as The Driver walked around the house and looked at the camera positions on the corner of the house, just under one of the roof's soffits; it appeared to be normal. He checked his cell phone for the time and saw he had to leave now to be at the gym for his final surveillance. Time enough to fix the camera later. The Driver hurried off, jumped in his green Honda, and drove out of the driveway.

The Driver arrived at the gym and checked the parking lot for the rusted Toyota. It wasn't there yet. That was a good thing. He liked to arrive and get set up. Have a cup of coffee ready, and his notepad as well, to take notes should something catch his eye. He parked in a different parking place than he had the previous day and waited. An hour later, still no Nick. The Driver wondered out loud, "Maybe the old man is sick? Perhaps he's been called in to work?" He drove to Nick's work and did a drive through of the parking lot. No truck here either.

"Ground control to Major Tom," The Driver mumbled. "Take your protein pills and put your helmet on."

The Driver stopped and thought to himself, *Where could he be?*

After checking a few of the local restaurants and finding no sign of the truck, he decided to head home and check the old man's debit card and bank account. Perhaps the old man had finally recognized it would be a bad idea and had bugged out. The digital record of his financials would show something if that were the case.

The Driver stopped in his favorite local restaurant, "Simmer", and ordered lunch to go. The restaurant specialized in serving only locally grown food that was also organic. His mouth watered as he spoke to Yvonne, the hostess, and ordered his usual beet salad and chicken waffles. He paid her and waited for the order to be prepared. When his order was complete, he nodded to her and thanked her again for their quick, prompt service.

The Driver arrived at the farm house less than 20 minutes later and entered the home whistling. It had been an interesting day; first the camera, then the gym rat had broken from his pattern of behavior. No matter, he would rain down havoc on the old man's parade soon enough.

The Driver unlocked the door and heard the alarm sounding on the exterior alarm system's monitoring panel.

"Now what?" he said out loud as he entered the large computer room filled with monitors. He sat in his La-Z-Boy Captain's chair and pulled up the alarm system on his monitor. The system had both motion and metallic sensors buried underground, creating an alarmed perimeter around the old farm house. Both sensor systems had gone off.

"That's not good," The Driver said. "That's not good at all."

He checked the sensor sector that had alarmed and realized it was the sector directly in front of the malfunctioning camera.

"Oh, shit," he blurted out. The realization hit him a moment too late. He turned, and there was Nick dressed in black, the barrel of a Para Ordinance GI expert .45 caliber handgun pointed at his head.

The Mongoose and The Cobra

"Hi there. I saw your profile on Tinder and thought I'd introduce myself. You're the profile 'Man seeks NSA encounter', aren't you?"

The Driver was speechless for a moment, then answered, "How did you get in here? I know my rights; you can't enter my home without a warrant!"

"Oh, let me guess, someone's attended a criminal justice class or two and thinks they know the law. Well, first things first, Mr. Lonely Heart." Nick tossed a roll of duct tape to The Driver and told him to wrap the tape around his left arm and the armrest of the chair he was sitting in.

The Driver said, "Screw you. I'm calling my lawyer. This is harassment. I'll have your job by the end of the day."

Nick's eyes narrowed; apparently, The Driver was very slow on the uptake. He fired one round into the chair, just missing The Driver's right ear and blowing a hole out the back of the chair before finally stopping embedded in the wood paneling.

"Just so we're clear. I'm serious about the Tinder ad; I'm not happy with how you've ignored my friend requests on Facebook either. You know the saying, 'Hell hath no fury?' Here I am, scorned and furious."

The Driver was confused and frightened. This guy was unhinged; he kept mumbling about social media and some dating site ad...what the hell was going on?

Nick repeated, "The tape! Get started, or the next bullet will find its new home in your right knee, you sexy animal."

The Driver started quickly wrapping the tape around his right arm, breathing rapidly in a state of panic. When he had finished, he turned to Nick and said, "There, it's done. OK?"

Nick rolled his eyes. "No attention to detail. Already, we're starting off on the wrong foot. Is this any way to start out our first date? Good thing we didn't meet in a restaurant. You undoubtedly would have wanted to take charge and order for both of us, and then done it poorly. All you 'Fifty Shades' men are so bossy."

The Driver was at a loss; terror had a stranglehold on his mind. He'd always manipulated the environment online and avoided personal contact with his victims. This was an encounter he had no frame of reference for. His brain was shutting down, and he was experiencing tunnel vision.

Nick approached him and tore off the tape from his right arm.

"First, Princess, I asked you to tape the left arm, but no bother; I understand what it means to be dismissed. No one listens until they realize I will not be ignored."

Nick started to wrap the tape around The Driver's left arm. When it was secure, he said, "Now, I'm going to leave your feet free. It's not that I don't like the idea of you being tied up and unable to resist my romantic advances, but I do like the idea of you having some freedom of movement while we make beautiful music together."

The Driver whined in a terror-filled stupor, "What the hell are you talking about? I'm not interested in men, and I put no ads on Tinder. Are you off your medication or something? What the hell is this?"

"Always play hard to get, don't we? No bother, we'll take some time to get acquainted before we get started. First off, my name is Nick. And you are?"

The Driver told Nick his name. "I'm Michael Spacy."

"Hi, Mike. Now, is that your real name, or is that an alias?"

"It's my name," The Driver answered, not admitting it was an alias, one of many he used.

"I understand. I too have a couple of names; one being William, the other Nick. Some people call me a space cowboy, some call me the gangster of love."

The Driver was more confused; the line sounded familiar, like maybe from a movie or something. This guy was psychotic, that was clear. He responded, "OK."

Nick smiled. "So what's in the bag? Eats, I hope. I'm starved. You see, I've been out in the field behind your house all night, waiting. I thought I'd thought of everything for our first date, but I forgot the pizza and wine." Nick opened the bag, then said to The Driver, "You don't mind, do you?"

"No, no, by all means, have some."

"Thanks, don't mind if I do."

Nick ate and smiled at The Driver as he watched. Finally, when the chicken waffles were gone, he placed the bag on the table near The Driver.

"Shall we begin now in earnest, Mike? Feeling up to the challenge of our first date?"

The Driver didn't answer. He was suddenly aware Nick was no longer smiling, and the look in his eyes was suddenly murderously serious.

"So, why have you been conducting surveillance on me? And be aware of this: I don't have a lot of patience for bullshit. Truth will get you a long ways, Mike, so think about your answers before you blurt them out. Why are you watching me?"

The Driver thought long and hard. This wasn't what he expected it to be like when he was finally apprehended. He'd been living on the fringes of the Dark Web for so long, he'd forgotten what it was like to live any other way. Finally, he answered, "I've been watching you to figure out why you're back in Moses Lake. I dropped you off on my bus route a few months ago; I know, because I checked the video from the bus to verify it. Now here you are, back in Moses Lake with a new name and acting like you've never been here before. It made me suspicious."

"Excellent memory, Mike. Yes, I was here, but you already know that. You work for that piece of human garbage, The Director, and are imbedded here, am I right? Keeping an eye on Moses Hole and reporting back to the man?"

"What? Who is The Director? What are you talking about? I can't tell when you're serious or not. Is this part of that whole Tinder thing?"

Nick sighed. "Time to get real, my friend; every wrong answer will begin to cost you. Please listen, for your own benefit. What is it you do here with all these computers? This is some big-time hardware for little ole Moses Hole. What's the deal?"

The Driver replied, "You already know why. I'm a hacker, you know this, and you're in my house without a warrant. I don't care who you work for; wearing your ninja pajamas doesn't mean shit to me. I'm a citizen…"

"Stop, stop, stop," Nick interrupted impatiently. "Did I not mention that wrong answers would cost you painfully?"

Nick removed a knife from the waist of his 511 pants and opened the blade until it locked into place. He placed the blade under the pinky finger of The Driver's left hand and shoved it slowly under the fingernail. When it was deep enough under the nail, he pried the nail off the finger and placed it on the table in front of the now hysterically screaming hacker.

"Now that you realize I'm no ordinary hookup on Tinder, perhaps we should begin again? What do you think? Do you have a little more clarity now that some pain has quietly entered the room? Or do you need further motivation?"

The Driver nodded in the affirmative; he was now sweating profusely and breathing rapidly. "OK, I'll be straight with you: my name isn't Michael."

"That's a good start. Continue."

"I'm a hacker. I've spent the last 20 years of my life hiding in plain sight, working a day job and appearing to be no one important. In my off time, I hack anything and everything and sell the information I find to the highest bidder. That's why all the equipment. I use computer muscle to overwhelm systems and extract information by force."

"Hacker? Seriously, you expect me to believe you watched me because you're a hacker?"

"It's the truth. I can prove it: Google my hacker name, and it'll come up. I go by several names online, but mostly I'm known in hacker communities as The Driver."

"The Driver? That's not even original."

"Ya, I thought it was kind of ironic since when I'm on my day job, I drove for Greyhound, at least until you showed up. I was sure the FBI or NSA had finally caught up to me when I saw you. I figured I needed to disappear; I'd been in one place too long or perhaps slipped up on my security protocols."

Nick sat silent for some time, watching The Driver's eyes and body language. The removal of the fingernail should have impressed on him the seriousness of his current status. The hacker's story flowed from him too easily to be made up.

"OK, Mr. Anderson, let's play a little game: I talk, and you listen. When I'm done, you'll have 30 minutes to tell me something about my little story I don't know. If you fail, you lose another fingernail. Are we clear?"

"Yes, clear. I'll need my hands free to type."

"You'll get one hand free; the other is mine if you fail. Keep in mind, Mr. Anderson, you have 19 more nails I can remove just as delicately. We can be here all damn day if you choose. I really don't care."

Nick sat down and told The Driver his story about Camp Baroota. He included all the details and people's names, including the drone strike on his mountain home. When he finished, he said, "Any questions?"

"Jesus Christ, is that real? I mean, I've seen some shitty operations the government has covered up, but nothing that diabolical. So that's real, then?"

"You tell me, Mr. Anderson. Thirty minutes, starting now, and please don't spend your time staring at the woman in the red dress. I am very real, and the clock is ticking."

Every five minutes, Nick reminded The Driver the clock was ticking. The purpose was to crank up his stress level; it worked. The Driver was sweating, his one hand dancing over the keyboard erratically. At twenty minutes left, he said, "Here it is, the plane crash, you're right, this did happen! Those sons of bitches!" The Driver kept at it while Nick watched. If The Driver was faking it, he was a very skilled liar. He was in an environment in which he was obviously very comfortable. The more he searched, the less he paid attention to his wounded finger. The hacker was in the flow. It reminded Nick of a conversation he had with Joanna during her doctoral program. She'd mentioned "Flow" and an article written by the Hungarian psychologist Mihaly Csikszentmihalyi. Flow was a highly focused mental state, similar to a basketball player's feeling of being in the zone during a game where they just couldn't miss a shot. Nick grimaced; he hated how he still remembered Joanna fondly, in spite of the fact she'd set him up to be killed in Baroota.

"HA! I got some shit here I know you never mentioned about the dirty little government hand job you were given!"

The Driver was elated, his damaged finger long forgotten. Nick thought, not for the last time as he watched the man, he was truly in the flow. Gone was The Driver's terror and anxiety. Here in this world, he ruled supreme. Despite being shot at and having his fingernail peeled off, here he was, fearless – hell, cocky even.

"OK, Mr. Anderson, show me what you got. Still five minutes left to go; are you sure you don't want the extra time?"

"HA! No, this is my world. No way you know what I've found," he said smugly.

"OK, spill it, my sexy man crush, and don't leave out any details."

"So you mentioned the drone strike – which by the way is illegal as hell on American soil, government bastards! I found the Web evidence of the fire. The strike had been covered up with false information. Typical government bullshit. But did you know? Drum roll, please…there was a survivor of the fire."

Nick was stunned. His face instantly betrayed the fact; no, he did not know.

The Driver laughed and laughed. "I told you I was the best! I told you I did this shit for a living, and a very good living, by the way." He slammed his free hand on the desktop. "Bada boom Bada Bing, bitches better recognize when The Driver is on the Web, no secret is safe!"

Nick asked, "Man or woman?"

"What?"

"Man or woman? The survivor, a man or a woman?"

"Oh, it's a man, and he's being housed in a nearby burn facility under 24-hour care. Now maybe you'll believe me. I am The Driver; I reign supreme on the Web. I wander around on the dark Web like a kid in a toy store. I wreck lives and take what I want! I am The Driver!" he finished in a deep voice, the rant similar to Smaug the dragon speaking to Frodo in the dwarf's Lonely mountain home.

Nick sat down, stunned. All this time, Jay had been alive. He had to be in bad shape, and yet he had survived.

"Can you tell me where he's being cared for? The survivor."

"Yes, I can, but since neither of us is who we thought the other was, perhaps you'd consider releasing me? I would prefer not to lose another fingernail or hear any more of your psychological warfare bullshit with Tinder and social media."

Nick thought it over briefly, then agreed. Now he felt stupidly brutal. "Sorry about the fingernail, man. The people I've been dealing with play a brutal game. I've had to be unquestionably brutal to get past their practiced façade. I'm deeply sorry...OK, so maybe not deeply. I mean, you did go to the diner and watch my friend, and for that you were going to pay painfully. So, consider the whole fingernail thing a debt paid. Don't ever mess with my friend, deal?"

The Driver nodded, a bit shook up by how this encounter could have ended. *He's still unquestionably dangerous, damaged, and unhinged,* The Driver silently thought of Nick as he cut the duct tape restraints on his remaining hand.

Nick sat lost in his thoughts while The Driver went to get a bandage for his wounded finger. An uneasy alliance was beginning between the two former enemies. The Mongoose and the Cobra now on the same team.

When The Driver returned, Nick asked, "So what big deal hacks have you done? Anything I'd recognize?" The Driver laughed and laughed. "Is the DNC email hack big enough for you? When WikiLeaks founder Julian Assange says the Russians didn't give them the emails, he isn't lying. I hacked Hillary's lame ass security long ago and used a Russian IP to do it. That shit was like taking candy from a naked baby. Trust me, the Russians had no idea what happened. I muscle fucked their servers and made them squeal while I downloaded the DNC's dirty little secrets. You don't mess with The Driver! I have mad skillz and the throbbing server muscle to make you sweat while you say my name over and over!"

Nick laughed and laughed at the description The Driver had given of his skills. He had to admit, he was starting to like this guy. The Driver was twisted and bent in his own unique way.

CHAPTER TWELVE

While Nick was on his "Tinder date" with The Driver, Nõn was on the other side of the world with the Asgarda. She felt a surprising kinship with the female warriors. She'd spoken to many of them and listened to their stories. They'd all experienced hardship and difficult times and had somehow prevailed. Still, no one had answered her question of why they'd maintained the façade of the first camp she'd been shown. She was hopeful the answer would make itself known if she was patient and listened well. This was a trait Nõn and Nick's professions shared. Listening not only to what is said, but what is not, and the insight both provide. It was this realization that made her a very talented reporter and writer. Nõn hadn't spoken to the Amazonian leader of the Asgarda since that first night. They' had watched each other as they each interacted with the Asgarda members, but no communication had occurred. There was an unspoken understanding between the two of them. They would speak when the time was right.

Night after night, the Asgarda would sit in small groups here and there, gathered around small fires and talking. Nõn would move from group to group with her interpreter and listen. It seemed each group had a different personality, and they had much different conversations. Some were jovial and pranksters, always looking for the next laugh. Others were much more serious. Each group had a leader, and sometimes the leader role changed, depending on the topic they discussed. Some leaders were very intense, others carefree. It was remarkable to see the difference. She knew on some level there was a reason for the groupings, but she couldn't quite put a point to their purpose. Finally, one night the reason became very clear.

The Asgarda had gathered at night around their fires and eaten the day's final meal. A moose had been killed, and the camp had been eating meat for several days following the hunt. Nõn's interpreter explained they had to be careful eating the wild game in Western Ukraine because of the Chernobyl nuclear accident. In spite of what the world thought, the plant hadn't been shut down after the initial accident. The damaged reactor had been shut down, but the remaining reactors had been online, and each had experienced some type of breakdown. The entire area of the Ukraine had been affected by the disaster. The Interpreter explained that in 2016 a radiation survey was conducted, and the results showed the radiation from the disaster had fallen in half during the thirty years that had since passed.

Nõn listened, thinking it had never occurred to her that the plant would have been allowed to remain in operation, much less after continued breakdowns. She made a mental note to suggest to Carrie at NPR an article be written on the aftereffects of the disaster. Suddenly, there was a loud commotion as the camp came to life. A group was approaching on foot, and sentries had sounded a subtle alarm. Nõn now became aware of another level to the camp. They posted sentries? They needed security? The depth of the Asgarda and their secrets was constantly being revealed the longer she stayed in the camp. The group immediately scattered and took up defensive positions, ready for battle, as Nõn was quickly hustled into a hidden defensive fighting position and told to stay down. She hadn't even realized the position existed until she was in it. It had been carefully constructed and camouflaged. She sat and listened as the camp was instantly silent. The discipline of the Asgarda was soundlessly apparent. A small band of women entered the camp, carrying a wounded comrade. The camp again transformed, and several of the women grabbed medical kits from their fighting positions. Nõn watched as they settled in and began to treat the wounded woman warrior. She recognized some of the wounds were bullet wounds, and others were from a knife attack. The wounds were very serious. The medics worked feverishly and did what they could to ease the woman's pain and treat her wounds. Despite their best efforts, she died after being in the camp less than an hour. To Nõn, the entire Asgarda myth, the woman warriors doing battle, became painfully real. She watched as the woman lay dying and realized the whole article she was about to write was about their struggle; not the novelty of these woman warriors, but the reality of their fight against whatever that was and with whom remained to be revealed.

Nõn watched as the women each displayed different emotions; some angry, others strangely solemn. As Nõn observed the crowd, the tall and muscled leader of the Asgarda came forward and knelt at the fallen woman's side. She whispered something softly under her breath and placed a small metal object on the dead woman's chest. She then spoke in a louder tone to the women surrounding her. They picked up the woman's body and removed it from the camp. There would be no laughter or talking in the camp for the rest of the night. Nõn didn't speak to anyone and didn't ask her interpreter any questions that night. She let the reality of the death she'd witnessed sink in.

The next morning, Nõn was woken up by her interpreter.

"The commander wishes to see you."

She dressed quickly and tried to gather her thoughts. Her sleep had been fitful and filled with dark dreams. Surprisingly, the priestess was back in her dreams, and the message felt ominous.

Nõn left her small tent and followed Katerna to a larger tent. They both entered and were met by Bexx, who rose and said, "Please come in and sit."

Nõn walked into the tent and sat on a log covered with an animal skin.

Bexx began, "I imagine now you realize we have many reasons for disguising the true intent of our group. I will explain, and when I am done, if you have additional questions, I will try to answer them." Nõn nodded.

"The woman who died last night was sent on a mission to attempt to infiltrate the Russian occupation of Crimea. The Russian federation has annexed Crimea after a brief military occupation. She died trying to disrupt their occupation. The reason for our deception is simple. We are training as Asgarda warriors, true, but we are also mercenaries, or if you prefer freedom fighters. The Russians have not learned of our camp or our true purpose. If they did, our warriors would no longer be as effective. I wanted you to see the camp and commitment we have made to the people of Ukraine before you write your article. Should the Russians learn of our true nature, it would make our missions incredibly difficult and deadly. Does that make sense?"

Nõn nodded. It made her article incredibly interesting to the readers – and if she chose to write the truth, incredibly dangerous for the Asgarda.

Bexx continued. "We have many camps; some train in hand to hand combat, some demolitions, some electronic warfare. Anything that can be useful in the battle against the Russians, we try to excel in. Historically, the men of Ukraine have fought in these wars; however, through simple attrition, we as a people have less men than women. The ratio imbalance is killing our people. Every year, two hundred thousand more people die than are born here. So not only are we at war with Russia, they simply have to wait us out as our population collapses. The women of Ukraine know this. We speak about it quietly amongst ourselves. The incident at Chernobyl has affected our men much more than the women. It was assumed that women's fertility would be affected by the radiation; however, it has been quite the opposite. Men cannot reproduce and are demoralized by their inability to defend our people and fertilize our wombs. In a word, we are a broken people. It is only a matter of time before we fall. So your article could be very disastrous for us, or perhaps a godsend. It is all dependent on the tack you take. Truly, no one knows the future, and we have discussed many times the possible outcomes. I cannot clearly see any direction that doesn't pose potential harm for us. No route is perfect, do you see?"

Nõn did. Every article she'd written had a double edge. One side brought awareness to an issue, which could be both good and bad. It was a difficult tightrope to walk.

"So now you know why we keep all of our camps a secret and only allow the public to know of the 'Face Camp', as we call it."

Nõn nodded.

Bexx continued. "This camp will be disbanded after you leave. We cannot risk your disclosure of our mission here. We will disband and be absorbed into the remaining camps. Do you have any questions?"

Nõn thought for some time. Finally, she said, "I do. Is this why at the fires there are small groups?"

"Yes. Each is a team, led by a team leader, each having their own style and personality. Each team member has a specialty." Nõn was reminded of the team at Baroota and Nick's description of them.

"I have much to think about," Nõn said. "Thank you for trusting me with this secret. I will do my best to honor your trust."

Bexx nodded. The meeting was over. Nõn stood up and left the tent. Her interpreter stayed behind.

That day, Nõn spent most of her time alone deep in thought. She was not only deeply affected by the Asgarda story, her dreams the previous night had been unsettling. The visits by the priestess were never joyful. The visions always felt powerful and overwhelming. She felt disjointed and out of sorts.

That night, the dreams returned. She woke covered with sweat, breathing rapidly. The message was clear. She had much to consider. The priestess had called her to her side and motioned for her to sit next to her. What that meant, she had no idea. But it was clear the priestess was calling Nõn to join her. That morning, Nõn decided to turn her phone on. She had turned it off to conserve battery life. She was surprised to find she had a strong signal in the remote mountain valley. Her first call was to Carrie. She gave her a brief rundown of the information she'd discovered on the Asgarda and explained there was much to discuss before publishing any article. She felt she'd be wrapping up soon and would let Carrie know when to book the return flight. She hung up and set the phone on her bedding inside the tent.

That night around the fires, the women had returned to their former selves; some joking and kidding each other, others more serious and quiet. Nõn listened to them, some speaking quietly, some laughing. As she listened, she thought about her dream and wondered what it meant. Her thoughts were interrupted by a buzzing sound. She looked up; they all did. The sound was gone, then returned, only to stop again. The buzz was very out of place in the mountains. Nõn was puzzled, then realized it was her phone. She apologized to everyone as she walked to her tent and retrieved the phone. Typing in the security code, she saw the phone showed she had a series of messages. Nick had messaged her. She stopped and didn't read the messages. She had too much to think about to deal with Nick right now. She shut off the phone and returned to the fires, noticeably shaken. She sat but fidgeted nervously. Bexx noticed the change in Nõn's demeanor immediately but said nothing.

CHAPTER THIRTEEN

The Driver determined Jay had survived the drone strike, but survival was a relative term. He was burned badly and had lost both legs and arms. He was, in effect, a torso and head only. The Driver could find no details on Jay's cognitive condition. Once The Driver understood Nick wasn't some secret government agent and was indeed in a shit storm himself dealing with trying to locate and kill The Director, he was on board immediately.

Nick was still reeling from the realization that Jay had survived the explosion. After a couple hours of reflection, he decided to pay Jay a visit.

"I'm going to go see what's left of Jay and see if I can find out anything at all about The Director from him."

"OK, man, good luck."

"Thanks again for finding this. Let me know if you can find out anything more, anything at all. Who pays his bills, who visits him, anything that might lead to The Director."

"No problem, man. If it's there, The Driver will find it, even if I have to pound the hell out of some virginal medical company's recordkeeping systems to do it."

Nick laughed. Every comment from The Driver involving hacking was some barely veiled sexual reference.

Nick arrived at the Burn Center at the University of Colorado Hospital twenty hours later. He hoped to see his nemesis, Jay. He'd come up with a cover story that was half-truth and half-lies. When he entered the unit, he asked if he could visit his friend, Jay Blackfoot. The receptionist explained that in a Burn Center there was a tremendous risk of infection for the patients they treated, so if Nick wanted to speak to Jay, it would be after following strict infection prevention protocols and in a sterile room adjacent to Jay's, and then only through an intercom system. Nick signed the necessary paperwork, then washed his hands and put on disposable scrubs and booties, along with a head and face mask. He walked through a series of rooms, each pressurized to ensure that when the door opened, a rush of air would escape the room and prevent any airborne infection from following Nick into the sterile environment.

Finally, before Nick was allowed to see or talk to Jay, he was warned by the nurse who had met him on the floor that Jay was in very bad shape. It would be difficult to look in on him if Nick wasn't prepared.

Nick had hoped for some "alone time" with Jay. He wanted to question him and perhaps provoke him into disclosing some details about The Director; instead, he'd be speaking to Jay through an intercom. This wasn't what he'd hoped for, but there still may be some value in the visit.

When Nick finally did see Jay, he had to admit he was surprised at his condition. Jay was lying in a bed of sorts, surrounded by tubes and machines, all trying to keep him hydrated. Gone were both legs at the hip, and both arms at the shoulder. What remained was burned and disfigured. Where his eyes had been were covered with bandages, and his lips were burned off as well, exposing blackened teeth. He couldn't see, speak or communicate. According to the nurse, he could hear, and their focus at the moment was to make him as comfortable as possible.

"Oh, wow, he's in bad shape, isn't he?"

"Yes, he is. Normally we'd encourage his family to allow us to let him pass by keeping him medicated and comfortable; however, that isn't his legal executor's wish."

"This kind of care must cost a bundle, am I right?"

"Yes, it's very expensive, and it's all paid for, no questions asked, according to our billing department. The doctors were advised to take whatever means necessary to keep Jay alive."

"That's too bad. I guess his family just can't let go. This isn't living. I wouldn't want to be Jay, living like this, no hope of anything meaningful in life."

"Yes, some people can't accept that their loved ones are better off moving on," the nurse replied, "but in Jay's case, he has a wealthy benefactor who has all legal and medical rights to his estate. It isn't his family keeping him alive."

Nick realized exactly what that meant: The Director was keeping Jay alive as punishment for his actions at Baroota. In doing so, he'd made a serious tactical mistake. Nick was fairly confident The Driver could obtain information from the facilities billing department that would lead them to The Director.

Nick asked, "May I speak to Jay?"

"Most definitely. Please do anything to help us brighten his mood!"

Nick pushed the talk button on the intercom and spoke.

"Hey Jay, how you doing, brother? It's me, your old friend Nick. Remember me? From that mission in the Darien Gap? Baroota?"

Jay noticeably perked up his head, slightly turning, blindly looking around the room.

Nick turned to the nurse.

"We had a special relationship. We both were sent on a dangerous mission off the books, you know, top secret, black ops kind of stuff. Jay has a remarkable and sarcastic sense of humor. We used to laugh and laugh in the darkest of moments. Oh man, the stories I could tell you. He really is a funny guy."

"Well, please feel free to speak openly with him. Listening is the only interaction he has left."

"Are you sure? I'm afraid our humor would be a bit harsh if you didn't know him. It sounds abusive, but really he enjoyed the dark jokes we made about each other."

"Please don't let me get in your way. Anything you can do to brighten his day, I would appreciate."

Nick pushed the talk button. "Jay, I'm not sure if you realize this or not, but buddy, you look like shit! I swear, you look like a huge piece of foreskin stretched over the ugliest dick I've ever seen. Seriously, man, like one whale was giving another whale a blow job and accidentally bit off the tip. You look like the ugly tip of a whale's dick, bro."

Jay started to rock back and forth, making gurgling noises.

The nurse watched and said, "I do believe he's laughing! I think you're right! Look at that, he's laughing." Jay continued rocking, and spit began to drip down his disfigured face. "Your sense of humor is atrocious, but this is the happiest I've seen him."

"Yes, we had a special bond only people who have been in battle and survived can understand."

"Oh, so you were both in the military together?"

"Yes, we served together on a few missions. Jay was quite the stickler for details."

"Oh, I can imagine. I'm an Army wife; I know all about what it means to be in the military."

Nick recognized this was his play. "You know, I'd really like to thank whomever is paying for Jay's care. It must be quite a hardship for them. I do appreciate that someone out there realizes that although he's severely physically compromised and his life will never be the same, he's not forgotten. If it were possible for me to get that information, it would stay just between us."

The nurse frowned as she thought the proposal over.

"Oh, and just as a suggestion: Jay absolutely loved cold coffee with lots of milk. It drove his waitresses crazy. Who demands cold coffee? Oh, and burnt to a crisp toast with no butter!"

This final act of "kindness" sealed the deal for the nurse. She said, "OK, but I could lose my job if it's ever discovered I broke the rules. Just this once. After all, we're all family, military family."

Nick pressed the talk button. "Jay, I'm leaving now, but I'll check in from time to time to see how you're doing. Try not to be too depressed about your situation. It could always be worse, ya know. Oh, and I left a little note with the nurse about how you loved your cold coffee and burnt dry toast. Anything else I remember to make you more comfortable, I'll be sure to make a list. Take care, old man. Time to hit a strip club and get a lap dance. I'll be thinking of you."

Jay, more agitated now, grunted, "...uck u!...uck u!"

The nurse laughed and said, "I think he's trying to say good luck to you!"

Nick laughed. "I think you're right. He always did put others before himself. He was selfless like that."

The nurse left, then returned with a name of the person assigned as legal executor of Jay's estate. Additionally, she handed Nick an address assigned to Jay's medical records. It was the physical address the bills were sent to. Nick thanked her and calmly walked out of the unit after removing the disposable sterile scrubs.

When Nick was back at the truck, he started breathing rapidly. The anxiety of finally having a breakthrough in locating The Director had hit him hard. He sat in the car, head against the steering wheel, breathing deeply, trying to calm himself. Could it really be this easy?

Nick opened the paper, and there was a name: Winston V. Firestone.

The address came back to a P.O. box in Hannah, North Dakota, listed to Cachibaché Enterprises.

Nick smiled and called The Driver.

"Sup, man? Any news?"

"The Driver is on the case! Of course I have news. How about you? Anything new?"

"Yeah, I have some information. You go first!"

"Nope, you first, Nick. The Driver is used to successfully gathering information against impossible odds."

Nick explained he'd discovered the legal executor of Jay's estate and the billing address for Jay's medical records.

The Driver was silent. "No way! Serious, you're just jerking my chain. What's the name? Go ahead, tell me the name."

"Winston V. Firestone," Nick replied. "The billing address is in North Dakota."

The Driver, now disappointed, said, "Yeah, I had the same intel. You suck, man. You beat The Driver to the prize. I don't do sloppy seconds."

Nick smiled and responded, "Brother, I am a nightmare walking, psychopath talking..."

64

The Driver responded, "Ya, I know all about the nightmare walking part. I've seen that shit up close and personal. My finger still hurts! By the way, what the hell did you do with my fingernail, you sick prick?"

"I kept it as a reminder of our first Tinder date, my friend. A memento."

"You're amazingly bent, but screw it, we're on a mission. Let's get this bastard. What's your next play?"

"My next play? Heading to Hannah, North Dakota, to check out that address. Do your thing in the meantime. Let me know all there is to know about Mr. Firestone and the meaning behind that word Cachibaché and Hannah, North Dakota."

"Have no fear, The Driver is here! Ready to muscle fuck any and all information systems, my servers are fired up and vibrating with lust..."

Nick hung up. He didn't want to hear the rest of The Driver's lame-ass sexual innuendos. Nick smiled as he pulled out of the parking lot. This must be how Nõn felt when he was on one of his hilarious, humor-filled tirades. He laughed and began to sing the lyrics again. "I am a nightmare walking, psychopath talking, king of my jungle..."

CHAPTER FOURTEEN

The drive from the Burn Center in Denver, Colorado, to the post office in Hannah, North Dakota, took approximately fourteen and a half hours. Initially Nick had been upbeat and hopeful he'd finally found The Director, but a couple hours into the drive, reality began to creep back in. The Director wouldn't be holed up in a town as small as Hannah was reported to be in the Google search Nick had conducted during the drive. No one in Hannah had the weight to order a drone strike on his home in Colorado. Hannah would be another rung in the ladder in the search for the prick. Slowly, the anger returned, seeping back into the cracks where hope had been. Nick glared out the window as he drove on into the night.

The Driver had called once or twice to update Nick on the information he'd obtained from his searches as well. There was no one named Firestone within a thousand miles of Hannah, North Dakota. The Driver had searched LinkedIn and a few other social media sites for the name and found nothing. The lack of any evidence of the name Winston V. Firestone told The Driver one thing: his information had almost certainly been scrubbed from the Web. That spoke volumes to The Driver of just who The Director was. Almost no one was able to completely remove all references of their name from the Web. The Driver would be forced to go deep into what hacker novices referred to as the Deep Web, or Dark Web. Real hackers understood this was media code for "I don't have a clue what I'm talking about and want to sound cool". The Driver would need to access "Tor Hidden Service Protocol." This allowed him to maximize his search while remaining anonymous. He wouldn't know what systems he'd accessed, and unless he made a critical error, they would have no idea who he was as well. The Driver laughed at that idea; as if he could be found, arriving by the back door, he took advantage of what novice security systems that were in place and rocked the information system's world until he was finished. Then lighting a cigarette, he left the system feeling violated, used and dirty. He smiled at the thought as he started his search.

Dr. Warsaw had arrived at the Cachibaché Facilities in North Dakota a few days before Nick and The Driver had started their Tinder date. She'd been given files on the first group of clients she'd be treating at the facility. The files were in-depth psychological profiles that had been illegally obtained. From them, Lennie gained invaluable insight into each client's deepest, darkest fears. Lennie loved the feeling of power she felt as she perused the personal information, diving deep into her future clients' most guarded secrets. The information she found would make manipulation of the clients incredibly easy and very emotionally satisfying to her. She made a few notes on possible "treatment programs" for the individual phobias of each of her future clients. The Director had been explicitly clear in what he expected her to accomplish: he wanted these people pushed to their emotional limits, psychologically tormented and tortured by their personal demons until they broke. If they died as a result of the experience, that was all the better. The sessions would be filmed. Clients were already lining up for the groundbreaking, revolutionary treatments. Unbeknownst to them, there were already prospective buyers lined up to watch the high-priced records of their treatments. There never seemed to be a shortage of people with the necessary monetary resources to support The Director's camps.

The first day Lennie arrived at the facility, she'd been given a tour by the head of security. The security officer was a tall, fit, middle aged man named Greg Schidel. He wore sergeant stripes on the collar of his black long sleeve 511 tactical Ripstop TDU uniform shirt. This was an immediate indication to Lennie that this man thought highly of himself and valued placing himself above the rest of the security squad. She made a mental note to use that to her advantage later.

"Well, Dr. Warsaw, I don't know if you realize this or not, but this facility is indeed rare. I'm told your work here is to be cutting edge and revolutionary, and that alone should make this facility unique. But did you know the entire facility used to be a 1950s missile silo?"

Lennie knew when to act impressed. She couldn't care less about the details of the missile silo, but if it mattered to the sergeant, she'd make the most of it.

"Perhaps, Sergeant Schidel, you should call me Lennie?"

Sergeant Schidel smiled. "Of course, Lennie, and you may call me Greg, but only when my men aren't around. I can't have them getting the idea that discipline will be lacking at the facility. Our work here is too important for lackadaisical attitudes."

Lennie smiled. "Thank you, Greg. It'll be our little secret. Could you show me the rest of the facility?"

"It would be my pleasure, Lennie!"

Schidel continued with his tour of the former Sprint Missile silo, now converted to a thinly veiled psychological behavioral modification facility.

"The entire facility is 36 acres surrounded by an eight-foot tall military grade chain link fence. The above ground facility is 2400 square feet of reinforced concrete capable of withstanding a nearby impact from a nuclear weapon. There are kitchen facilities, living quarters and a security desk and turnstile. Also, we have a full weapons armory. Your patients will be housed in the below ground facility, the former Launch Control facility for the missiles. It's twelve thousand square feet, with fifteen-foot high ceilings. The area is all on one level and is separated into several different offices and rooms. Those are the rooms where your patients will be housed and 'treated'. The outside walls of the below ground facility are made from concrete thirty-six inches thick and are heavily reinforced with rebar. Should emergency egress be required, there are two seventy-five foot tunnels, each nine feet by nine feet. They were built to allow personnel and vehicle access and are secured by heavy duty blast doors. The long and short of it is this facility is secure from attack, and should a patient try to escape, they won't be able to unless my security team allows it. Your program is in good hands here. The Director wanted me to make sure you understood you had a free hand here. Nothing leaves this facility unless we allow it – not even sound."

"So where were the missiles located?"
"There are 12 silos on the property. They're 11 feet across and 35 feet deep. Each has a heavy steel door covering the tube."

"Really?" Lennie was suddenly sincerely interested in seeing the silos. The dimensions of the silos were a perfect fit for several of the potential therapy sessions she'd envisioned. "Are the tubes accessible? And would the results of the patients' continued therapy be able to be recorded?"

"The Director has directed me to make this facility fit your needs, so if you'd prefer to use those tubes for your therapy, I'll make it happen. Cameras included. As soon as is humanly possible."

"Please show me the silos. They sound perfect for what I had in mind."

A half hour later, Sergeant Schidel and Doctor Warsaw were standing in front of the silos. "Greg, these are perfect for what I had in mind. How soon would you be able to get each wired for video observation?"

"For you, Lennie, I'll have it completed by week's end."

"Thank you, Greg. That's so sweet of you."

They smiled warmly at each other.

CHAPTER FIFTEEN

Nick had been in Hannah, North Dakota, for two days now, and so far it had been a bust. He found the post office and asked if there was a way he could find out who had purchased the P.O. box. "No, the information is protected," he was advised by the postal worker. "Only a legally obtained warrant can produce the information." Nick was stuck. He was so close; there had to be a reason The Director had purchased a P.O. box here and had Jay's medical bills sent to it. Frustrated, he drove around the area looking for anything that might be a clue. Back in the street, they called it "shaking the tree to see what falls out." Here, Nick couldn't even find a tree to shake. There was nothing. He looked in the local phonebook for Cachibaché or any references to Firestone; there was nothing. He checked the local cemetery and hospital as well; no Firestones in either place. He sat down in a café in the same building that housed the post office and thought to himself, *How do I draw someone out into the open using only a P.O. box?*

A half hour later, after sitting at the café and having a burger, Nick had an idea – a really good idea! He called The Driver.

"Hey man, it's Nick. I need a favor."

"Shoot, brother. The Driver is ready. My servers are oiled and swollen with anticipation, my…"

"Yeah, yeah, Jesus, I get it. Can we just press on without you raping and pillaging the Internet with these lame-ass innuendos?"

The Driver was silent. "Fine! What is it you need?"

"I need a letter or a package, something sent to the P.O. box here in Hannah. The town's population is only 20 people, so it isn't like I can surveil anything or anyone and not be noticed. Hell, it's a ghost town. Only thing missing is a bald kid sitting on the front porch with a banjo! I can't blend in. Everyone here knows everyone else and has had their sisters' dads' babies. I'm screwed on this end. So, my idea is you send a package that has a tracker in it. Then when you mail it, you send it certified mail. Whoever picks it up will have to sign for it. That goes into the post office computer system, and you'll be notified it was picked up. When you get the message, text me, then I can follow them back to wherever or whatever Cachibaché is. Does that make sense?"

The Driver was silent for a moment, then in an elated voice began speaking. "Brother, I'm already on it! I sent the package after you cock-blocked me back at the hospital. I had to get out in front, my man; not a fan of sloppy seconds. The Driver is always first to the show, prepared to go, rockin' and poppin', slammin' and slidin'. Pulling that hair and making you scream my name. Sealing the deal, making sure you feel my…"

"Jesus! Man, stop. I get it, I get it. You're the sexual god of the Internet! When will the package arrive? Please?"

"The package arrived this morning, brother. I sent it priority mail express. It arrived, and the anticipation has already begun. Will the package fit? Will it be enormous? Will it take her breath away?"

Nick grimaced. Listening, he thought, *I really owe Nõn an apology if this is how I sound.* "OK, man. Can you let me know when the package is picked up? As soon as it is, call me or text."

"There will be no doubt when the package is picked up, my friend; just look for the hot female in the area, sweating uncomfortably and smiling, flush cheeks, breathing…."

Nick hung up. Talking to himself, he mumbled, "I really should have taken off another fingernail; peeling just one has barely taken the wind out of his sails." Then the thought occurred to him: *What was The Driver like before the painful manicure?* Nick cringed at the thought.

Lennie had many duties as the Cachibaché facility manager, and one was going into town. Sergeant Schidel explained to Lennie he would have liked to accompany her to the small town, but it was not an option. The Director had strict rules for the security crew. The town was small, and they had to be discreet. There could be no unnecessary attention drawn to the facility. Men in uniforms, short crew cut hair, and athletic builds tended to draw attention. Too much attention. She would have to make the trip on her own. They were expecting a group of patients to arrive tonight, and the facility would begin its operations in earnest after the intake process had been completed. The cameras were nearly installed on the twelve silos, as Schidel had promised.

Lennie arrived at the post office at about 12:30 in the afternoon. Upon retrieving the mail, she found a package had been sent priority express. She went to the counter, showed the clerk the slip, and signed the electronic signature pad. She then went out of the post office with an arm load of mail and the package. Placing them in the back seat of the Chevy Trailblazer, she closed the door and went into the small mom and pop country store to buy food and cleaning supplies for the facility.

Nick smiled as he realized The Driver had really been upset by his human intelligence gathering beating the electronic intelligence gathering to the punch. The Driver took pride in his work, and he had real potential as an ally. He'd already saved at least one day by mailing the package.

Nick didn't have to wait long. A grey Chevy Trailblazer pulled into the small one horse town's post office parking lot, and a middle-aged woman got out of the driver's door and entered the post office. A few moments later, she came out carrying an arm load of mail and a package. As she loaded them into the Trailblazer, Nick watched and waited for The Driver's message. The woman went into the store and came out with several bags of groceries and put them in the back of the Trailblazer as well. As the Chevy drove off into the distance, Nick's phone buzzed. He looked, and the text was from The Driver. The package had been picked up.

Nick fired up the rusted 'Yota and pulled out. No point in rushing; there was no way he could lose the Trailblazer, since it was the only other car on the road. Twenty total citizens made covert surveillance easier in some respects, and much harder in others.

Nick followed the Trailblazer from a distance that normally would have been unthinkable. The Trailblazer traveled North on 91st Ave to Town Line Road and turned right. She travelled about two minutes more, then turned right on 95th Ave Wales and traveled south. Nick was about 45 seconds behind her. She turned left on Cavalier County Road Hwy 55, and Nick fell in behind her a few seconds later. Left and right, the Blazer negotiated the back-country roads. Finally, the Trailblazer pulled into a long concrete drive off the roadway and approached a chain link fence-enclosed compound. The woman exited the vehicle and typed in a code on the electronic key pad that controlled an electronic gate. The gate rolled open, and the Trailblazer entered the compound. Nick had pulled over and watched from a half-mile away. When the vehicle was finally inside and out of sight, Nick pulled up to the compound. It took a while for the reality of what the compound was to register.

Nick picked up the cell phone and called The Driver.

"You won't believe this, man: I think Cachibaché is housed in an old missile silo. Pull up any old missile silos in the area of Dresden, North Dakota. I just followed the package to an area that is obviously a former military installation. The vehicle I followed drove into a three-car garage that's part of a concrete building. There are large pipes and concrete buildings that look like fortified fighting positions. They have portholes for small arms engagement."

The Driver asked, "How do you know what a fortified fighting position looks like?"

Nick replied, "I used to sit in one. I worked nuke security for several years a long time ago. I know what I'm seeing. This is military, and it's old. It has to be a missile silo or launch command and control facility for a field of missiles."

"I'm on it. I'll have blueprints for the installation, and a topographical map as well. Never fear, my friend; The Driver is always ready, pumped up. I'm popping little blue pills now…"

Nick hung up on The Driver. He needed to think. Whatever was going on in the abandoned silo, The Director wanted it safely tucked away, impenetrable. It wouldn't be an easy task to breach the compound. The Director had upped the ante on his camp security. This would be no quick hit and run operation.

Nick brought the 'Yota to a stop as he surveilled the exterior fencing. After making several mental notes, he finally "flipped a bitch" and headed west to begin the long trip back to Moses Hole.

By the time Nick returned to Moses Lake, he'd dug deep into his memories to recall the tactics security forces had used to defend the missiles and systems that had been in place to protect the compounds. Most likely, all the security systems had been removed when the compound had been scrapped. He did recognize the error that had been made when the portholes had been installed in the fighting position's cement walls: they'd been installed backwards. Not much had changed since this place was built. The contractors who install the equipment today have no idea how it is to be used. Portholes that were installed backwards funneled any incoming rounds into the target; it was the same mistake over and over.

CHAPTER SIXTEEN

When Nick arrived in Moses Lake, The Driver was waiting with blueprints and photos of the inside of the facility. The silo had been for sale for many years, and The Driver had done a Web search to locate the pictures used in the listing. He also explained to Nick, The Director had purchased one of only four Sprint missile silos that had ever been built. The Sprint system was an early anti-ballistic missile system. The missiles were radio guided and used solid rocket fuel. The system had an incredible acceleration rate, reaching Mach 10 in 5 seconds or less. The Driver was impressed by the technology of the system and rambled on and on about the workarounds the engineers had come up with to achieve their goals.

Nick couldn't have cared less. He knew that unless they were incredibly lucky, they would never gain access to the buildings, much less find out anything about The Director's intentions with the site. A missile silo by its very nature is designed to be impenetrable. It seemed to Nick the closer they came to finding The Director, the more difficult the task became. Baroota was merely located in one of the most remote places in the world, but once you arrived there, your only obstacles were the jungle, gun runners and narcotic traffickers. A missile silo was a whole different game. The more Nick thought about it, the more the task seemed impossible.

Nick tried to explain the obstacles they were up against to The Driver; however, The Driver was unable to comprehend the difficulty. In his world, there was nothing that wasn't hackable if you had the right skills and enough time. It was unimaginable to The Driver that anything this old wasn't breechable. As they talked, Nick was suddenly quiet.

"What? Why so quiet all of a sudden?"

"I just remembered an exercise I did when I was in the military. There were so many of them, we trained constantly back then for threats that never, ever happened. This one was an exercise against a mock nuclear weapons convoy. They had a camera crew come out to show how capable the security forces were in protecting the bombs. We had to wear MILES gear, which was basically a military version of laser tag. To make a long, tedious story short, our four-man team killed off the entire 15-man convoy security team and stole the nuke in under 4 minutes. They stopped the exercise, and the film was immediately classified. Understand, they felt it would be an impossible task to do, and if it were possible, it would take at least an hour to accomplish. Nope, 4 minutes and done, the nuke is ours, the brass wasn't happy. We were able to accomplish it because we understood their tactics and used them to our advantage. We knew every weakness they had, and how they would deploy. If we can gain that depth of understanding of the facility and its routines, we may have a chance. It will take a lot of co-vert surveillance, but it's possible. We'll have to know their routines as well as they do, every single little nuance."

"Sounds like this kind of surveillance is right up your alley, Nick! Will anyone lose a fingernail when this is over, or is that for special clients only?"

Nick smiled. "Dude, you are so sensitive. If you had any idea of how medieval I was about to get on your ass, you'd be grateful I stopped and gave you the thirty-minute litmus test to pass."

"Ya, for example? Like what, Mr. Badass?"

"Hmm...well, imagine what you could do with a piece of det cord, duct tape and a machete. The mind boggles."

The Driver was quiet. "OK, man, OK. Gonna have to take your word for it. This is your department, not mine. Do you realize what I had planned for you?"

"No, what?"

"A complete meltdown of your life, finances, credit cards and credit rating, warrants for crimes you never committed, driver's license revoked. You were about to be royally screwed by The Driver. So, I guess we're both glad the other backed off, huh?"

Nick raised his eyebrows. "Ya, I guess so."

Nick had made a list of things to accomplish on the first three-day surveillance of the silo and had returned to Dresden, North Dakota, the nearest town to the silo. A quick Internet search of the local government website revealed the county had a sheriff's department comprised of five full-time deputies and one K-9 officer. Hopefully, he'd be able to avoid them. Five deputies for an entire county made the odds of being discovered minimal. Nick broke into an abandoned garage and hid the 'Yota there and began the two-mile trek to the silo's exterior fencing.

Three days later, he left the area. He'd learned a lot. He'd watched security patrols and timed their routes, there were no sensors on the fencing or buried around the perimeter. The security patrols were predictable and switched out on a regularly timed rotation. They were doing everything in a regimented manner, which made it extremely exploitable. The last night he was present, he watched while the security team removed a naked man from what Nick thought was one of the old missile silos. They dragged the man into the facility. Obviously, The Director had been busy. The security team seemed to consist of a group of only four men, armed with semi-automatic handguns and a radios; he saw nothing else. Nick had a small sliver of hope. It might be possible to take control of the compound if he had some help and a lot of luck. He reached for his smart phone and sent a series of texts to Nõn. He texted, "I've made an ally of the driver of the green Honda (I'll explain later). I found out Jay survived the drone strike and went to see him. Located another camp in North Dakota." Then the final text said, "I think we can take this camp by force if I can get some help. Please advise, will you come?" He waited for an answer.

Back in Ukraine, Bexx had been watching Nõn and the change in her demeanor since she'd turned her phone back on. One night a couple of nights after the texting incident, she approached Nõn as she sat by a fire alone.

"May I sit with you?"

"Yes. Please do. I am most grateful for the company."

After a few moments, Bexx got right to the point.

"I have noticed that since your phone buzzed, you have been unsettled."

"Yes, I have some text messages there waiting. I am not ready to open them. I am afraid of what they will ask me to do. There are decisions I will have to make. I made a promise to a man I know that if he asked, I would think about returning. I am not ready yet for him to ask that of me."

"I see. This man, he is your husband? Boyfriend? Lover?"

Nõn laughed out loud. "No, no, I do not think he even realizes I am a woman. He…we have been through a lot. It is a story no one would believe, but it is true."

"I think I would be interested in hearing this story, if you would like to tell it."

"It all began with a dream, I have a spiritual guide, a priestess who told me in a dream to follow a wolf through a desert. In the desert, there were three pyramids. It took me a while to understand the dream, and eventually I came to realize the wolf was this man who has texted me. I followed him in spite of my desire to do anything but what he asked. He is infuriating, juvenile, and absolutely insane with rage. Somehow, he saved us both; actually, I guess we saved each other, but without him I would not have survived. He sees the world differently than you or I. Nothing about him is predictable. Just when you think you understand him, he shows you, you know nothing about him at all. Anyway, he is hunting another man who tried to have us killed. He will not stop until he finds him. Finds him, then destroys him."

"Please tell me everything that happened, and tell me more about this man/ wolf of yours."

Nõn told the entire story of Baroota from her perspective, finishing with the trip to Ukraine.

Bexx was silent for several minutes, staring into the fire. "This wolf of yours, he continues the hunt now, and you think he has texted you requesting your help again?"

"I am afraid so, yes, that is what I expect to find when I open the messages. He will not stop until he is dead or kills this man. He lost everything that mattered to him. He has nothing left but this obsession to destroy the man we call The Director. On the other hand, I do have a life, and a promising career. I love writing, and I am a good investigative reporter. I have no wish to go back to that life of hunting."

Bexx stared into the fire. "When you do make your decision and decide to read the texts, I have a request."

"I would be happy to consider your request; you have been very helpful in allowing me to see your life here, and I feel I should do something to repay you if I can."

"I want you to tell your story to the camp, the entire thing, from the dreams in the beginning to the texts you have yet to read. I want my Asgarda to understand you as you do them."

Bexx stood up and didn't wait for a reply. She turned and walked into the night.

Nõn understood the request wasn't a request and she'd been given no option but to comply with it.

CHAPTER SEVENTEEN

T he first week of patients in the compound had been a remarkable success. After the initial in-processing and paperwork had been completed, Lennie oversaw the removal of all personal items from her prospective patients. The reason for this was clear. She wanted no possibility of anyone hiding a cell phone or any communication device of any kind. She explained that this was a necessary and required part of the treatment they were about to receive. When the in-processing was complete, each patient was shown to their room and given a small meal. They were then left alone. Internal closed circuit cameras allowed the security staff to observe which of the patients passed out first from their drugged meal. When they were all incapacitated, they were stripped and then removed from the facility to one of the twelve missile silos in the field outside of the former launch control facility. Sergeant Schidel oversaw the placement of each of the first four patients into the silos. Lennie had left specific instructions that they had to be unharmed during their transportation to the silos.

The following day when the patients awoke, they were in unfamiliar surroundings, cold, hungry, naked and disoriented. Day one of their desensitization treatments had begun. Much to The Director's excitement, none would survive the therapy Lennie had devised. He'd definitely picked the right woman for the job, in spite of her disgusting habits. She'd been able to maximize the information in the files she'd been given on the patients' psychological profiles, with alarming results. Two of the patients died within hours from cardiac arrest. One had suffered and aneurysm, and the final patient had died while perched on a four-inch I beam attached to the water tank five stories above ground. Lennie had come up with the idea to maximize that patient's fear of heights. He awoke, hands bound behind him at waist level, standing in bare feet on the 4-inch wide platform, fifty-five feet above the ground. His will to survive had been the strongest. He'd somehow remained perched, in spite of the constant North Dakota winds. The final day of his life was spent in a desperate attempt to somehow crawl down from the I beam without the use of his arms or hands. He failed, but the pointless battle for his life had been filmed in its entirety. It had the highest bids of any of the patients' films, which made The Director exceedingly happy. Once the patient's bodies were collected, they were taken to a far corner of the thirty-six acre compound and placed one on top of another in a 20-foot-deep narrow grave that Schidel and his men had dug using a backhoe. The grave was then filled. The plan was exceedingly efficient in The Director's eyes. The money was beginning to roll in, and his tireless efforts were being rewarded.

Nick arrived back in Moses Lake and immediately began to set up a table top scale model of the facility based on Google maps photos of the facility and pictures The Driver had been able to pull off the Web. To The Driver, the idea seemed childish.

"Why the hell are you creating a miniature version of the facility?"

"It's necessary for tactical planning, my friend. It's called a table top exercise and is used worldwide by military commanders to visualize the area they're going to conduct operations in. Mental preparation is just as critical in these types of operations, as is physical."

"OK, well should I buy a G.I. Joe with the Kung Fu grip for you to imagine yourself with? Or perhaps a He-Man action figure would be better; not sure, though, if there's a He-Man character as old as you."

"I'd prefer a John Wick, if it exists."

"Who?"

"Never mind."

The time had finally come for Nõn to read the texts Nick had sent. Her dreams had been consistent, and the message sent by her spiritual guide hadn't wavered. There was an urgency in the plea for Nõn to join her. What that meant, she had no idea, but since she'd left Moses Lake, the dreams had begun again. Nõn felt that was in itself a sign she was somehow on track by being in Ukraine.

Nõn approached Bexx and asked if they could talk alone. Bexx motioned to her to follow, and they walked off down a path away from the rest of the group.

Nõn explained the content of the texts and that Nick had asked her to return. He'd found another camp. He said it was a difficult task and he needed help to have any chance of successfully shutting down the facility.

"And what does he expect you to help him with?"

"I do not know. I am a writer, not a tactician. I have no combat experience. But he asked me to return."

Bexx was quiet, her eyes dark and withdrawn. "Walk with me." She motioned for Nõn to follow. "Will you address the Asgarda tonight, then?"

"If you would still like me to, yes, I had planned on it."

"Yes, I would like you to do so. Have you answered your texts yet?"

"No, I have not. I planned on doing so very soon."

"Would you wait until after you've briefed the Asgarda?"

"May I ask why you would like me to wait?"

"You may. I have much to consider. I need time to address my team and the rest of this cell of the Asgarda. I cannot explain right now why I am asking you to wait. I want the rest of my team to make their own decisions."

Nõn was puzzled by what that meant exactly, but after thinking it over, she realized it had already been several days since she'd received the texts; a few more hours wouldn't matter one way or another.

"I will do as you ask."

"Thank you. We will speak again tonight, then, at the campfire." Bexx turned and walked away.

Later that night, all the Asgarda had gathered at Bexx's request. They'd built one fire instead of many. Finally when they were all there, Bexx called Nõn forward and began to speak

"Our guest will be leaving soon. She has been with us many days and has gathered our stories. She will be writing about this cell of the Asgarda, and this will bring much needed attention to our cause. It will also bring unwanted attention from the Russians. Our cell will begin shutting down, each team will be folded into another cell of their choosing. Our fight will continue. I wanted you all to hear the reason our guest must now leave. We are the Asgarda, and our fight is here, protecting Ukraine. We are not alone, however. Hear her story." Bexx motioned for Nõn to begin.

An hour and a half later, Nõn had finished her account of her life and the complicated path that took her to Baroota. Following her dreams and the suggestions of her spirit guide. When she described Baroota and her realization that Nick was the wolf in her dreams, Bexx paid special attention. Nõn detailed how they'd survived Baroota by, as Nick had described it, "seeing things with new eyes." She described his incredibly juvenile manner and irritating jokes. Several of the women asked, "Is he your man?" She laughed and laughed as she replied, "No, he does not even recognize I am a woman. We are bonded by the hunt at Baroota; nothing else. He sees me as a fellow warrior, in spite of the fact that I do not want to be one."

When she finished, the camp was silent. Bexx silently made eye contact with each member of her team. Their communication was unspoken. None of the remaining Asgarda knew of their plans.

As the fire died and the teams withdrew into their tents, Bexx and her team stood fast around the fire. She stared long and hard into the fire and finally looked at Nõn.

Nõn had sensed this meeting at the fire meant more than Bexx had let on; there was much more to this woman than she allowed the Asgarda to know. Nõn watched and waited, then finally, staring back into the fire, Bexx began to speak.

"I have spoken to my team and let each of them make their own decision. We have agreed as a team. We will follow you, and if we can help in this operation, we will help. When you text your wolf, advise him he will have our help in this endeavor."

Nõn replied, "What about passports, and identification for international flights?"

"We are always prepared to leave and take this fight to another place. Our preparations are always done in the mindset of planning for the worst and how to survive whatever is coming. We are prepared to leave as soon as you are."

Nõn nodded. Apparently, Bexx wasn't going to be dissuaded. Her mind was made up.

Nõn walked back to her tent and turned the phone back on. After the phone's software had booted up and ran its set up protocols, she began to text.

Nick had been lying in a small depression in a field outside the facility for a couple hours. This was his third trip to Dresden, North Dakota, and by far the most disturbing. He'd witnessed the security team removing a naked man from one of the missile silos on the previous trip. This trip, Nick had watched while apparently drugged or unconscious body after body was brought from the facility to the missile tubes. He counted eight bodies in all as he watched. The security team was apparently the same group he'd witnessed doing patrols before. He began to name them. Lurch was at least 6'5", and very fit. He'd be difficult to subdue. The next he named Gomez, because he looked like the character Gomez from the Addams family. Falling in line with the motif, the final guard Nick named Pugsley. He was Fat and complained a lot. Additionally, he had a slight hitch in his gait. He limped on his left leg. The bodies' placement had been supervised by a tall, thin man and the dark-haired woman. The woman had an exceptionally large forehead, and her hair line started mid-skull and had obviously been dyed jet black. She was a cross in Nick's mind between Morticia and a Bene Gesserit from Frank Herbert's "Dune." Morticia won out as her assigned name. The remaining man wore sergeant stripes and had no other peculiar features. He was just the sergeant.

Nick watched as the bodies were placed and the silos sealed. The security team left, as did Morticia and the sergeant. A few hours later, the screams for help began.

As Nick listened, his phone buzzed. He rolled over and checked the screen. It was Nõn.

Nõn explained she'd be coming, and since he'd said he'd need help, she was bringing mercenaries from Ukraine. Her assignment from NPR had been to do a piece on them, and she'd explained their situation. The leader of the mercenaries had asked to be provided transportation. They had the passports and necessary identification. Nick was hesitant at first. He normally had worked alone. To have a bunch of Russian Marlboro men taking over this mission wasn't exactly what he had in mind from the text he'd sent. He sent back a response explaining that. It seemed strange to him that he'd spent most of his time in the military training to fight Russia and Russians. This was ironic; now Russian mercenaries were asking to help him. He needed to think this over. So, he waited on the reply text. Finally, he responded.

"Yes, they can come. I'm forwarding you a number to call. He calls himself 'The Driver', and he can arrange tickets and travel arrangements for all of you. I'm at the facility now, and I can hear people screaming from inside. The Director is definitely in charge of this camp as well. It looks ugly. Advise your mercenaries this is no joke, they'd better be prepared to bring their 'A' game. No Russian bullshit. This is my operation. Make that clear. I don't wanna have to go all Rocky Balboa on their giant Russian asses."

Nick pushed send.

Nõn rolled her eyes on the other side of the world as the text arrived. She wasn't sure she had the patience for this ridiculous juvenile mentality again. She'd mentioned she was in Ukraine, and Nick had read Russian. She smiled when she realized she'd left out the small detail that the mercenaries were women. What he didn't know, wouldn't hurt him, she decided. Time for Nick to feel the sting of being the brunt of a joke.

Nick texted The Driver and began to detail what Nõn had said. As he was about to push send, he realized here was an opportunity to take the edge off The Driver's constant sexual innuendos. He erased Russian mercenaries from the text and started giggling as he typed. When he was done, he was beside himself with evil laughter. Finally, he pushed send.

"Yo, Driver, I have some amazing news, brother! Nõn, the waitress you stalked at the restaurant, is in Russia and wants to rescue 6 Russian girls. She was there doing a piece on RussianBrides.com. These women need a place to stay, and I thought perhaps The Driver could put them up for a month or two. Thoughts?"

On the other end, The Driver sat stunned. No way his luck was this good. Russian brides? Could Nick be serious? The Driver couldn't reply quick enough.

"Yes! Yes! The Driver will secure first class seats a.s.a.p. Nothing but the best for these prospective Russian conquests! My servers are already aching with anticipation! I'm on it. Send the information, brother. The Driver will deliver a special package to each and every one of these poor damsels in distress."

Nick was beside himself with laughter. The Driver had bit, and bit hard. Time to slowly and painfully reel him in.

Nick forwarded Nõn The Driver's number and told her to arrange travel with him. The rest of the day went exceedingly fast. In spite of the screams from the silos, Nick was in high spirits. This would be an epic prank on The Driver.

Moments later, Nõn received Nick's text and began to collect the information needed from each of Bexx's team members to obtain the airline tickets.

CHAPTER EIGHTEEN

Nick began to plan for the next mission to the facility. With a team of six, in addition to Nõn and himself, they would need a much larger staging area. He located an abandoned barn large enough to contain the vehicles they would need, as well as equipment. He began to make a mental list of weapons, ammo, and tactical gear they would need. Being Russians, Nick assumed the team would be most comfortable with the AK design of assault rifles. He decided on the CAI Drako AK 47 pistol. It was a close combat weapon. He looked up a list of potential suppliers and decided on Atlantic Firearms. The gun was currently on sale there and could be on its way as soon as he secured an approved FFL dealer to act as a go-between.

Meanwhile, The Driver was in high gear. He'd secured seven first class tickets for Nõn, Bexx and the team. They would arrive in Spokane in just under twenty-eight hours. Fragrant scented candles and soaps were being purchased. New beds and bedding, satin sheets, feather pillows. The Driver left no detail to chance. He had a new Rinnai water heater installed in the farmhouse so there would be an endless supply of hot water for his Russian beauties. He bought an extra fridge to hold the additional food seven extra people would require. When Nick arrived back at the farmhouse, the building had been transformed into a 15-year-old boy's version of a bachelor pad. Nick was beside himself with evil, sadistic glee. The Driver had taken the bait and ran with it.

Nõn and Bexx had been seated next to each other on the plane, which gave them time to speak quietly while the others enjoyed the luxury of first class accommodations. Nõn had a few questions for the Leader of the Asgarda.

"I have a question?"

"Yes?"

"Why are you leaving Ukraine to enlist in a fight that is not yours? Ukraine obviously is a more pressing battle."

Bexx was quiet for a moment. "Yes, that is a legitimate question. Between us, I am not from Ukraine. I am from the former Soviet state of Georgia. My country was invaded by Russia several years before the current Ukraine crisis. Our military conducted preemptive strikes on the Russians, in spite of overwhelming Russian military superiority. The Russians used that aggression as an excuse for war. To make a long story short, I came to

Ukraine to help stop the Russians again. This time, they advanced so rapidly and took Crimea before any resistance could be realistically formed. The writing is on the wall here in Ukraine. NATO will do nothing until it is too late. I am not waiting for the inevitable outcome. When I was a child, I lived in the United States for some time. I was a high school student there until I was forced to return to Georgia. My father had sent us away when the Soviet Union collapsed in the 1990s. He wanted us to be safe and felt we would be in the United States. I returned to Georgia after my father had been killed by Abkhaz separatists. The entire country was a mess." Bexx was quiet again for several moments. "Anyway, I was forced to return to Georgia, and when I arrived home I entered a war zone. It was very brutal. Many people died needlessly. Does that explain my motivations for joining you?"

"It does."

"Now I have some questions for you, if you would consider them."

"Please, do ask."

"Explain to me how you came to know that this man Nick was the wolf in your dreams?"

Nõn explained the dream itself again, and then the tattoo on Nick's chest, along with the Viking symbols on his shoulder. There was nothing else it could have been. And given the fact they'd been the only survivors from Baroota, she felt her dream had been a prophecy and correct.

Bexx nodded. It made sense. "Please tell me about this man we are to join in battle. What is he like?"

Nõn rolled her eyes and began. "Well, he can be incredibly frustrating, and he has the most annoying sense of humor. He is hard to take seriously until you realize that under all that juvenile façade, he is incredibly angry. The way he tortured and eventually killed our captors in Baroota. They were exceptionally bad people with no doubt, but watching him made me realize he had thought long about retribution, revenge, and what he would do to those that had wronged him in the past. It is like there are two of him; one that is incredibly damaged that is barely contained by the other, juvenile and annoying. Nothing about him is what it appears. Many times, I thought he was wrong in Baroota, but he was not. He saw the camp with such clarity, he knew exactly what to do to dismantle the operation there. It was all so subtle, juvenile, and yet brutally effective. He accomplished much, with nothing more than childish pranks. I am afraid of him, to be honest."

"Afraid of him? Afraid he may harm you?" Bexx said, mildly angry.

"No, never. He would never harm me; quite the opposite. I am afraid of what lies beneath that façade. When you meet him, you will see what I mean. He is stoic, he never lets you know what he is thinking. You think he is mad about one thing, and it is another thing entirely. If the dark side of Nick ever escapes, I do not want to see what happens. I have seen him when he is still in control of himself, and it is disturbing. Should he ever lose control, I do not want to be present."

Bexx was quiet. She understood what Nõn was driving at. The war in her home state of Georgia had been bloody. She'd witnessed many horrors and seen men driven mad with rage at the tortures their enemies had bestowed on fallen comrades. There were no winners; only carnage and damaged psyches. This told her much of Nick's personal history that Nõn hadn't understood.

Nick had located a FFL dealer in Moses Lake called Red Dawn Tactical and ordered the seven CAI Drako AK 47 pistols, along with four thirty-round clips each. In his mind, he imagined the team would be at least grateful for the familiarity with the weapon and its capabilities.

The day had come to pick up Nõn and company from the airport in Spokane. The Driver had rented an 18 pack van from the local Hertz car rental. Nick began the long drive to the Spokane Airport, whistling as he imagined The Driver's face when he realized he'd been punked again.

Nick arrived at the passenger pick up area of the Spokane Airport for Nõn and the team. As he waited, he wondered how things would go with the Russians. Would they be open to his plan of how to tactically take the compound? In his mind, he pictured Dolph Lundgren, Jean Claude Van Damme, and Jason Statham getting off the plane and walking through the lobby of the airport, a toxic cloud of testosterone billowing behind them. Shirts much too tight, as were their pants, obviously meant to show off their superior genes. He couldn't wait to see The Driver's face when the team exited the van at the farmhouse. All the fancy satin sheets would get some questionable looks for sure, not to mention the perfumed soaps and candles. The Driver was about to sooo be punked by Nick. Nick could hardly contain himself as he smirked at the many visual images that crossed his mind's eye.

When Nõn finally did walk into the airport waiting area, she was alone. There was no group of testosterone-filled mercenaries in tow. She walked up to him and said, "Hey, Nick!"

"Nõn," he nodded, "how was the flight?"

"It was long. I am beat. Can we go now?"

"Sure. What happened to the mercenaries? Did they change their minds? Were they stopped by immigration or TSA?"

"No, they're right here."

"Where? I don't see anyone." Nick looked through and around the crowd of women that had stopped and surrounded Nõn.

"Nick, meet Bexx. And this is her team. She's the leader of the Asgarda, a group of women warriors from Ukraine. They think of themselves as the Amazon warriors of old, reborn."

Nick's expression was uncommitted; stoic as usual, he gave away nothing. The anticipation of his prank was suddenly gone. "Wait – is this The Driver's idea of a joke? You said Russian mercenaries."

"I said Ukraine mercenaries; you heard Russian mercenaries."

Nick could see Nõn was indeed serious. He looked at Bexx and showed no emotion whatsoever, and the stern faces of the Asgarda stared back at him. He turned, saying, "Follow me" as he put on his sunglasses and walked toward the building exit.

Bexx looked to Nõn and whispered, "You didn't tell him that we would be women?"

Nõn shrugged and shook her head no.

"I think it best, then, that he doesn't know we speak English either. Agreed?"

Nõn smiled and nodded yes.

"We will have the woman who was your interpreter speak for us."

Nõn again nodded.

Bexx spoke to the group in a language Nick could only assume was Russian as he walked towards the exit. The group laughed and spoke excitedly amongst each other.

Nick unlocked the van and started to walk to the other side of the van, when Bexx stepped into his path.

"Yo Nõn, can you tell Xena the Princess Warrior to get the hell up out of my grill?"

Nick could feel the heat coming off her body in waves. He looked up at her eyes; she must have stood at least 6'3", with shoulder length raven black hair. Nick stammered, trying to say something witty but finally waved backwards, motioning for her to move. She smiled and said something he didn't understand and moved out of his way. He grimaced and said in a low, quiet voice, "This shit is gonna be hell on Earth."

Nick said nothing for the first half hour of the drive, then finally he said to Nõn, "Do any of them speak English?" Nõn said she didn't know, she'd used an interpreter the entire time she was in Ukraine; this was partially true.

"OK, well you could have let me know you were bringing Xena Princess Warrior, the Powerpuff Girls, and Buffy the Vampire Slayer. And I guess this one is The Interpreter, since she's mad doggin' the hell out of me right now. Sup, Mz. Interpreter? Does someone need a hug? Not feeling feminine fresh after your long flight, I see." Nick winked at her.

Nõn replied, "Yes, she's The Interpreter, and what does their being women matter to you?"

"It matters because I'd set this up as a prank! The Driver is a hacker, a crazy skilled hacker, and about the single biggest pervert I've ever met. I told him you'd be bringing girls rescued from RussianBrides.com. He's been sporting wood ever since! I expected hard core Marlboro men. Russian mercenaries! Instead, it looks like a Victoria's Secret magazine puked up all over my van. Jesus, Nõn! And what's with Xena? Why does she have to get all up in my grill? Breathing on me and shit! Tell your interpreter to tell Xena to stay the hell…never mind! Never mind! Jesus!"

The remainder of the drive was filled with the girls speaking animatedly to each other. Nõn turned from the front of the van and made eye contact with Bexx, then raised her eyebrows, meaning, *See! Exactly what I told you.* Bexx nodded in return, and a slight smile crossed her lips. She then turned and looked out the window as the van cruised on down I- 90 westbound towards Moses Lake.

CHAPTER NINETEEN

T he van arrived at The Driver's farmhouse, and the team members all exited the vehicle. The Driver came out of the house smiling. "Man, do I ever owe you big time," he said to Nick.

Ever the opportunist, Nick agreed, "You do owe me," then under his breath he said, "you have no idea how much you owe me. This is so not the outcome I'd imagined."

Nick introduced the girls to The Driver. "This is Xena, Buffy, The Interpreter, and the Powerpuff Girls. And this is Nõn. You remember Nõn, the waitress you were watching from the diner?"

Nick looked at Nõn and nodded, then said, "Ya, he was a customer, the green Honda guy."

She looked at The Driver, stunned. "BLT, fries, decaf?"

The Driver smiled a sheepish smile. "That was me, yes."

Nõn swallowed, looking at Nick, then at The Driver. "And you're alive? This couldn't have been pretty. Are you OK?"

The Driver held up his hand and showed her his bandaged finger.

Nick reached out for her hand and handed her a small prescription pill bottle. "gift for you."

Nõn looked inside; there was a single fingernail. She cringed.

Bexx watched the whole exchange as the girls gathered around The Driver. Nõn was right, Nick would never hurt her; however, he apparently had no issue hurting any threat to her.

Nick smiled. "Debt paid for daring to surveil you."

Nõn replied, "He was there the whole time? Right in front of me?"

"Yes. When I realized that, it was clear you were right. This isn't your fight; you needed to write, not follow me. This is my arena."

Nõn looked at The Driver and said, "I'm sorry for your finger."

The Driver made the most out of the situation, while The Interpreter pretended to inform the girls of the conversation. The girls immediately began to pay attention to The Driver, the tones of their voices sympathetic as they kissed his hand and face.

Nick looked on, disgusted. This wasn't what he'd imagined the meet-and-greet between The Driver and the Russian mercenaries would be. He'd imagined a much different scenario.

The Driver asked the mercenaries to follow him into the house as he showed them to their rooms and explained where everything was in the kitchen.

Nick, surly as ever, went to his room and closed the door.

Nick listened glumly as the conversation continued outside his door. He set the alarm on his phone for 5 am and covered his head with a pillow. He'd hoped to get up early and begin his morning workout. Since he'd located the camp, he'd quit his job and devoted his total focus to training for the assault on the facility.

The next morning, Nick woke up as the alarm went off and headed to the bathroom to prepare for his morning run. He was grateful for the silence in the house as he walked quietly down the hallway, passing the closed doors to now no longer empty bedrooms. As he opened the door, his eyes were stung by a cloud of steam rolling out of the room, engulfing him. There stood Bexx, just opening the shower door. She didn't bother to cover herself as Nick looked on. Stunned, barely awake and now looking at Bexx as water dripped off her body from the shower, it took Nick a moment to collect himself. Finally after he realized more than a few moments had passed of him staring at her, he mumbled, "Uh, sorry," and closed the door. Bexx smiled and began to towel off.

Nick walked back down the hallway and collected all his belongings from his room. He wrapped everything in a big bundle and angrily headed down the stairs and out the door, mumbling angrily under his breath, "Don't need this shit now!" He headed to the barn. Dropping the bundle into the straw, he moved into a stall in the barn, ensuring the distraction of the mercenaries wouldn't derail his focus on The Director. He then went for his morning run.

When Nick returned, Bexx was in the field beside the house. She'd set up bales of hay approximately one hundred meters away and was now shooting a compound bow The Driver had purchased but never used. Nick watched as he walked, cooling down from the run; Xena had world class skills with the bow, there was no doubt. Arrow after arrow pierced the bull's eye. She too was aware of his presence as she recovered the arrows and returned to her starting place. Smiling, she decided to do a tactical drill with the bow and began an assault on the bales of hay, shooting on the run, then reloading while rolling to the right, she came up and shot again. Then rolling to the left coming up, running to cover as she shot on the run. She continued until she no longer had arrows. She walked to the bales to check her target.

Nick watched as she conducted the drill. It had never occurred to him a bow could be used in this way. When she finished, he turned away and walked into the barn, the image of her earlier in the morning still burning in his head.

Nick continued on with his routine, trying to ignore Bexx and hers.

He hit the heavy bag, speed bag, then finished his morning with a Kata routine with an ancient oak nightstick he'd carried for 30 years or more. The moves smooth and well-practiced, he started slowly, then built up speed until he was a blur of motion, strikes, blocks, foot sweeps, parries, then he slowed back down to the smooth, practiced ending. Bexx watched quietly from the front porch as he slowed. When he stopped, she went into the farmhouse and the day began.

Nick finished with three sets of pull-ups off the load bearing "I beam" that ran the length of the barn. He then cleaned up using cold water from the faucet used to water animals that had been housed in the barn.

An hour later, Nick tried to salvage something of the day with the Asgarda by presenting them with the weapons he'd purchased from Red Dawn tactical. He'd laid them out on a table, each with its own magazines and ammo. When the Asgarda saw the weapons, they reacted exactly the opposite of how Nick imagined.

"What are these?" asked The Interpreter.

"Romanian AK 47 pistols, excellent for close combat engagements." Nick spoke clearly as he smiled, waiting for their reaction. "I bought them for you, for all of you. When you're ready, I'll show you how to make tactical slings for them."

The team milled around the table, and one of the Powerpuff girls picked up a gun and looked at it disapprovingly. Nick watched, astonished. Day one with the mercenaries was going to be a long one.

The Interpreter finally explained that the Asgarda trained with ancient weapons, swords, arrows, knives, scythes and hand-to-hand combat. They didn't use guns. They were silent in their attacks, preferring stealth and slyness to brute force.

Nick clenched his teeth and took a deep breath. He then growled, "Wonderful! Well, we had a saying on the streets: 'Only a dead man brings a knife to a gun fight.' You all need to wake the hell up! You're in America now; everyone here has a damn gun, every housewife, grandmother, and 4-year-old on a swing in the park has a gun in their pocket. You show up to this fight with your ancient Kung Fu Panda bullshit, and you'll be buried with it."

Nick looked at Bexx. "You better get your people in line, this shit won't do. I won't be responsible for their deaths because they refuse to adapt. This isn't some bullshit Dallas Cowboy cheerleader tryouts. Your Asgarda cheerleading squad needs to unass the short skirts and pompoms. The people at this facility are real. They're torturing their victims as we speak, and they have no problem adding your candy asses to the day's menu."

Nick scowled at Nõn as he stormed out of the now quiet room, swearing and knocking a chair out of his way. He headed to his faithful 'Yota and fired up the motor. He drove away and didn't return for several hours.

The Driver had started his morning by making breakfast to order as each of the Asgarda woke. The exact opposite of Nick, The Driver was in man heaven. His previously empty farmhouse was now filled with beautiful, formidable women, and they loved how he'd pampered them.

As the conversation went around the table between the Asgarda, The Interpreter asked, "Why do you call yourself The Driver?"

The Driver began to explain he was a hacker, a first-rate hacker, and he was rambling on about himself when Buffy the Vampire Slayer piped up. Speaking to the group, she explained that if this was THE DRIVER, he was a very famous hacker. She was the group electronics specialist, and herself formidable in Web assaults. The Interpreter asked the hacker to detail his latest deeds, which he proudly did. Buffy talked excitedly and said this was what all the rumors on the Web said in chat rooms and blog threads, and it was common knowledge The Driver was rumored to be the one behind the DNC hacks and had made it look like the Russians had been the guilty party. He would be a formidable asset to any cause he joined. She looked at him approvingly, as did the rest of the Asgarda.

After breakfast, The Interpreter spoke to The Driver for Buffy and asked if she could see his computer room. The Driver was more than willing to show off his "Bat Cave." Hours later, The Interpreter came out of the room, bored beyond belief. Bexx asked, "How's it going in there?"

"I am no longer needed, she is in her world; I guess their world, actually. I have no idea what they are doing, but she did tell me that he is indeed The Driver. I am afraid that we may not see her for several more hours."

Bexx nodded. She instructed the remaining Asgarda to prepare for their morning routine.

When the Asgarda had finished their morning workout, Bexx told them to assemble near the barn. She had them construct a circle of straw bales 12 feet in diameter. Each of them knew what was expected. This was their fighting circle. They trained in a twelve-foot circle they thought of as their "bubble of death." Should an enemy enter the twelve-foot bubble, they'd entered a zone in which the Asgarda would quickly destroy them. As the first two women entered the circle, Nick returned to the farm. He sat in his truck and watched as the women began to battle in the circle.

Nick was familiar with the concept of the bubble. He'd spent a career in a world where "the bubble of death" was much smaller. He watched and took mental notes. *Do or Die*, he thought as he got out of the truck and retrieved the ancient oak riot baton from behind the seat.

He approached Bexx and asked to join the circle; however, he asked that the four remaining Asgarda all attack as one. In one assault, he would be the focus of their attack. Bexx agreed. She already had an idea of what he was capable of in the circle; now she would see if he was as skilled as he thought. On the other hand, her Asgarda needed to be humbled. They were already getting too accustomed to the softer lifestyle The Driver had made possible.

The women entered the circle, and Nick stood in the center. The Asgarda spoke amongst themselves about who would go first, and one made the comment that the arrogant man would think differently of them after they beat him bloody. Bexx looked on grimly. The cockiness of her team was concerning. They had no idea of his skill or abilities and had never seen Nick fight anyone, but they assumed they were superior in skill and ability. This was not a good thing. Confidence, yes; arrogant cockiness, not a good thing for a warrior.

Nick nodded to Bexx that he was ready, and she gave the command to begin. The Asgarda were armed with wooden staffs, swords and knifes. Nick began spinning, attacking, and knocking them out of the circle before Bexx had finished speaking the command to begin. In less than ten seconds, the circle was clear of all the Asgarda warriors and only Nick remained, breathing heavily.

Nick spoke angrily, "You must be prepared for anything in this fight. You hesitate one half-second, and you *will* die. This enemy won't use wooden swords or toy guns. There will be no command to begin; it'll just begin without warning. You must be prepared for anything!" He pointed at the ground and looked at Bexx angrily.

Bexx walked into the circle and faced Nick and drew her sword as she faced him. The Asgarda were picking themselves up from the dirt and brushing off the straw as they began to cheer her on. Her eyes now cold and hard, she raised the sword over her shoulders into what Nick recognized as a head defensive stance. They locked eyes, and for a moment he considered fighting her; however, he'd already come to the realization on the drive he wouldn't fight her. Ever.

Nick stepped out of the circle and said one word, "No." He walked away from the group, hoping his point had been understood. The women looked at Bexx, unsure of what to think of the events that had happened and looking for her guidance. She called two of them into the circle and began to spar with them.

CHAPTER TWENTY

Several days had passed, and the Asgarda had grudgingly accepted the use of and training in the Romanian AK 47 pistols. Nick had instructed them in basic dry fire drills, then worked up the ladder to live fire. Each of the Asgarda had a custom made tactical sling and now carried the weapons everywhere they went in their daily routine. Bexx had demanded their complete compliance with Nick's instructions since the humiliating demonstration in the Asgarda's combat circle. She reminded them of Nõn's account of Baroota and how what Nick had said to Nõn had seemed trivial at the time, but later saved their lives. There was to be no argument about the weapons.

Table top exercises were conducted with the entire team as a whole, then later with each team member individually. Nick required each team member to explain what their roles would be in the assault, then questioned how they would react should the plan go south. There had to be contingencies for everything. A reaction for every action. Finally, the time had come that the plan was clear to everyone. They'd practiced the assault using hay bale mock ups of the interior of the facility, practiced compromising the chain link barrier using various methods, should one or the other fail. At last, Nick asked the group if there was anything that had been missed, did anyone see anything that needed to be addressed? There was nothing. They were ready.

That night, Nick threw a party for the Asgarda. He explained, "Tomorrow, we'll be going into battle; tonight, we'll celebrate." The Driver had taken a poll of what the Asgarda would prefer to eat and drink on their last meal before their plan went into motion. He then had it all delivered, paid for courtesy of hacked credit card numbers and accounts he'd obtained off the Web. Somewhere, an unwitting husband would be trying to explain to his suspicious wife that he hadn't purchased enough food and vodka to supply a weekend frat house party. The Driver laughed at the image in his head as he ordered the supplies for the celebration.

The party was planned to start that night as the sun went down. Nick was the self-appointed bartender and drink slinger. He made sure everyone's glasses were kept full and everyone was happy. For Nõn, he poured whatever nonalcoholic beverage she desired. She never would be comfortable with being intoxicated. It was a lesson she'd learned well as a child: never ever let your guard down, and never allow someone to have control over you. He respected that. The Asgarda could learn a lot from her. When Nick came to fill the first glass for Bexx, he took it from her and returned after filling it. When he handed it to her, he held it for a moment. He made sure she held his eye contact as they communicated silently. Bexx was puzzled by the look he gave her until she tasted the clear liquid in the glass. It was water; only water. She looked at Nick, and he stared back with a purposeful look. Just as Nõn had said, assume nothing when it comes to Nick. Bexx was learning.

The party continued for several more hours, with Nick pushing alcohol on the Asgarda team. As she became more drunk, The Interpreter admitted to The Driver that she had a secret! The Driver was curious and asked what it was. "Shuuuuuhsh," she slurred as she looked around, then said, "We all speak English! Every one of us, but Bexx doesn't want Nick to know." The Driver smiled. "Don't worry; your secret is safe with me." He absolutely loved that he had another tiny bit of information Nick was unaware of. The Driver then smiled, realizing as he watched Buffy she'd played her part very well, but he'd suspected her comprehension of the Web hacks he'd taught her had been a little too insightful for someone who didn't understand a single word he'd spoken. The women told stories to each other as the alcohol loosened their inhibitions and the fire they'd built slowly burned down to glowing coals. Bexx quietly asked the interpreter to repeat a story she was about to tell so Nick would understand her. It would be the only story she translated that night.

"When I was a child, my father was in the army of my homeland of Georgia. Many of you assumed I was from Ukraine, and I let that assumption stand. When the Soviet Union fell, my father sent my brother and I into the woods near our home. My father was fearful that we would be targets of the Abkhazia separatists. There were several hundred acres there of wooded and wild land. We were frightened and had no idea what to expect. I was older, so I took care of my brother as best I could. We were in the woods for several days, we kept track of the number of days by making notches on a stick. When we had 12 notches, we started to worry. That night I saw a wolf, old and grizzled, just outside the firelight of our camp. I don't know how long he had watched us, but that night I became aware of him. My brother wanted me to kill him; he thought the wolf would attack us when we slept. I saw something different. I watched the wolf, and I saw curiosity. He looked hungry, so I cut off a piece of meat from a rabbit we had cooked and threw it out to him. He carefully snuck up and ate it. This went on for several nights. We both started to feed the wolf, my brother and I. It was very odd; we had been taught to fear the wolves in the forest. The government frequently went on hunts to wipe out wolf packs that had grown too aggressive and attacked people in our town as they walked at night. However, this wolf never attacked us." Bexx stared into the fire as the Asgarda and Nick listened. He watched her intently, waiting for her to continue. The Asgarda also listened; Bexx had never spoken of her past, not once, and they were very interested in what she had to say.

Finally, she continued. "Eventually, by throwing the food shorter distances to the wolf, we were able to coax it into the camp. I could see that it had been a beautiful animal at one time. It was now scarred and beat up, there were fresh wounds from a fight it had recently been in. It watched me as I watched it. As incredible as it sounds, one night the wolf came into our camp with a rabbit and laid it down near me. It then stepped back and waited. We cooked the rabbit and ate it, feeding a large part of it to the wolf. He stayed in the camp that night, near the warmth of the fire. We became more and more comfortable with each other. The wolf kept us fed, and we kept it warm by the fire. One day it came into camp with another rabbit, and then the wolf lay down next to me beside the fire. I was terrified and elated at the same time. The wolf was much bigger than he seemed at a distance. I dared to run my fingers through its black pelt. The wolf growled, deep and threatening. Its teeth bared, and I stopped. I waited and stroked its back again. The wolf growled and bared its teeth but never snapped or bit me."

Bexx, unaware that Nick had become noticeably agitated as she told the story, continued. "The wolf began to gain weight, and we felt safe with him around. We imagined him as our protector. We benefited from each other. He liked our fire, we needed the food he brought. One night the wolf got up as we sat by the fire; he was agitated, staring into the night, listening intently. Suddenly he snarled at us, growling fiercely. He drove us out of the camp and into a nearby tree. My brother begged me to shoot it, but I couldn't. The wolf went back to our fire and waited. Three more wolves appeared on the outskirts of our camp. They were ragged and beaten down. Our wolf had once looked like that; now he was muscular and healthy. Our wolf snarled at the three intruders, and the fight began. It was horrible to watch. He was outnumbered, and they came at him as a single group. He killed two almost immediately but was severely wounded. He and the third wolf fought a long time before he finally killed that one as well. My wolf had been mortally wounded in the fight. He was dying. I told my brother to stay in the tree, and I climbed down. I walked carefully to my wolf." Bexx's eyes were moist now, and she paused. "I sat next to my wolf and thanked him for protecting us; in my child's mind, he had driven us off to protect us from the pack. I pulled his body closer to the fire and stroked his back as he lay dying." She paused for some time, remembering the event. "Two days later, my father came and found us. 'Tamriko' he said, 'you must leave here now.' He made us get on a plane and come to the United States. That was the last time I saw my father alive." Bexx looked around the camp at each of her Asgarda warriors. "Now you all know my real name and where I am from. I thought that since tonight was our last night before the mission, you should know the truth." Without warning, Nick threw a log onto the fire and stormed out of the camp, shaking his head. The group, puzzled by his curious reaction to the story, watched as he animatedly paced in the darkness. Bexx assumed he was angry with her for telling the story, and possibly making the group question whether or not they should follow her because of the disclosure of not being from Ukraine. That fear had always been in the back of her mind as well. Eventually, Nick did return to the fire and said nothing. Something in the story had struck a nerve in him that was obvious.

When the Asgarda were good and drunk, Nick spoke quietly to Nõn and explained his plan. He wanted her to know what would be the real plan should the entire operation go south. He asked her to repeat everything he'd said in detail until he was satisfied she understood.

"I can't ask you to enter this fight. I told you a couple of days ago I shouldn't have expected you to enter this fight. I meant it." He looked at the women drinking and laughing around the fire. "I can't ask them to enter this fight either. Xena and I will go. I work better alone, you know that, but if she agrees to come, we'll go together; I trust her. We'll be OK."

He then returned to the party for the final round of drinks. Filling everyone's glass one last time, he called out, "Last call for alcohol."

He didn't bother filling Bexx's drink another time with water; she hadn't emptied it from the last round. Bexx followed his progress from warrior to warrior. Finally, he stopped and looked at her long and hard. He placed two fingers on his wrist where had he worn a watch, the meaning would be clear. He tapped once, then nodded his head to her. *Do you understand?* he asked, raising his eyebrows questioningly. She nodded yes once.

Nõn and Bexx put the intoxicated team to bed and made sure everyone was taken care of. Nõn came to Bexx and quietly said, "Good luck to you both. I hope to see you in two days. Remember what I told you about him; nothing will be what it seems." Bexx nodded, and the two women hugged. Bexx then went to her room to prepare for the trip ahead. She had an hour before she'd meet Nick at the rusted truck. She felt her heart beating rapidly. This had been a fight she'd imagined as a team. Her and her team. Now it would be just the two of them.

An hour later, Bexx arrived at the truck. Nick was impatiently pacing back and forth. He said nothing as she loaded her equipment. He'd already loaded his. She got into the truck and watched as he paced outside the truck. She assumed that he too was nervous about the mission; her second assumption of the night, and she'd already been wrong twice. Finally, he got into the truck and started it, then backed quietly out of the driveway and off into the night.

CHAPTER TWENTY-ONE

The Director was more than pleased with the progress that had occurred at Camp Cachibaché. There seemed to be no limit to Lennie's ability to devise diabolical ways to torture her "patients." Her methods were simple, brutal and effective, and more importantly extremely cost effective. She seemed to have a knack for devising seemingly effective and simple ways to inflict the most amount of psychological stress on the patients. Most were highly compromised before they arrived, already subjected to years of pharmaceutical abuse by their doctors. Lennie just removed that crutch, then created an environment for them to experience their worst fears and watched as they crashed and burned, gloriously and gruesomely.

Now that Lennie had proven herself and the camp was functioning, The Director wanted to add an additional layer of protection to his investment.

"Arthur, would you bring the files that arrived this morning?"

"Yes, sir."

Arthur brought the files and laid them on The Director's desk.

"Thank you, Arthur, that will be all."

Arthur left the room and quietly closed the doors. The Director needed a team separate from the security team already in place at Cachibaché to protect his investment, much like the spy in plain sight at Baroota. He wanted an additional set of eyes on the events at the camp. He opened the files and began to search for the team he felt could pull off the job discreetly, but able to address any issues with immediate urgency.

Nick had driven about an hour now; they hadn't spoken a word since they left. It seemed pointless. Bexx didn't speak English, and he didn't speak whatever language she spoke...Russian? Slav? He had no idea. He'd Googled Ukraine languages and found out there were at least 13 recognized languages spoken. The official language was Ukrainian. The unofficial language was Russian, and then there were a dozen or more thrown into the mix. That was all great, but he was tired; he needed to listen to music, or talk, something, anything to break up the white noise of the motor grinding out the miles to North Dakota. Finally, Nick slid a CD into the CD player, and Godsmack broke the silence for a while. He grew tired of the music quickly, until "Serenity" came on. Nick turned to Bexx and said, "Listen to this song. I like it a lot." She just stared at him, emotionless, as she listened. When the song was over, he flipped down the visor above the passenger seat and pulled out another CD from the CD holder hidden there. It held maybe 7-8 CDs, the ones he liked the most.

He slid out the first one, and a moment later Seether's live version of "The Gift" came over the car stereo. Nick pointed to his ears, then to Bexx, and said, "Listen." These were painfully illuminating songs Bexx would never have imagined would be in his library. She listened as song after song was selected and played for her and Nick sang the lyrics. Finally, he was silent and shut off the CD player. Bexx flipped down the visor and pulled out CDs, examining them one at a time. One was a homemade mix that hadn't been named, and she held it up, eyebrows raised, the unspoken question: "How about this one?" She wanted to hear what songs he'd made for his own mix. Nick shook his head no, not that one. Bexx wondered why as she put it back.

Nick said nothing for another hour, then realized they needed to get gas. The truck had a limited range, with a maximum gas mileage of 19-20 miles per gallon, and he had to pay attention to the gas gauge. The tank held a maximum 17 gallons of gas, and at 150 miles on the tank already, he began to get nervous and looked for a place to fill up. They found a place that was open in Coeur D'Alene Idaho and pulled over to get gas. He pointed inside the store and asked if Bexx needed anything. Food? A drink? Bathroom break? She nodded and walked into the store. Once Nick had filled up, he also went in to get a drink and hit the restroom. A few minutes later, they were back on the road, each with a drink and some snacks.

Several more hours later and a couple more stops, and they found themselves at a small gas station in Mosby, Montana. The gas station had seen better days but was new enough to take credit cards at the pump. Nick refueled while Bexx went into the small convenience store. Nick entered the store a short time later to find Bexx face-to-face with one of the locals, while another man was circling her, looking her up and down. The guy behind the counter laughed nervously as he watched. The men had watched her walk in alone and thought they could take advantage of the situation. Nick listened as they spoke to her.

"Well now, aren't you a purty li'l philly!" said the guy in front of her, toothpick hanging from his gap-toothed tobacco-stained mouth.

"Ain't she, though? She just looks like if she were proper broke, she could be ridden all damn day."

The man behind the counter continued to giggle nervously.

The circling man said, "Let's get a good look at you. Come on now, show us something we wanna see."

Bexx was accustomed to being catcalled. In Ukraine, men were easily as cocky and ridiculous. She tried to get into the freezer to retrieve a cold drink, and as she did, the circling man grabbed her ass.

Nick walked down the aisle towards them. "Is there a problem here?"

"No, no problem. Just admiring this li'l philly's ass-ets, thinking we might close and lock the door and take her out for a bit of a ride."

Nick laughed. "Not today, gentlemen. Not today. She's with me."

Nick grabbed her arm and pulled her away from the two men, placing himself between them and her. Bexx really didn't need his help; she'd dealt with men like this her whole life, and she could handle herself. She was surprised at Nick's protectiveness. She decided to play along to see how this unfolded.

Nick backed her up and out of the door, talking to the two men as they backed out of the store. They walked to the truck slowly as the men came to the door, continuing to talk to Bexx, about Bexx, saying what they'd like to do with her. Nick opened her door and motioned for her to get in. He locked the door and closed it after she did and walked around to the driver's side, glaring at the men. They laughed and closed the door of the small country store. Nick got in the truck and asked, "Are you OK?" Bexx said nothing. He pointed at her and gave the thumbs up, then a questioning look. She nodded yes. Nick took a deep breath and stared out the windshield of the truck, then glared at the store and took another breath. Sitting there for a moment, his breathing started to increase slowly at first, then more and more urgent. He slammed the truck into reverse and started to back out of the lot, then stopped. Bexx watched as the anger began to build and his breathing became more rapid. Finally erupting, he spoke.

Fuck it! Nick slammed the truck into 1st gear and pulled forward. He came to a sliding stop in the gravel outside the store. Nick reached across the front of the dash to the glove box and opened it. Inside, there was a set of brass knuckles. He pulled them out and put them on. He also grabbed a large black Gerber lock blade knife and shoved it in his pocket.

"These Buck Owens, Hee Haw, country boy can survive motherfuckers need a tune up," he said to Bexx. "You stay here," Nick said. "Stay! You got that? Stay!" She nodded; the transformation of Nick was a little bit disconcerting. Bexx had to admit, she was a bit curious where this would end. He left the keys in the truck and kept it running and started to get out. He said, "Five minutes. I'll be back in 5 minutes. Stay here!" He slammed the door hard and started to rapidly walk to the store, muttering to himself. "Redneck banjo playing punk ass motherfuckers. Oh, she just needs to be proper broke, huh? Well, fuck you! Shit breathing, gap tooth, can't read or write, sheep raping motherfuckers. We'll see who needs to be proper broke."

Nick opened the door to the store, then closed it. He stopped and locked the door and flipped the well-worn "Open" sign to "Closed".

Bexx waited. She didn't know what to think of the sudden explosive rage she'd observed in Nick. She thought for a moment, then reached up to the CD holder on the visor above her head. She took out the CD he'd said "no" to and slid it in the CD player. A moment later, "Ride of the Valkyries" by Wagner cued up as Joan Sutherland began her operatic rendition of the classic. Bexx raised her eyes, thinking, *Really? Opera?*

Inside the store, another very real battle raged while Joan sang about the Valkyries surveying the battlefield, looking for fallen warriors brave enough to return to Valhalla.

Several minutes later, Nick emerged from the store carrying a digital video recorder that had been the store's sole security device and the drink Bexx had been unable to purchase. He was transformed from the stoic and mildly angry Nick into something else Bexx couldn't describe. He walked quickly to the truck and threw the recorder in the back. He got in the truck and found the music playing. He stopped for a moment, mesmerized. Listening, breathing hard, he started to apologize to Bexx. "Sorry, I'm sorry. That was stupid. I shouldn't have let that get to me. I'm sorry." Nick looked into the mirror and saw that there were several drops of blood smeared on his face. He started to wipe them off, muttering, "Proper broke, my ass." As he spoke, Bexx reached towards him. "What?" he said aggressively as she pulled back. She motioned for him just to trust her, then she slowly reached to a fold in his shirt and retrieved a large bloody tooth hidden there. She held it in front of his face and raised her eyebrows, questioning. Nick, embarrassed now, said, "Huh...umm...oh well...a souvenir. I guess something to remember Mosby, Montana, by." He took the tooth from her and threw it in the 'Yota's ashtray, slamming it shut.

Nick pulled out and continued on towards Dresden, and the facility. Bexx looked out the window silently as they drove, a small, playful smile crossing her lips.

The rest of the trip was uneventful as Nick carried on entire conversations by himself and Bexx listened quietly, never letting on that she understood every word. It was odd to her how different it was to listen only and not speak as he talked. His one-sided conversations went directions she never would have imagined existed, and they were incredibly revealing. Finally, they arrived at the old abandoned barn he'd decided was to be their base camp. It was nearly 4am when they'd unpacked the truck and settled in. Neither had slept since they left Moses Lake just over twenty hours before. Nick wanted to set a watch, but as soon as he lay down, he was out. Bexx watched him fall asleep instantly, his face curiously relaxing. She watched him sleep for some time before she fell asleep herself. When she awoke the next day, she had no idea what time it was. She looked, and Nick wasn't in his sleeping bag. She looked around the barn and found him nowhere near. She got up quietly and walked around the barn. She found him in a stall in the back of the barn. He was naked, washing the blood from the fight in the store off. He scrubbed with soap and washed and then poured cold water over his head. Bexx said nothing; just watched. It was her turn to catch him unaware as he bathed. She noticed some new bruises from the fight, the numerous scars and tattoos, and in particular the tattoos Nõn had described. He was curiously fit for his age; that spoke to the endless pent up energy, a result of his barely manageable anger. When he was nearly finished, she walked back to where they'd been sleeping quietly and waited for him to return. She didn't know how he'd react to knowing she'd been watching him bathe. It felt way too intimate a moment, considering the fight they were about to enter.

Nick returned to the main open area of the barn and said, "Good morning. There's water in the back if you need to wash up. We'll rest for the remainder of the day, then prepare for our assault tonight. I'll have food ready in a few minutes." Bexx stood silent, playing her quiet part. Nick motioned for her to follow as he took her back to where he'd been bathing. He returned to the front while she washed up. When she returned, they ate, then she sat down and waited. Nick scratched out the design of the missile site in the dirt of the barn's floor and looked at her eyebrows up. "Understand?" She nodded. He detailed his plan slowly, asking with shrugs and always speaking in English, hoping she understood. When he finished, she was even more afraid than before. This plan was suicidal. She looked at him as he calmly walked her through the plan. He showed no sign of anxiety. She, however, was now truly afraid. His entire plan was to take the missile facility by stealth, ambush one guard at a time, kill one, wait for the next, kill him, then the next and the next, until they gained access. They would be close when he took them. Her job was to flank them and if something went wrong to use her bow to silently take out the guards as Nick fought him.

Nick finished and looked at her now wide eyes. Her breathing had increased. He could tell she was afraid, but she wouldn't back out. She looked up at him. He sighed and said, "Look, I know it looks crazy, but I've done this before. I don't know how to explain this, but I have a weird knack for this kind of attack. You have to trust me on this. I can't manage a team of six of you and watch everything, take care of everything. I can't be responsible for your team if anything goes wrong. I don't think that way. It sounds ugly, I know, but I learned long ago I'm…" He stopped and was silent. "I'm so glad you can't understand me right now. It's been nice to talk and not worry about you judging me; it's been strangely therapeutic." He took a big breath and continued. "I'm frighteningly lethal on my own. I guess I was born for this. It frightens me how good I am alone as an… assassin." He was quiet. "Anyway, trust me. We'll be fine. I got this…I really have got this." He could see she was still afraid, so he took her hand and placed it on his chest. His breathing was slow and deep. His heart beat slowly and surprisingly; to her, the depth and strength of the beats in his chest felt reassuring. She started to calm down. He really was relaxed.

Nighttime finally came, and they left the barn and walked silently along a path. Nick was apparently sure of where he was going. Soon enough, she learned he was; they'd arrived at the facility.

Nick had brought a weird combination of items that made no sense to her. A long steel pipe about 2" thick and 12-14 feet long, a roll of bubble wrap, and a weird looking cap thing that looked like a skin colored shower cap. He kept the bubble wrap, cap and a pair of bolt cutters in a large bag, along with one of the Romanian AK-47 pistols and four-thirty round clips. The gun made sense, but none of the rest of it made any sense to her. He threw the bag over the fence after he cut the half-inch aircraft cable that encircled the perimeter, woven into the fabric of the chain link fence. He tossed the bolt cutters over the fence as well, then slid the pipe through the chain link fence a couple links above the ground. Once it was nearly halfway through the fence, he lifted his end. The space the pipe created was just enough to crawl under. He motioned for her to go under. Once Bexx was clear, he dropped the fence and motioned for her to repeat it from her end. She did, and he quietly slid under the fence. He pulled the pipe through, then lay it against the bottom of the fence. They were in just like that; quiet and effective. Nick smiled as he whispered..."Pretty simple, huh? I learned that in the military. It's quite effective and simple. We had to train like we thought our enemies would; actually, the Russians would." He smiled. "That's how they thought the Russians or any terrorists would sneak into our nuclear areas. Simple, quiet, and effective." He picked up the bag and bolt cutters and said, "Let's go." Bexx was surprised to see Nick was actually having fun. "Now we wait. The guard rotation has to be perfect for my plan to work."

They waited in silence for a while, and finally Nick spoke again. "This reminds me of a mission I went on in the military. There was a mock P.O.W camp outside of our base. They used it to train pilots in escape and evasion should they ever be shot down over enemy-held lands. The trainers there wanted to run a scenario where our team rescued the pilots to see their reaction. Basically, they wondered if the pilots would choose to escape or stay in the cells they were kept in. I was the team leader, and we agreed to the plan, but we wanted to do our own surveillance of the camp and plan our own rescue. The higher-ups decided that would be too risky and scrapped the plan. They were sure their P.O.W camp guards would catch us and a fight would erupt. We had a reputation on base – our squadron did, I mean – as brawlers. There were a lot of other squadrons that wanted a piece of us. Anyway, the commanders called it off, but we went anyway, unsanctioned. Seemed like that made it more real to us, with no authorization. By 'we', I mean me and one other guy from the team. We snuck under three fences one after another using the pipe method, then we low crawled through the occupied camp past guards smoking and spotlights searching the area. We got into a secure area where the pilots were being held in mock cells, then left a simple message: 'The mighty 92nd S.P.S sends you our best'. Then I wrote the time and date we entered, and a smiley face. We then left the camp the same way we went in, at times laughing so hard, we nearly peed our pants." Nick was laughing at the memory as he told her. "A week later, my team and I were before the commander. He wanted to know who had left the note. No one confessed. He was furious at us, but we'd made our point. We were that damn good. The guys who were working that day were all reprimanded. We didn't care. We answered their challenge. Anyway, my point is this feels the same. We'll be fine, Bexx; just trust me on this. In this arena, I'm positively lethal. Small group tactics, quiet, covert assassination, I can stand with the best in the world."

Bexx listened and realized he had no fear at all; he was completely at ease. He believed what he said.

Finally, the guard rotation lined up in the sequence Nick had been waiting for. He motioned for her to stay down and only come if it went bad. Nick started to crawl up the small crease he had them lying in towards the approaching guard. The guard Nick called Pugsley had a noticeable hitch in his gate; probably an old injury, or maybe arthritis…Nick didn't care. He watched as the guard stopped a few feet from where he was lying motionless. Nick had chosen this night for a reason: it was a new moon, the night was positively ink black. Only the stars shown in the sky. That was just enough light to silhouette the guard as he stood at the end of his assigned patrol route. Just like clockwork, the guard stopped and lit a cigarette. Nick slowly rose to his feet and stepped forward towards the guard. When he was close enough, he withdrew a large close quarters combat knife that had been strapped to his calf and drove it quickly into the guard's throat. The guard died quietly and quickly. Nick quickly pulled him back to where Bexx had been lying and watching. Nick began to strip the guard, then himself. He unwrapped the bubble wrap from the bag and began to wrap it around his torso. He smiled as she watched. "Sorry about the nudity, but ole boy is a bit soggy in the mid-section. I need to look like him when I take out the next guard." Next, Nick dressed in the guard's uniform and picked up his still lit cigarette. He shut off the guard's radio and returned to where the guard had been standing. A half hour later, the next guard approached. Nick whispered to himself, "Gomez, and right on time." Gomez called out, "Hey, fuck nuts! Answer your radio!" Nick pulled out the radio and waved it in the air, indicating the radio had died as he now walked with the same limp the dead guard had. He approached Gomez slowly, head down, still smoking the cigarette. Gomez said, "You stupid fucker! If Sergeant Schidel catches you smoking out here, you'll get fired; you know the rules. No smoking on the compound." Nick shrugged and continued to close the gap, with Gomez saying nothing. Bexx watched quietly, realizing Nick was incredibly calm. The limp, the bubble wrap, the uniform…it all was working just as he'd planned. Moments later, Nick drove the knife into the Gomez's throat, silencing him as well. Two down, two to go. Nick motioned to Bexx to join him, then they pulled the guard's body back to the depression and lay him next to the first guard. Nick whispered, "Next is Lurch. That's why you're here. Lurch is huge, and strong. I'll only be able to take him alone if I'm very lucky." Nick motioned. "You flank out to the right and wait. When he comes out, I'll take the same approach as I did with Gomez, smoking and acting like my radio is dead. When I get close, I'll attack. If that doesn't work, I'm depending on you to take the shot with your bow and drop the big bastard. Got it?" Nick motioned to her to flank and then come up, acting like he had the bow and was shooting an arrow. "Yes?" Bexx nodded yes, then carefully started off into the night.

Less than a half hour later, the door to the facility flew open and Lurch exited with his gun already drawn. The other two guards had gone silent and hadn't checked in on their rounds. Something was wrong. Lurch allowed his eyes to adjust to the night, then slowly began to look for the other guards. He saw a lit cigarette off in the distance. He felt some relief; at least the stupid bastard was consistent. Smoking on the job was going to get him fired. They all knew he smoked when he did his patrols; they could smell it when he came back in the facility. Lurch relaxed a little bit and headed towards the lit cigarette embers. His gun was still out, and it still felt wrong that both guards had suddenly gone quiet. He walked towards the fat guard and called out to him. The guard turned and slowly walked towards him, waving his radio, indicating it was dead. Lurch nodded and looked for the remaining guard. "Have you seen Scott? He's out here somewhere." Nick was too far away when the question was asked to close the gap, so he faked an answer and began to cough, hoping a sudden smoker's cough attack would allow him to close the gap. The tactic worked, and he was able to get within striking distance of Lurch; the problem was, Lurch was already armed, his gun drawn. At best it would be a knife against gun fight, at worst gun against gun, and the surprise they needed to breach the facility would be lost. The plan had gone to shit just that quick. Nick would have to take Lurch with incredible quickness and violence to avoid being shot. Just as Nick was about to attack, Lurch stopped and said, "Who the fuck are you?" He pulled the gun up and pointed it at Nick's chest.

Bexx had watched the exchange from the darkness. Nick had closed the gap so he was within striking distance, then something went wrong. Lurch realized Nick wasn't the fat guard. His gun came up, and he had Nick within his sights. She quietly brought the compound bow up and sighted the large man's head as the target. Hopefully, he wouldn't involuntarily pull the trigger when her arrow found its mark. She released the arrow.

Nick was screwed, and he knew it. Hopefully, somewhere out there Bexx was watching and knew what to do. The answer to his question came just as the thought crossed his mind. An arrow came out of the darkness and pierced the huge man's head. He dropped immediately to the ground.

Bexx carefully approached from the right flank as Nick was stripping the large man of his uniform. He motioned to Bexx and said, "Your turn." Nick ran off into the night and returned with the remaining bubble wrap. Nick motioned for her to strip, then wrap the bubble wrap around her chest and shoulders. Lurch was massive through the chest and shoulders. Bexx was near his height, but not his size. The plan was beginning to make sense to her. They would take advantage of her height and Nick's now apparently overweight body to gain access to the facility as a team. Nick quickly wrapped Bexx's shoulder and chest as he said, "Sorry Lurch has pecs, not breasts – amazingly perfect breasts, honestly – but still, they won't help us now." He smiled. "I'm so damn glad you don't understand me, girl, because this would be embarrassing…you are hot as hell." Nick smiled, then helped her get dressed in Lurch's uniform. He then put out his cigarette, and they started towards the facility door. Nick stopped suddenly and whispered, "Wait, where's the shower cap?" Nick headed back to the clothing she'd left and returned with it. He told her to kneel, then he put the cap on her head and began stuffing her raven back hair under it until it was all covered. He then put on the uniform ball cap and looked at her. Nick smiled; the similarity would be good enough for the ancient cameras. Or at least he hoped. Nick approached the door and knocked hard. *Boom! Boom!*

CHAPTER TWENTY-TWO

Unbeknownst to Nick and Bexx, the scene inside the missile silo was remarkably disturbing. If it hadn't occurred as it had, they wouldn't have been successful in breaching the facility. Lennie had begun a new series of treatments for the latest batch of patients.

While Nick had been driving across Montana, and Bexx had been pulling the bloody tooth from the folds of his shirt, Lennie had been setting the stage for her latest desensitization therapy sessions. Schidel's security team had removed the patients one by one from the silos and placed them in their respective rooms, each containing the necessary items to provoke the reaction their files suggested would occur. One room was crawling with spiders that had been delivered that morning to the post office, another with snakes Lennie had brought with her when she arrived at the facility. She had a special sexual attraction to the snakes that she'd never admitted to anyone. Another room held a single dog, chained to the wall. The dog hadn't eaten in several days, and Lennie had kept it in that room for anyone who had a canine phobia in the last several groups. It only took one dog, vicious and large, to incite panic for those who held the fear. Room after room held its own special surprise, each unique and effective.

Once the patients were in place and the screams for help began, Lennie always found herself strangely sexually aroused by the patients' terror. This session was no different. As the screams became more frantic, so did her need. She reached out to a possible solution to her problem.

"Sergeant Schidel, could you come to my office for a moment, please?"

"Right away, Doctor Warsaw," Schidel answered. He'd been waiting on Brian to check in on his security patrol. The man was impossibly undisciplined, frumpy, and had a limp that set off something deep inside Schidel's psyche. Schidel saw himself as the perfect physical specimen. He had no patience for physical weakness, and Brian had many weaknesses. One, the gimp leg; two, he smoked. Schidel could tolerate neither. He wanted Brian gone, but that would have to wait. There wasn't a huge pool of human resources in northern North Dakota to draw upon, so for the moment he was stuck with the chain smoking, gimp Brian.

"Echo 1, status?" Schidel spoke into the handheld radio.

Silence was all Schidel received. He looked at Larry and Scott and said, "I need to go help the doctor. One of you go out and take a radio to that lazy bastard so he has no excuse for not answering."

Schidel opened the large steel door and headed down to the "Cave of Pain." That was the security team's nickname for Doctor Warsaw's level of the facility.

When Schidel arrived at the "Cave of Pain", Lennie was writhing around like a cat in heat. He knocked at the door, and she said, "Enter" in a deep, lusty voice. He walked in and found she was sitting at her desk, glaring at him. "How may I be of assistance, Lennie?"

"Greg, please shut the door and lock it, and turn off your radio."

He raised an eyebrow at the request but did so.

Lennie rose from her chair and began to undo the tight bun she'd kept her hair in and shook it loose, letting it fall around her shoulders. Greg entered the office as she started walking around the desk towards him. She took awkward strides; step-pause, step-pause, step-pause, as she imagined herself looking like a sexy lioness stalking her prey…instead, she looked ridiculous. Greg watched her and thought, *She's wack…she's finally snapped.*

"Do you like Star Wars, Greg?" she asked.

"Um…ya, sure…I guess so. I always did like the Klingons."

"No, no, Star Wars! Princess Leia, Chewie, Han Solo – you know, Star Wars!"

"Oh, yeah. Sure, it was OK."

"More than OK," she replied, "it was HOT!"

"Uh huh," Greg replied, unsure of where this was headed.

Lennie continued. "I always loved the idea of Princess Leia being interrogated by Darth Vader. He wanted to know the location of the rebel base, and the princess refused to tell him."

Greg didn't know what to say. He was feeling incredibly uncomfortable.

Lennie continued. "The only problem was, Princess Leia was such a prude. I always imagined her being a shameless little slut. A princess slut who secretly wanted to be interrogated by Darth Vader."

"Um, Lennie…Doctor Warsaw? Are you OK?"

She continued. "Can you make that sound for me? The one where Darth breathes in his mask, in and out, in and out?"

Greg made the sound.

"Yes! That's it. Now say, 'Tell me the location of the rebel base, you slut!'"

Greg, making the breathing noise, said, "Tell me the location of the rebel base, you slut."

Lennie spun around and pulled down the black pants of her business suit and bent over the desk. "No, I will never tell you the rebel base location,

Lord Vader, no matter what you do to me with your light saber." She panted with anticipation.

Greg was stunned for a moment. He thought to himself, *No one would ever believe this story.*

Lennie waited, then finally turned her head and said, "Keep making the breathing noise, and take out your light saber, Lord Vader. I won't tell you a thing, no matter how you punish me."

Greg said, "But wasn't Darth Vader Princess Leia's father?"

Lennie gave him a wicked look and said, "Precisely!" She then began to scream, "No, not the light saber!" She pinned her own hands behind her back and spread her legs.

Greg rose to the occasion, so to speak, and did his best to make breathing noises while he took her from behind with his "light saber." He prayed none of his security team found out about this event; he'd never live it down if they did.

While Darth was warming up to the idea of the incestual interrogation of Princess Leia, Scott had gone out to find Brian. Larry was now monitoring the radio. Scott radioed in that he'd found Brian and it looked like his radio was dead, then there was nothing from either guard. Larry had a bad feeling about this and tried to raise Schidel on the radio. He too failed to respond.

Larry waited for a few moments and repeated the calls to Brian and Scott, asking for their status. He called Schidel again as well but received no answer. There was no way he could have known Darth was in the middle of interrogating that slut Princess Leia and she was finally about to disclose the site of the secret rebel base.

Larry unsnapped his gun and left a note for Schidel that the entire facility was experiencing radio difficulties. He'd gone out to check on Brian and Scott. Larry unholstered his gun and opened the facility doorway, stepping out into the nighttime air.

Larry walked a few feet and saw Brian smoking in the night. Larry called out to him, and Brian started limping towards him.

At about the same moment Darth was about the seal the deal with Princess Leia, Bexx had sealed Larry's deal. He dropped instantly as his central nervous system was shut down by the brutal intrusion of her arrow.

Darth grabbed Princess Leia by her hair and snapped her head back. Now totally engulfed in his role, he growled, "Tell me the location of the rebel base, you slut!"

The sudden motion of her head snapping back caught the princess off guard. Her top and bottom dentures slipped out of her mouth and flew across the desk as she cried out. She meant to say, "Yavin Four," but without her teeth it came out as "Yawin hoor."

Schidel tried as best he could to hide his disgust, but well, you know, it isn't every day Princess Leia's teeth fly across her desk at the moment you seal the deal. She turned and smiled at him, further cementing in his mind that this horror story would never be told, to anyone, ever. She had one grey tooth visible in that smile; the rest of her mouth was a cavernous, empty black hole. Schidel grimaced and did his best to make a graceful but rapid exit from her office.

Schidel arrived in the security office a few moments later; he was relieved to see no one was there and didn't read Larry's note. No one would ask where he'd been. Outside the facility door, he heard two loud knocks. *Boom! Boom!*

Schidel pulled up the ancient camera system and looked at the image. The grainy image showed Larry and Brian standing together, waiting to be let in the facility. He wondered what had happened as he pressed the button, releasing the electronic lock. "Brian" opened the door, and the two guards entered the facility.

"What the hell has been going on?" Schidel said loudly as he tried to purge the image of Lennie's dentures soaring across the desk. He kept his head down and his eyes closed so tight, he saw bright spots. Finally, he looked up at Nick and Bexx and said, "Oh shit!"

"Hello, Sergeant. Schidel, is it?" Nick said, looking at the shiny steel nametag Schidel wore on his neatly pressed shirt. "I am the fly in the ointment, the ghost in the darkness, the monkey in the wrench. I am the Wild Card! You can call me Nick. We're about to become very close, you and I." Nick held Schidel at gunpoint and handed him a set of handcuffs he'd taken off Pugsley. "Put this on your left arm, then secure that arm to your chair." Schidel slowly did as he was told. Nick continued. "Excellent; you secured the correct hand. I can see you're paying attention. The last guy didn't pay attention. I said left, but he secured the right. People today! You know they just don't listen; talk, talk, talk, and no listening. Now I'm going to secure the other arm, and then we'll begin. The tall one next to me, her name is Xena. She doesn't talk much and doesn't speak English, so you're stuck with li'l ole me. Personally, if I were you, I'd prefer she questioned me. She is hot as hell, don't you think?" Schidel looked at Bexx and said, "I guess if you're into that sort of thing." Nick's eyes glazed over, his voice suddenly menacing. "Meaning? Schidel, before you go down some path you'll regret, I encourage you to be respectful, very respectful. The last guy who spoke harshly to her...mmm, mmm, mmm, trust me, you just don't want to go there. This can be bad – and judging from your demeanor, it probably will be – or this can be Hell. You'll pray for bad, if we go to hell, I promise you.

Now, you were saying?"

Schidel saw Nick meant what he said. "I just mean all muscular, tall and shit. She's too tall and buff for me. Nothing wrong with that, if you're into it."

Nick glared at Schidel for a minute and said nothing. "Wise choice of words, Sergeant, actually I am. She has no clue, of course. You can't imagine what it's like to ride for twenty hours in the cab of a small Toyota pickup with her." Nick paused, smiling. "Sorry, again I digress. We're here to talk, you and I. Your boss hired me a few months back for some off the books Black Ops mission. He hired me because I was supposed to bring an element to the mission that was unpredictable, a fresh set of eyes on the problem. What he didn't count on was he got exactly that. Dismantling the last camp was child's play. A piece of det cord here, a couple rats there, and the whole house of cards came tumbling down. Your boss upped his game with this camp, though. This one took some effort. Imagine my surprise when I realized this was an abandoned missile silo, made to be impenetrable. I actually had to work at this. Unfortunately for your boss, and I guess for you as well, I've had some experience at this. So, I have some questions for you, Sergeant. Have you met The Director?"

Schidel answered, "Schidel, Greg A., rank sergeant, Social Security Number..."

Nick started laughing. "Oh my God, you can't be serious! Greg?! Like Greg Brady?" Nick started to sing the Brady Bunch theme. "Da da da da dada. Here's the story of a boy named Greggy, who was too stupid to answer a question he was asked. He had ten toes and ten fingers, and then he lost just one." Nick picked up the bolt cutters and clamped them down on the pinky finger on Schidel's right hand. Schidel screamed as the bone and sinew popped and crunched. The finger hung there lifeless. The bolt cutters weren't sharp enough to completely remove the finger. Nick sat watching Greg scream, his face emotionless while Greg writhed in pain. Finally, when Greg started to calm down a bit, Nick contin-ued. "See what I mean? That was one; there are 19 more, and then things start to get really medieval – I mean really painful. You don't want to go there, trust me. Mister Happy comes off an inch at a time, and for some people that's over quicker than others. I'm guessing for you that'll be over quicker than most. But who knows? Never judge a book by its cover, they say." Schidel looked at Nick in horror as he realized what he meant. "Again, I'm asking a simple question. Have you met The Director?" "Schidel, Greg A., Social..."

Nick screamed, "Do I look like I'm someone you really want to fuck with? Seriously, the piece of shit you work for took everything from me. I will take you apart piece by piece if that's what it takes to get to him, do you understand? It doesn't have to be this way, Greg. It really doesn't. You're just a rung on a ladder, Greg. Wake up!"

"Schidel, Greg A...."

"All right," Nick said quietly, "have it your way, Greg." Nick turned to Bexx. "I wish you didn't have to see this." He motioned for her to leave. "Come back in a while? Please, you don't have to watch this." She shook her head. No, she was staying. She stood up straighter, shoulders squared. Body language saying what she would not: she was *not* leaving. Nick sighed. "Greg, remember I gave you the chance." Nick pulled out a small iPod shuffle from the bag and plugged in the headphones. "Brought this so I don't have to listen to you scream like a bitch. Shit is about to get real, Greg...one last chance...you really don't want to know what's behind door #1. Trust me. Take the deal and make Monty happy."

"Schidel..."

"Yeah, I got that. Let's see what you say after my boys Sen Dog and B Real finish Cypress Hill's 'Rise Up!' Ya know, Mike Tyson says everyone has a plan till they get punched in the face; that's when you find out who's a fighter."

Nick cued the iPod, and Tommy Morello started making the guitar talk like no one else ever could. Nick ripped off Greg's shoes and picked up the bolt cutters while Sen Dog and B Real teamed up for the dark lyrics "This life that I live, it ain't for the weak." Nick clipped off the big toes of both of Greg's feet like he was pruning a couple of small tree branches. He could feel the bones crunching through the handles of the bolt cutters while Greg screamed, his face turning purple. Nick heard nothing. Sen Dog belted out, "I go psycho, crazy Michael Myers." Nick picked up the toes after hav-ing to use his knife to cut the flesh and tendons the bolt cutters wouldn't. He then placed them on the table in front of Greg and broke into an air guitar solo as Tommy made his axe scream. Finally, the song was over and Nick spoke. "Two down, Greg," he said. Nick cued up Breaking Benjamins on the iPod, and their song "Breathe" began. "I like this song, Greg. It gets me all fired up." Greg was begging Nick to stop, but instead Nick sang the song. *"This will be all over soon, pour the salt into the open wound."* Clip, clip...small toes on both feet gone, laid on the table. Nice and neat. After again cutting the tendons and skin off: *"I see nothing in your eyes, and the more I see, the less I like."* Nick whispered, *"Is it over yet? In my head? I'm going all the way, get away, please."* Nick started on the thumb of the right hand. *"I know that I can't ind, the ire in your eyes, I'm going all the way, get away, please! You gotta ight just to make it through, 'cuz I will be the death of you."*

112

Two more digits lined up on the table. Bexx tried to keep a straight face. It wasn't the torture that bothered her so much; Nick was singing and had the most awful singing voice she'd ever heard.

Nick removed his ear buds and saw Greg had passed out.

The room was quiet. Nick went to the first aid kit on the wall and retrieved two capsules of smelling salts. Breaking them, he placed them under Greg's nose and made him breath the foul-smelling scent. Greg snapped back to life.

"Welcome back. Your dreams were your ticket out. Now do you take the deal, or do we go for door number two?" Nick said.

Greg watched Nick with a terrified stare.

"Now that you understand what I mean when I say I will literally take your ass apart piece by piece to learn what you know about The Director, let's start again. Have you met The Director?"

"Yes! I've met him." Greg gasped, sweat running down his forehead and into his eyes.

Nick smiled. "Finally. So he is a man. Do you know his name?"

"Firestone. Winston V. Firestone."

"And where did you meet him?"

"In Washington, D.C. I had to interview for this job there. I was contacted by his secretary and offered a job."

Nick smiled; now they were getting somewhere. He looked at Bexx. She just looked back. She'd witnessed torture before in Georgia, during the war. She showed no emotion at all. It was ugly, always was; Nick's singing voice, however, was unbearable.

"See, Greg? No need to go all Geneva Convention, G.I. Joe, Mission Impossible on my ass. Just answer the question, and we're all happier."

"What was The Director's position? What job does he hold?"

"I don't know. I really don't know. I was just told to report to a hotel, and a car picked me up and drove me to this government building. I was told to take the elevator to the top floor, then walk to my right. The Director's office was the last one on the right."

"But you're sure it was in D.C.?"

"Yes. Definitely. I was housed in a hotel in Virginia, the car picked me up, and we drove in on the belt outside of D.C. The building was like every other building in the area: old, nondescript, nothing special about it. Just plain old government business building."

"No signs outside indicating what agency or department it contained? I've been to D.C., Greg. Every building has some kind of sign telling everyone 'This is the Department of Housing, or the G.S.A.'"

"No, nothing. Seriously."

"OK, Greg. Anything else you can remember? Anything at all?"

"He drank whiskey, expensive stuff, and had a strange habit of holding his whiskey glass with a cloth."

"Anything else?"

"No, but Princess Leia – uh, I mean Doctor Warsaw, she may know more. She's in the lower levels of the facility with her patients."

"Did you say Princess Leia?"

"Please don't ask. This whole day has been a nightmare."

"Yes, it has, and for that I'm sorry – but I did warn you, Greg. I really did. Monty offered you a deal, but NOOOO, you just had to take door number one."

Nick smiled. "Princess Leia, huh? Guessing there's more to that story, huh? OK, just between us guys, and thanks for the heads up."

"OK, Greg, one more question: who else is here? Any more security? Maintenance crews? Anyone else besides Morticia – err, I mean Princess Leia?" Nick smiled.

Greg winced at the memory. "No, no, just her and I, and her patients."

"How many of the patients?"

"There are eight."

CHAPTER TWENTY-THREE

Nick probably should have realized The Director would have had a contingency plan in place after he dismantled Baroota so effortlessly. He'd observed Camp Cachibaché on at least three different occasions and saw no other levels of security present. The team that had arrived and was now present, The Director had sent them to the camp covertly the day Nick had been picking up what he'd thought were Russian mercenaries from the Spokane Airport. This team had a different mission than the facility security team. They were instructed to lay low, observe and report back anything unusual. They'd been a sniper/observer team and worked several private contracts. They had explicit instructions not to make contact with the facility and/or security team. They were to operate autonomously and evaluate the camp, and if necessary they were armed to deal with emergencies. If an emergency did occur, they had instructions to contact The Director before taking any action. An emergency was definitely occurring.

"Zeus this is Falcon one, over."

"Go ahead, Falcon one."

"Yes, sir. The host has an infection; two, actually. Arrival at approximately 0500 Zulu."

"Copy that, Falcon one. Any fatalities?"

"Affirmative, sir. One down. What are your orders?"

"Falcon one, let it play. I want to see the integrity of the facility in real world threat."

"Copy that, sir. Falcon one out."

An hour later, the team reestablished contact.

"Zeus, this is Falcon one."

"Go ahead, Falcon one."

"Host has been penetrated. Three down. I repeat, three down. Unknown interior fatalities."

"Copy that. Total infections in play?"

"Still two, sir."

"Copy that, Falcon one. Stand by until situation changes. Should more infection arrive on site, advise me. Until then, observe only. Do you copy?"

"Wilco. Falcon one out."

Inside the facility, Bexx and Nick had cleared the interior first floor. Taking Schidel's keys, they now had access to the armory and all locked doors in the facility. As they began to descend into the lower levels of the facility, they started to hear the screams of Lennie's patients.

Nick spent the next day asking questions of the patients. How had they been contacted? Who had driven them to the facility? Every question he could think of, no matter how obscure, the answer was always the same. All remaining roads led to Doctor Warsaw. She was the sole remaining link to The Director. Nick let her simmer in her room while he gathered information from the patients. He promised help was on the way, and when it arrived they'd be driven to the local authorities. Until then, they had to sit tight and wait. Nick didn't want the local sheriff coming in and questioning who had killed the three dead guards until he and Bexx were several hundred miles away.

With the facility secured, Nick decided to check the remaining thirty-six-acre compound around the facility. Bexx chose to remain inside the facility and keep an eye on the people they'd rescued from Lennie's treatment program. He grabbed the Romanian AK 47 from the bag and slung the tactical sling over his head and shoulder. He loaded it, inserting one of the thirty round magazines into the weapon.

Nick left the facility and started a clockwise search of the acreage, looking for any sign of something suspicious. He looked around the exterior fighting positions, and the water tower. He carefully started up the metal ladder until he was about halfway up, then he could see the trap door to the tower was padlocked, a precaution Schidel had taken just in case one of the patients left up there to suffer somehow made it back to the tower. They would still be contained, with no way to get down. Seeing the padlock in place and locked was good enough for Nick. No need to get any higher. He carefully climbed down the ladder, shaking as he went down. If Nick had been Lennie's patient, this would have been his Achilles' heel; heights terrified him. Nick continued the search of the compound and was nearly finished when he caught a scent on the wind. It smelled like cigarette smoke. He turned quickly into the wind and tried to pick up the scent again; nothing. He was facing the water tower and thought, *That's where I would be if I wanted to watch the entire site.* He watched the tower for several minutes and saw nothing. It was probably nothing, and besides, he'd been smoking Pugsley's cigarettes; maybe he'd just caught a whiff of that scent. Finally, he turned and went back to the facility.

The Driver rented two 2017 Ford Transit F-350 12-passenger vans, and they started the drive to Dresden, North Dakota. Nick had told Nõn to leave in 24-36 hours after he and Bexx had left, or whenever the Asgarda had recovered from the party. The trip was uneventful, for the most part. The Driver and Buffy drove in one of the vans, talking computers and hacking stuff, while the rest of the team mysteriously chose to ride with Nõn in the other. The trip was pretty much uneventful until they reached Mosby,

Montana. There, they were stopped by the local sheriff at a roadblock. The Driver had already spoken to Nõn about their cover story should they be stopped. They were coaches of a Ukraine women's MMA team headed to a match in Chicago. That way, the girls wouldn't be required to speak and he and Nõn would be the only ones interviewed. Just in case. The Driver was wise, Nõn realized as they approached the roadblock.

"What happened, Officer?"

"Do you have your license and registration, ma'am?"

"Yes, of course. Here it is."

The deputy examined the documents, then returned them. "And why are y'all traveling through the great state of Montana today, ma'am?"

"Oh, we – I mean this van and the one behind me, we are traveling to an MMA match in Chicago with our team of women MMA fighters."

"These girls are MMA fighters?"

"Yes, and quite good. They are from Ukraine. I and the man driving behind us are their coaches."

"I see...so he'll have the same story as you when I question him, correct?" The deputy motioned to the van behind Nõn.

"Of course. May I ask what happened? Why are we being stopped?"

The deputy grimaced. "A horrible thing has happened. A couple of our local boys were attacked in a gas station up the road a spell. According to the one victim who regained consciousness, a man and a woman entered the store and left. The man returned a short time later and for no apparent reason attacked them. They are messed up something awful."

Nõn was smart enough to act shocked, but she had a suspicion she knew exactly who the attacker was. It was Nick, and something had set him off.

"Are they all right? I mean, will they be OK?"

"Ma'am, I've been a deputy in these parts for 15 years now, and I've never seen anything like it. We don't know for sure what happened, because the attacker took the surveillance equipment when he left. But what I do know is that I have three victims. The store owner, and two customers, all three were beaten unconscious. The store owner got the least of it. The other two...well, they're in bad shape. I've never in all my years...he castrated the two of them, ma'am. Beat them unconscious, then castrated them and put the...umm...parts in a jar on the counter and wrote on a piece of paper 'Proper Broke'. Now what the hell does that mean, I ask you? Those boys will never be the same regardless."

Nõn said, "That is horrible! I am so sorry for those poor men. I hope you find the person who did this, Officer."

"Thank you, ma'am. You and your team be careful, the world has gone bat shit crazy."

She waited while the deputy spoke to The Driver, and when he was done he waved them on. The girls in the van were curiously silent, looking at each other with startled looks.

Nõn knew exactly who the assailant was, there was no doubt. She wondered what had set Nick off this time. She texted Nick.

Just drove through Mosby, Montana, and was stopped by the sheriff. Apparently, someone castrated two men at a gas station there and left. Do you know anything about that?

She pushed send.

He replied, *Call me.*

"Hello, how is the great state of Montana?"

"Good. Apparently, you had a run-in with some locals?"

"Not a run-in so much as a tune up. They just…well, you know… needed an attitude adjustment."

"So you castrated them? And then left their testicles in a jar on the counter?"

Nick sighed. "Well, I looked around for a hyena, but they're a bit hard to come by in Montana. The shop owner had no dog, so it seemed the least I could do. Besides, why are you all up in my ass about it? Where do you think I came up with the idea?"

Nõn closed her eyes; she was now sorry she'd ever shared her story with Nick. "Does Bexx know what happened?"

"No. How could I tell her? She doesn't speak English, remember? And I wasn't going to drag her into the store afterwards to show her they were now the newest members of the Heaven's Gate cult. You can tell her when you get here, since you're so worried about Bo and Luke Duke. Trust me, they weren't some good ole boys never meaning no harm. They earned this little session of same day surgery."

Nõn had no idea who Bo and Luke Duke were; Nick's obscure references always baffled her. "Who are Bo and Luke Duke? Was that their names, the men you castrated?"

Nick sighed again. "Never mind. Text me when you're close. We're inside, and all is well. Just waiting on you to arrive."

CHAPTER TWENTY-FOUR

Nick was making a list of the things that needed to be done once Nõn arrived with the team. He wanted to be out of the facility as soon as possible.

They needed to collect all documents in the facility, and if possible have The Driver and Buffy check out the hard drives on the computers. They needed to know what and who they were up against. Hopefully, the information they obtained would help them come up with a plan. The next step in the hunt for The Director wasn't clear to Nick. So far, it felt like every time he thought he had a break, it was just another layer peeled off the onion. They would clean out the facility's armory, and just as they were prepared to leave they would release the patients. His plan was to drop them off at an abandoned barn or shed at night, then call the local sheriff to re-port some suspicious activity. When the sheriff finally wrapped their heads around the story the patients would be telling, Nick, Bexx, and the entire team would be long gone. At least that was how he saw it going in his head.

Nõn and The Driver arrived at about 3am and set up a camp of sorts in the same barn Nick and Bexx had been in a couple days earlier. They briefly slept, then when everyone was awake and had eaten, Nõn called Nick.

"Nick, we are in the barn and ready to come to the facility."

"OK. Explain to everyone that we're going to strip the facility as best we can of anything we can use. Priority is intelligence gathering, any phone numbers, cell phones, paperwork and computers. We'll take the ar-mory as well. They have a stock of weapons and ammo we can use. When the facility is purged, then we'll remove the patients who are here and take them to an abandoned barn near Nekoma; it's a small town a few miles from here. I have directions already for whoever transports them. Once they're in place, I'll make an anonymous phone call to the local sheriff and they'll be picked up. Then we un-ass the area and head back to Moses Lake. Any questions?"

Nõn had a couple of questions. "In our planning sessions at The Driver's house, you mentioned there was a woman there; Morticia, you called her. Is she there?"

"Yes, she's locked in a room."

"What do you plan to do with her? And are there any survivors from the security team?"

"There's one survivor: The Sergeant is here. He isn't happy or comfortable, but he's alive. As far as Morticia, I don't know yet. She appears to be our only tie to The Director. I don't want to give up on that, but the idea of leaving her alive…I don't know, Nõn. If you saw what she was doing here, the things she did to these people, I can't think of a way to kill her slow enough."

"It is that bad?"

"Yes, it is. She basically put them into the worst situation they could be in, taking advantage of their worst fears, and left them there until they died from fear."

"That is bad. Have you spoken with her?"

"No. I don't think she'd survive the conversation. I know I'm too angry to think clearly, so I've left her alone, at least for now. When I must make the decision, I will. For now, it's unclear."

"OK. We will be there in 5 minutes."

"The gate will be open. Bring both vans; one for intelligence and equipment, the other for the patients."

When the vans arrived, Nick had the gate open. Buffy and The Driv-er were still in a van by themselves, and Nick told them to go to the entrance tunnel on the west side. It was open, and they were to drive the van into the tunnel. When the time came, they would load the patients and drive them to the abandoned barn in Nekoma. In the meantime, he needed their expertise in gathering computers and electronic intelligence.

The Driver and Buffy were clear on what needed to be done. Nick closed the gate and walked back to the facility as the vans drove on ahead. He told everyone, "If everything goes according to plan, we'll be out of the facility and on our way home by midnight." Nick whispered out loud, "And when does anything ever go according to plan?"

The next few hours were pretty frantic. The first van was loaded with everything that had any value. The team had entered the facility un-aware of the interrogation of Schidel. The sight of his various fingers and toes lined up on the table in front of him took them all by surprise. They stopped for a moment, trying to imagine what had happened and how. They looked at Nick uneasily; he smiled. "Welcome. Ladies. Anyone up for a pedi or mani?" Bexx broke their trance by issuing orders in their native tongue.

"Move!" she said. "What did you think we were going to do here, Asgarda? Hold his hand? Sing songs? Torture him with kindness? You have your orders, get it done." No one moved.

"NOW damn it!" she commanded.

The team scrambled, making her orders happen as best they could. Nick watched and smiled; Jesus, this woman had stones. Strong and pragmatic, nothing fazed her. She was as quiet as a church mouse when he went to work on Schidel, and she never batted an eyelash. He understood the significance of that. This was nothing new to her. Her account of the time spent in Georgia during the civil wars of the 90s were real.

The team started gathering anything that looked like it may be worthwhile and loaded it into the back of the van. Buffy and The Driver had come up from the basement after securing the outer doors of the tunnel and also began their tasks.

The Driver saw Schidel and the fingers and toes lined up on the table and shuddered. He held up his hand, the bandage now gone, and showed Schidel. "Been there, brother…been there."

Nick rolled his eyes. The Driver was such a drama queen. Things were rolling smoothly inside the facility. Nick pulled Bexx to the side and waved over The Interpreter. "Special K tell her I need to know what she thinks we should do with Morticia."

"Why are you calling me Special K?"

"Your name is Katrena right? So, Special K, sounds better than The Interpreter don't you think"

She rolled her eyes.

Special K spoke to Bexx for some time.

"He still has no idea you speak English?"

"No. Let's keep it that way for now."

"Understood. You heard his question. What would you like me to say?"

"Tell him I'll take care of the woman in the basement. I gathered from the interrogation of the patients and the man in the chair she's the only one here who may have actually met The Director. When the time comes, I'll remove her from the basement and walk her to the van. I'm afraid he'll kill her if she says the wrong thing or makes some offhand comment. He's very unpredictable, much more so than I imagined. I don't think he can be trusted to be logical now."

Special K spoke to Nick and explained Bexx would handle the psychologist he called Morticia. When the time came for them to move her, Bexx would bring her up from the basement.

Nick said, "I agree, that would be best. I'm not sure she'd make it out the door otherwise. Explain that to her, and tell her thanks."

Special K replied, "She knows."

When the facility was cleared, the team gathered outside. Nick and Nõn were standing face-to-face, talking while the team finished loading the last of the computers.

"Well, we're done here, Nõn. We didn't find The Director, but we did shut down another camp. In a day or two, the sheriff will find this place. The Director won't risk coming back."

Nõn was silent for some time. Finally, she said, "Nick, I am done. This is the last time I help you. I cannot be a part of this anymore. Those men you castrated, that man in there with his toes and fingers lined up on the desk, I cannot and will not condone this anymore. I think that is what my dreams have been trying to tell me. I need to get back to who I am."

Nick nodded. She was right; this was never her fight.

As he started to tell her just that, a small gnat flew into his nose. He shook his head, his eyes watering, and tried to blow the gnat out. Turning his head to the left, he placed one finger against the nostril opposite the now frantic gnat and blew hard.

The observation team had taken turns sleeping in four-hour shifts, one up while the other was down. Should anything happen, they'd wake up and go back to work. The Director had been clear not to engage the infection of the facility until the situation changed. At 7am, it changed. The spotter was up; it was his turn to watch while the sniper rested. The male had exited the facility and opened the electronic vehicle gate. A few moments later, two vans arrived. He spoke to the drivers of both vans. One went on ahead to a delivery tunnel and entered the facility underground. The other one drove to the front door of the facility, flipped around, and backed up to the door. The occupants got out and entered the facility.

The spotter counted eight additional people in the two vans. The first van carried two people; one man, one woman. The second van carried six women.

The observation team talked for a minute, watching, then made the call.

"Zeus, this is Falcon One, over."

They waited.

Arthur had received the call from the team. The Director was in a meeting with the president's national security advisors and couldn't be disturbed.

Arthur said, "Falcon One, this is Zeus, go ahead."

"Zeus, 8 additional infections have arrived at the facility, in two unmarked vans, 7 women and one man. They've entered the facility and are loading the vans with equipment. Please advise."

"Falcon One, understood. Continue monitoring, stand by for instructions."

"Falcon One, standing by."

An hour had passed. The sniper team was getting anxious.

"Zeus, this is Falcon One, still on standby. Please advise."

The Director had completed his meeting and made a few phone calls. When he was finished, Arthur advised him of the call from Falcon One.

"Falcon One, this is Zeus. Advise situation at your location."

"Zeus, the van is loaded in the front of the building. They appear to be prepared to leave soon. Please advise, over."

"Falcon One, you have permission to engage. I repeat, engage at your discretion. I want no one to leave that facility. Advise when task complete, Zeus out."

The spotter settled in and began the process of calling out targets. "Wind, 340 degrees, at 11 kph. Target 12 o'clock. Male standing in front of black female."

"Copy that, target acquired. Standing by." The sniper took the bolt action rifle off safety and stared down into the scope, the crosshairs resting comfortably on the back of Nick's head. The sniper began the process of breathing deep as he watched the crosshairs rise and fall, traveling up and down Nick's head over one hundred yards away. The sniper slowly applied pressure on the trigger. When the shot came, the spotter watched through binoculars. The area where the heads had been exploded in a red mist of brains and blood as the bullet traveled its deadly path. He called out, "Direct hit! Two down with one shot!"

Bexx had been milling around, aware Nõn wasn't happy about the actions taken at the camp. She overheard Nõn saying she was done, then she mentioned the men he'd castrated in the gas station. She was surprised Nick had reacted so strongly to them harassing her. She turned and looked at Nick, a surprised look on her face. He hadn't mentioned what had happened in his one-sided conversations with her as they drove to North Dakota. She wasn't sure how to feel about what Nick had done. Others had stood by and watched while she'd been gang raped in Georgia; they did nothing. She sought out her own retribution then and made sure those men would never harm another woman. Not once in her life had any man ever raised a hand to protect her. She was confused by his violence. It was at once both alarming, and somehow she felt grateful as well.

As she pondered the events at the gas station, she was instantly covered in a red mist. Both Nick and Nõn dropped to the ground as a shot rang out and the bullet found its target.

Time slowed down for her; Bexx had been here before many times. They were under attack. She looked in the direction she thought the shot had come from and saw nothing. Her movements felt awkward, every physical action felt much too slow and much too difficult. She tried to move, and nothing happened. Another shot rang out, and Special K spun; she'd been shot in the right shoulder. The bullet barely grazing her, but drawing blood.

The Asgarda Commander began to shout out instructions to the team, telling them to take cover and locate the shooter. She ran herself and grabbed Special K, pulling her behind the motor side of the van. Another shot rang out. And then another. From the pace of the shooting, Bexx understood it was most likely a bolt action sniper rifle, not an assault rifle. The shooter would then most likely be far away, and high. She scanned the horizon and guessed the water tower would be the most likely location for a sniper. The team would have to assault that location to survive.

Speaking rapidly, she called out, "Sound off! Who is hit?"

The team called back one at a time. All four remaining team members were still up, and no one had been shot. Not yet at least; that was good news. She asked how many had the Romanian AK 47s. There was silence. She asked again, "How many damn it?" The reply finally came. "None." They'd left them in the barn, feeling they weren't necessary since the facility had been taken. The only weapons they did have were the ones they usually carried, knives, short swords; nothing that would make engaging a target over 100 meters away possible. She realized they'd made a grave error. Nick had been right: bringing a knife to a gun fight was a quick way to die. The armory was inside and had many weapons, but it would be nearly impossible to get the keys from Nick's body, being now 10 meters away, then make entry into the facility with a sniper watching their every move. They had very few viable options.

"Commander, what should we do?" one of the team called out.

Bexx saw no other option but to wait until darkness; they had no weapons and no way to take the sniper out.

"Stay put until it is dark, then we move. Understand? Do not move, do not give the sniper a target."

"Understood." The waiting game began. There were no more shots fired for some time.

CHAPTER TWENTY-FIVE

As Nick turned to blow the gnat from his nose, he was knocked to the ground as something hit his head from behind, instantly knocking him out. He had no idea what had happened. Slowly, he began to regain consciousness and opened his eyes. His head was ringing; it hurt bad. His head felt like it was on fire, like an elephant had stepped on it repeatedly. At first he couldn't understand what he was seeing, then slowly his mind pieced together the image in front of him. It was Nõn – or had been Nõn... her head was gone, pieces of flesh hung lying here and there. A flap of her right cheek was sitting on her chest. There was part of her lower jaw still attached to her body; the rest was a mixture of blood, teeth, bone and pieces of hair scattered all over him and the area around them. He lay there and looked at her. The reality of what had happened was setting in. He heard voices calling out in Russian. The team was still up and alive. He heard Bexx calling out; she was somewhere close, her voice much clearer and loud, even and calm. He listened and closed his eyes. He realized he needed to know the extent of his injuries. He could see, but could he move? He tried to move and found he could. Slowly, he brought his hand to the injury on his head. He was bleeding, heavily; the head wounds always did. Pulling his hand back to his eyes, he saw his own blood, but he realized somehow no brain matter. The bullet had been meant for him, but as he turned to blow out the gnat, it had grazed him and killed Nõn instantly. He looked at what had been Nõn again. The darkness was coming, he felt it; there was no stopping it this time, his body flooded with warmth, he fell into the darkness and was only occasionally aware of quiet sounds and some motion. He felt like he was floating.

Bexx had been motionless for some time when she and the rest of the team heard an odd sound. It started as a deep grunt, like a large bull was somewhere nearby and had snorted. It came again louder, and then again louder still. She was afraid of what that meant. Did the snipers have animals to flush them out from behind cover? How much worse could this get? Another louder grunt that sounded more growl than grunt. She looked under the van and saw Nick was rising to his feet slowly. Her eyes widened. How could he be alive?

Nick finally rose to his feet, then took a tremendous breath and let loose the most primal and frightening sound Bexx had ever heard. To describe it as a scream or growl didn't come close to the sound that now left his body. It was more like a long, painful roar. His entire body tensed, arms thrown backward, his legs and back rigid. The roar impossibly continued. Everyone in the area stopped and listened, thinking, *What the hell was that?*

The spotter called out, "Target 12 o'clock. It can't be, I saw him go down. I saw them both go down. You had a direct hit. I saw the brain matter. He cannot be up."

"Re-acquire target, now. Put him down. Now! Do you copy?"

"Copy that, target reacquired." The sniper looked through his scope as Nick turned and faced the tower. Nick was covered in blood, fresh blood. He'd definitely been hit, but he was back up. The sniper felt a cold chill run through his body as he pulled the trigger; the shot rang out, and still the bleeding man stood glaring at him through the scope.

Nick's body spun and glared at the tower. Deep down, something had taken over. A shot rang out as he felt a brief whoosh of air cross his cheek; the second bullet had missed. Nick brought the Romanian AK-47 to his shoulder and started running and firing on the tower. Suppressive fire was his only option to keep the sniper down while he advanced. Screaming barely decipherable words, he ran, rapidly closing on the water tower.

The spotter called out, "Re-engage! I repeat, re-engage! Target is ap-proaching rapidly."

The spotter watched…the image couldn't be real…the man was closing incredibly fast…no one could run that fast and shoot. The wound on his head was clearly visible, blood was flowing down his right shoulder, and yet he continued to fire at the tower and run.

The second burst of suppressive fire hit the sniper. One round took off the trigger finger of his right hand and disabled the rifle as well, destroying the trigger housing. It had been an incredibly lucky shot, one that happened more often than people realized. Nick kept advancing, the tower growing larger.

Bexx took the opportunity to call out to the Asgarda, "ON ME! NOW!"

The team sprang from the field and sprinted to her position as they watched Nick charging the water tower. She yelled, "Get to the facility doors! See if you can get inside! The Driver is still in there somewhere!"

Nick had almost reached the tower when the sniper came on the radio. "My rifle is down. Can you bring him down?"

The spotter was equipped with a handgun. He fired several rounds at Nick as he approached the tower, but he was too far away for the handgun to be effective. Neither of them had faced anything like this before. As a sniper/spotter team that had always had the luxury of leisurely engaging their targets, their shooting skill was as a team and in a slow, methodical practiced method. They had no experience in tactical, close combat shooting; on the other hand, that was all Nick had ever done, small group tactics, advancing on an enemy position and taking it out.

Nick had reached the tower. Bexx could see he'd crossed the field in-between the facility and the tower and was now climbing the tower. They may survive this after all if he could take out the sniper. He was close now to doing just that.

The spotter watched as Nick slung the AK over his shoulder and started climbing the steel legs and cross beams of the tower. In less than 10 seconds, he was at the top of the tower. There was nothing he could do to help the sniper now. He watched as Nick climbed over the railing, then brought the AK to his shoulder as he began to search for the sniper. A moment later, several shots rang out and the spotter grimaced, closing his eyes. Nick had killed the sniper.

Nick reached the tower and started climbing the steel legs that held the massive structure. The ladder was useless; it led to a padlocked door he'd have to lift to gain access. He had to climb the structure's exterior to get to the sniper. His fear of heights now gone, the only thought that remained was destroying the sniper.

The spotter listened as the sniper screamed out over the radio, then it went silent. A moment later, he saw Nick lift the sniper's body over the walkway rail and throw him off the tower. Nick then flipped over the rail and began to climb down the steel frame, swinging from cross beam to cross beam. A couple seconds later, he hit the ground, then the whole scene became surreal. The spotter watched in horror. He had seen death many times. They had been a team, he and the sniper in many bad situations, but he'd never witnessed anything like he was seeing now.

Nick hit the ground and removed the AK from his shoulder. The image of what was left of Nõn burned in his mind, and his anger was overtaken by emotions no words could describe. He pulled the now dead man's arm up between his legs and lay down. Shoving on the wrist and snapping the arm at the elbow, He repeated the move on the remaining arm. The spotter heard the crunch and pop as the elbows came out of their sockets. Nick removed the man's shirt and began ripping at his chest with his bare fingers, scratching and clawing. A moment later, the spotter watched as Nick began to snap the now exposed ribs from the shooter's torso one by one. He was ripping the man apart; literally.

Bexx watched as Nick cleared the top of the tower. She heard the shots, then a body fell from the tower. She watched Nick crawl down the tower, then disappear in the grass below. She felt relieved. The sniper was dead. They may yet survive this.

Just then, The Driver opened the door to the facility. "Hello, girls, what did I miss? You all look like you need some of The Driver's special attention! Banging on the door like that, you act like it's urgent. Slow down, ladies; there's plenty of The Driver to go around!"

Bexx had the women armed and ready to go conduct a sweep of the area around the facility in moments, using weapons that had been in the facility's armory. She told the team medic to treat Special K, then accompany her to the tower. Nick had been wounded, there was no doubt about that. If he was still alive, they would do all they could to keep him that way.

As the spotter watched Nick rip the sniper apart, he also saw he was now outnumbered and the team had armed themselves and were advancing towards him and the tower, using a movement he recognized as bounding over watch: one group watched for a target while another moved. It was time to go. The spotter got the hell out of the area surrounding the facility. Once he was clear and felt reasonably safe, he called in, "Zeus, this is Falcon One, over."

"Go ahead, Falcon One."

"Sir, the operation is compromised. Sniper is down, I'm egressing the area."

The Director blinked a couple of times. How could he be hearing this correctly?

"Say again, Falcon One."

"I repeat, operation is compromised. Sniper is dead. Whoever this is that's entered the facility, I want no part of them. We had them, sir, two down with the first shot. I saw the heads explode myself. Then moments later, the man was back up and advancing on the sniper. He killed the sniper then ripped his body to pieces. Do you copy? The operation is over, I'm conducting emergency egress. I'm out. I want no part of this. Falcon One is out." The radio went dead.

The Director sat the phone down and looked out his office window. Camp Cachibaché was no more.

CHAPTER TWENTY-SIX

When Bexx and the medic arrived at the water tower, they stopped for a moment, trying to make sense of the scene. Nick sat in the grass, covered in his own still flowing blood and the dried, caked mess of what had been the sniper. Broken bones were strewn about the immediate area. The sniper's body was contorted and twisted in unnatural ways, his legs and arms bent in awkward directions. The stench was unbearable. Nick had ripped the sniper's intestines and lungs from his chest cavity. Finally, Nick had sat down, heaving, gasping, trying to breathe. His body was shutting down from the exertion and loss of blood.

Bexx had seen this in battle before, usually only in intense hand-to-hand confrontations where enemies were forced into a primal battle for their own survival. Their minds forced into an animal combat that made no real sense, they tore their enemies limb from limb.

She told the medic to wait while she approached Nick. Slowly, she crept up and called out to him.

"Nick?"

Nick sat breathing heavily, rapidly.

"Nick?"

Nick looked up at her, his eyes blank, gasping for air, sweat flowing into his eyes. He didn't want her to see him this way. He put his head down and closed his eyes and fell over on his side.

The medic ran up, and they immediately went to work on his injuries. The medic first cleaned the head wound and dressed it quickly in a bandage. She then checked his body for broken bones or other gunshot wounds; she found none. Checking his hands, she stopped and held them out for Bexx to see. Nick had ripped the fingernails off all the fingers of his left hand, and all the nails but his thumb on the right. "That had to hurt like…" the medic said. "I doubt he felt anything at all," Bexx replied. "Stay with him. I will go get the van, and we can take him back to the facility to clean him up better and check him again for any injuries we may have missed." She sprinted across the field to the facility, watching out of the corner of her eyes as the team continued searching the remaining land around them.

When Bexx returned to the tower, the team had arrived. They all knelt, trying to help the medic and taking fleeting uneasy glimpses at the body of the sniper.

Once inside the facility, they took Nick to one of the security team's rooms and sat him in a shower. They had to clean him off to be able to see any injuries. The blood and dirt combined with whatever else had come out of the sniper's body had to be removed. Once he was cleaned off, the medic gave him a shot of morphine, then rewrapped the head wound. Once Nick was as stable as they could make him in the facility, Bexx ordered the team to prepare to vacate the facility as soon as possible. She wanted them ready to go in 10 minutes. Period. She went to the basement and retrieved Lennie while Buffy and The Driver loaded the patients into their van. The plans had changed; they were all to meet up at the barn. Once they arrived there, new plans would be made.

The Driver left the facility, and the team was loaded. Lennie was bound and gagged and put into the van. Bexx had started the van and sat for a moment, thinking. She turned the van off and told one of the team members to bring Lennie and follow her back into the facility.

Schidel sat in his chair, afraid they were going to leave him there to starve or die from dehydration. He was relieved when Bexx came through the door with one of the women and Lennie in tow.

Bexx turned to Lennie and spoke.

"You will be questioned when we arrive back at our home base. I want you to understand this. If you lie to us, if you withhold anything from us…as this man has done, this will be just the beginning of your punishment."

Bexx walked to Schidel and said, "You lied to us. You said there were no other teams at the facility. One of our comrades has been killed because of that lie. Do you have anything to say?"

Schidel, still not too quick on the uptake, didn't understand the seriousness of Bexx's question.

"You speak English? Hahaha, I knew it."

Bexx removed his eyes in an obviously well-practiced move that left them still attached by the nerves and small muscles that controlled them. He screamed as they dangled on his cheeks. Bexx turned and looked at Lennie, making sure she understood the message. She then ripped the eyes from where they hung and put them on the table next to the rest of his now brutalized body parts.

Bexx approached Lennie. "Do you understand me?"

Eyes wide, Lennie nodded enthusiastically. "Yes!" As the now blind Schidel screamed himself hoarse, they left the facility.

Bexx told the Asgarda warrior to put Lennie back in the van, then closed and locked the door to the facility. She took the keys to the facility with her. It would be some time before anyone opened the door. It had, after all, been designed to be impenetrable.

Once at the barn, Bexx called the Asgarda to her. They planned to leave as soon as the sun went down. The Driver and Buffy would drive the patients to the second barn Nick had picked, as planned. They would return, then they'd all leave together. They had to be careful on the trip back. The incident in the gas station in Mosby had made law enforcement step up their stops of out of state cars. Someone would have to drive Nick's beloved 'Yota back while the rest of them traveled in the vans. Special K volunteered to drive the 'Yota. She would no longer be needed, since Nick was out cold on the morphine. Bexx directed that they'd bury Nõn in a simple grave inside the barn. There would be no ceremony and no gravestone. The Asgarda had buried many of their own over the years of conflict and understood this was all they could do for Nõn at the moment. They had to be on the move as soon as possible.

Hours later, the patients were dropped off and the team was on the road and with a new itinerary. Instead of 20 or so hours, the new plan would take 32-plus hours. They couldn't risk the more direct route through Montana.

When they arrived in Moses Lake, the first priority was to go through the documents, computer hard drives, and all data they'd taken from the facility. The Driver and Buffy were in charge of making all the random bits of information absorbable in a logical, functional timeline. Everything was looked at from every possible angle. It took them about a week.

Meanwhile, Nick was recovering. The medic had weaned him off the pain killers, and he'd started to slowly make some recovery. He had splitting headaches from the bullet injury, and his hands and body were battered and bruised. He didn't talk much to anyone; when asked if he was all right, he would just nod his head. Talking seemed pointless to him for the time being. He had a lot to process. He could remember everything that happened at the facility and struggled to make sense of how it felt. After Nõn had been killed, he felt like a passenger in his own body; something else had overridden Nick as he understood himself to be and stepped to the front. He felt pushed to the back, only an observer of whatever or whoever it was now running the sideshow called Nick. It was a very unsettling experience.

The day finally came that Nick felt strong enough to go back to the gym. He loaded up his gym bag and walked to the 'Yota. Getting in, he found the keys had been left in the ignition. He turned the key and listened as the starter motor engaged the flywheel and the motor came to life. Nick smiled; it seemed to him the 'Yota was welcoming him back. *Where to Boss? Are we going to the gym?* He turned around and backed out of the farmhouse's gravel driveway.

As Nick walked into Ali's gym after a several week absence, she looked up from a magazine she was reading and commented, as only Ali could, "What the hell happened to you? You look like shit!"

"Thanks, appreciate the reality check. And here I thought chicks liked scars."

"Scars, sure – but holy shit, man, have you seen your head?"

"Ya, I have. It feels a lot worse than it looks, if that means anything to you."

She continued. "Where the hell are your fingernails? What the hell happened?"

"I picked a fight with the chick at the Korean nail parlor and lost."

"I'll say you lost." Ali looked at him for a moment. "So, is it over now? You get your retribution?"

"No, not yet. Still working on that one. Do I still have the option to do better living through pharmacology?"

"We do, but as usual, it's pay as you go. It's all about the Benjamins. Same volume?"

"Sure, please. Same price?"

"Same price. As usual, when you pay me in cash, I make the order. Try not to bleed all over my equipment. You look like shit, man."

Nick smiled. This was Ali's way of saying, "Welcome back." Nick slowly started back into the workout routine he'd been doing, his head ached badly, but he pressed on working through the pain.

That night when he returned to the farmhouse, Bexx had called a meeting with him and the Asgarda. Buffy and The Driver had compiled all the information and still had no real clear direction to go in search of The Director. They needed a different perspective. Nick listened and said nothing. The roles had switched in the group; this had been Nick's show, now it was Bexx who ran the show. Through Special K, she discussed the information when she felt Nick needed to be involved.

Finally, Special K spoke to him. "Bexx would like to know if you are up to interviewing Doctor Warsaw?"

Nick thought about that for a while. "I can interview her, but I do it alone. No interference."

Bexx was silent for a moment, then spoke through Special K, "I want her to be unharmed. I want her alive. Can you interview her and not cut off any toes or other body parts?"

Nick locked eyes with her for several moments. He didn't like being told what to do by her, or any woman for that matter. She'd been useful at the camp, but in his mind this was now even more his personal vendetta. Especially after Nõn's death.

"What the hell do you care if she loses a few fingers, or an ear?

She will talk quicker and more honestly when the bullshit façade has been stripped away. Nothing does that quicker than pain."

The Asgarda were uneasy with this confrontational tone. No one had ever spoken to their leader like this. They waited to see what would happen.

Bexx replied, "I want her alive and unharmed. Is that clear?"

Nick smiled. "Ya, clear. It's clear. Alive and happy, fresh as a daisy! A gift box of her favorite feminine deodorant spray – a month supply, even. Jesus! Well, no time like the present. I promise I won't harm her. But do not interfere with me. Is that clear?"

Bexx nodded.

Nick got up and went to the barn where Lennie had been chained in a stall.

CHAPTER TWENTY-SEVEN

Nick walked into the barn and picked up an overturned chair that had been there for some time. He brought it into the stall Lennie had set up as hers. He sat and looked at her, saying nothing for several minutes. He wanted to take her out of her comfort zone by saying nothing, just watching. At first Lennie spoke to him with standard small talk, carefully designed, patterns of speech she'd learned in her years as a therapist.

"May I help you?"

Nick said nothing.

"Is there something I can do for you?"

Still nothing; he just glared. He hated her. Hated the sight of her, the way she moved, smiled uneasily and carefully touched her hair, smoothing it back, even though it needed no smoothing.

"I see you're hurt. That's unfortunate. Would you like to talk about what happened? Are you grieving?"

Nick sat stone cold angry and quiet, watching every nuance of her behavior, her patterns of speech, the way she framed her questions, the way she tried to assume a counselor's role in this very one-sided conversation.

Finally, she said, "OK, I will just wait for you to be comfortable to speak with me."

Nick spoke finally, after several more minutes.

"Tell me about The Director."

"Where would you like me to begin?"

"At the beginning, Princess Leia. How did you meet, why, where? Leave nothing out. You talk, and I'll listen. What was your job, why were you hired? How long have you worked for him? How much were you paid? Every single dirty little detail."

"Hmm…well, let's see now. I was contacted by his secretary and offered a job."

"What was his secretary's name?"

"Arthur."

"Continue."

Lennie recalled every detail she could remember about the couple of days she spent interviewing and staying at the hotel. She left out the part about chewing on her toenails and pulling out her dentures to remove the toenail wedged in-between her teeth. But for the most part, she was completely accurate and detailed.

"What was The Director's name?"

"Firestone, I think. Winston V. Firestone."

When she finished, Nick said, "Is that it?"

She said, "Yes, as well as I can remember. If something comes up, I'll be happy to make a note of it and make sure you're made aware of it." She smiled.

Nick thought as she smiled, *her teeth are too perfect, her hair too smooth and pulled back in a bun at the top of her head.* She wasn't afraid at all. She was entirely too comfortable. That made him more angry. He decided to change that, and quickly.

Lennie was aware Nick's demeanor had changed. He smiled, took a deep breath.

She was immediately very afraid. The change in him was sudden, and she felt he'd made a decision.

Bexx had been speaking to the Asgarda as they sat around the fire, quietly discussing what their next possible plans could be. They'd nearly forgotten about the fact Nick was in the barn speaking to Lennie, conducting his interview. They were reminded rather abruptly that he was interviewing her as a loud, long scream came from the barn. They ran to the barn, Bexx in the lead, afraid of what he'd done to Lennie.

When they arrived, Nick was leaving the stall, a huge handful of black hair in his hand. He smiled at Bexx as she ran up to him.

"Don't worry, I kept my promise. She isn't harmed...not permanently, at least."

Bexx looked in on the now cowering woman and saw Nick had cut off her hair in large, crude cuts. She was nearly bald in some places, and jagged pieces were longer in others. She continued to scream.

"...hat man is ebil...he is thatan...get thee out, thatan...I cas thee out of my word."

Nick laughed. "Satan? I cut your hair, and I'm Satan? What did you do to those people in the missile facility? You tortured them! They died, you bitch."

Lennie replied, her mouth now empty of her false teeth, "I am a thiensis. It was aww wone in the ame of thience and thychological therapy. I am a twained forenthic thychologitht. You are, in my pofessionao opinion, a wery isturbed thychopath."

"So now I'm Satan *and* a diagnosed psychopath. Diagnosed by a self-proclaimed forensic proctologist with a lisp. It must be my lucky day." He dropped the hair and the set of dentures she'd lost during the struggle in front of Bexx. "I kept my word; she's unharmed."

Nick stormed off, walking back towards the farmhouse.

The next week was very tense around the farmhouse. Nick was recovering physically, but not mentally. He'd become unbearable. Shoving the Asgarda out of his way when he walked into the house, he took food off their plates when they ate, basically doing anything he could to provoke and antagonize them. The situation had reached a breaking point. The Asgarda had spoken to Bexx repeatedly and expressed their anger at Nick's disrespectful actions and attitudes. Finally, it all came to a head, and she knew she would have to do something.

Bexx came to The Driver and asked him and Buffy to take the rest of the team to Moses Lake to rent a couple of rooms at a hotel and stay there until she called. The team needed a night or two to blow off some steam.

The Driver listened and replied, "Meanwhile, you're here alone with Nick? Do you think that's a good idea? Seriously, I mean, he did pry off my fingernail. What makes you think he won't go 5150, Loony Toons, bat shit crazy on you?"

Bexx thought for a minute. "I can explain it to you, but it would be better to show you." She called the team together and asked The Driver to connect the DVR from the incident at the gas station to a monitor. She told him to locate the day they'd entered the store and stop the recording. When he'd done so, she told the team her plan and that she needed to confront Nick alone. The team immediately protested. She waved her hands and said loudly, "Tishina!" The team fell silent. "What you are about to watch is the incident at the gas station. I want you to pay particular attention to Nick and his behavior." She nodded to The Driver, and he started the recording. There was no audio, so the room was completely silent. They watched as the men cornered Bexx, then saw Nick approach and smile, removing her from any danger, placing himself between the men and Bexx as they backed out. Motion sensors switched the recording to the outside camera. Nick opened the car door for her, then locked it as she got in and closed it. They watched as Nick got into the car, glaring at the three men standing at the door of the store laughing and heckling them. The truck backed out. A minute passed, and the truck pulled back in, coming to an abrupt stop. Nick's demeanor now had changed. He was dangerously angry. He walked rapidly into the store, then stopped, turned around, and flipped the open sign to closed and locked the door. The next few minutes were filled with the team making involuntary sounds of disgust. The Driver's face was ashen; all the blood had drained from his face as he realized finally how incredibly fortunate he'd been that night he and Nick had come face-to-face. Finally, Nick removed the DVR from behind the counter of the store and the screen went dead.

Bexx said, "Like all of you, this is the first time I have actually seen what happened. All of that was over me, because those men spoke rudely to me. Afterwards, Nick apologized to me over and over, not realizing I understood. He apologized to me for feeling embarrassed at his rage. Rage he felt because they had been rude to me. So you see, I will be fine. I need you to go to town with The Driver and wait until I ask you to return."

The team agreed to do as she asked. As they were loading the clothes they would need for the trip, Special K asked Bexx, "What do you plan to do?"

Bexx asked her to walk with her, away from the rest of the Asgarda.

Bexx turned and spoke plainly. "Bottom line is, I cannot have this breakdown in discipline. Our unit functions because we each have a role and an understanding of what is required of each of us. While Nõn was alive, she was our go-between with Nick. She is gone, and there is no understanding of his role anymore. We deal with our disagreements by solving them in the circle of combat. Nick refuses to fight me there, so I will change the rules. He will come to understand his role and submit to the team."

"And if he doesn't choose to submit? Then what?"

Bexx looked hard into Special K's eyes. "He will submit. I won't give him a choice. Simple as that."

Special K nodded. She had no doubt of her leader's ability, but Nick was an unknown. "I would feel better if you had backup, if one of us stayed just in case."

"If I need backup, then I don't deserve to lead any of you."

Special K nodded. "Good luck to you, then."

"I'll see you in a couple of days. Enjoy your time in the city."

The team drove off with The Driver in tow, leaving Bexx and Nick to sort things out.

As they drove off, Special K explained to the rest of the team what Bexx had said to her. The van was quiet. No one knew what to expect when they returned.

CHAPTER TWENTY-EIGHT

Nick woke up the next morning to a quiet farmhouse. The normal sounds of the Asgarda warriors had been replaced by silence. Since they'd returned to Moses Lake, he'd taken what had been Nõn's room while he recovered. He listened for a while and thought, *Maybe they finally took the damn hint and left.* He wanted them to go. He didn't want them to be drawn into his death match with The Director.

Nick got ready for the morning trek to the gym and headed out to repair the physical damage from Camp Cachibaché.

Bexx listened while Nick walked through the now quiet farmhouse, mumbling to himself. Surly as ever, he cursed under his breath, said, "Good riddance," and then "No great loss" tossed in with several curses, and a final "Russian mercenaries, my ass; more like pre-menopausal hosts of The View, candy ass wanna bees." Finally, he left the house and started his beloved 'Yota. She closed her eyes and thought, *Maybe I should have listened to Special K. Too late now.* She did have one last avenue to explore before she was all in and the real battle began. Bexx showered and dressed and went to the barn to take Lennie breakfast.

"Good morning."

Lennie replied, "Good morning to you as well."

"How did you sleep?"

"Good. Had some nightmares about Nick cutting off my nose and ears, but that's probably more precognition than dream. It's only a matter of time, isn't it?"

"I guess that depends. So far, you're alive. How would you feel about going for a walk when you're done eating?"

"To what end?"

"Humor me."

"May I have a hat or something to cover what used to be my beautiful hair?"

"Yes."

The two women walked out of the barn, and Bexx didn't speak for some time. Finally, she said, "I told everyone to leave. There is no one left here for the next few days except you, I and Nick. I am hoping you may be able to put aside your fear of him and help me look at him from another perspective. Your training is what I am asking for, not the rest of it."

"By the rest of it, I'm guessing you mean the treatments I was conducting on my patients."

Bexx stopped. "Let's be clear, you are still very much under my control. The only reason you are not dead back in the facility is because of me. So drop the pretenses. I know what you are, and you know what I am. If I chose not to protect you, Nick would have killed you instead of cutting off your hair. So can we speak plainly and honestly, or do you want to go back in the barn and take your chances?"

"What is it that you need help with?"

Two hours later, Nick returned to the farmhouse and saw Bexx walking with Morticia. He pulled into the driveway and turned off the 'Yota as he watched them talking back and forth, Morticia waving her hands animatedly and Bexx nodding.

"Tick, tock, tick, tock…can you hear that, Morticia? It's a big, toothy crocodile coming for the rest of your ass." Nick smirked, glaring as the two women continued to speak.

The day passed with Bexx not speaking to Nick, and vice versa; like two predators stalking each other, each was aware of the other but pretended not to be watching.

Finally night came, and Bexx built a fire in the fire pit outside the farmhouse and waited. The discussion with Lennie had given her much to think about, but really no new insight into Nick. The only thing she'd admitted was that in a few short moments, Nick had sized her up and knew exactly what would do the most harm to her mentally and still keep his promise to Bexx. The fact that he found a way around what Bexx had intended spoke volumes to her. She advised Bexx to be careful; Nick would be watching for any advantage, pushing whatever buttons he could to anger her.

Nick finally came out of the farmhouse and sat down by the fire, saying nothing. The chess match began. Nick moved first.

"Yesterday when you spoke to me, you spoke through Special K most of the exchange between us, until I pissed you off and challenged you in front of your beloved group of carpet munching wannabe Amazons. Did you realize you replied to me in English? Without using Special K? You took the bait, hook, line, and sinker. You've been listening to me the entire time and lying. Today, you walked with Morticia and spoke with her as well. I watched you both speaking back and forth. You speak English. You speak English very well." Nick glared at her.

Bexx took a deep breath. This wasn't a hopeful start. She ignored the comments.

"I have been hiding things from you, yes, and you from me as well. You did not tell me what happened in the gas station; meanwhile, I had to listen to you sing random songs from your very limited CD collection for

20 hours and not rip my hair out. Your singing voice is awful. I wanted to scream at you to shut the hell up, but I didn't. Trust me, it was not a pleasant experience."

Nick looked into the fire, refusing to acknowledge her. There were no comments from either of them for some time. Bexx stood suddenly, and Nick was immediately up as well, prepared for the attack. She held her hands up and said, "Relax, I am just standing up. Would you like a drink?"

"No, I can get my own."

Bexx returned with a beer for each of them and tried to hand it to him. He refused it.

She sat down closer to him in the circle around the fire.

"Tell me about your wife."

Nick sat staring into the fire for several minutes. He rolled his eyes and stood up. "If we're going to do this, then do this the right way at least." He walked away into the house and returned with a bottle of red wine and two glasses. "In Vino Veritas," he said. "Do you know what that means?"

She shook her head no.

"In wine there is truth. You want to do this? Speak the truth, quid pro quo, Clarice? You really want to dance with my demons? I wouldn't advise it. But we already know smart isn't something you do very well, is it? Pretty, tall, athletic, but dumb as a box of Russian rocks"

She ignored him and took the glass and held it up for him to pour. He did pour, filling each of their glasses nearly to the brim. "First off, I hate not filling a glass. It makes me feel poor, like I have to be careful and take less in case there won't be any tomorrow. Screw that. Live for today." Nick took a swallow of the wine.

"Your wife. Tell me about her, please."

Nick stared again into the fire. Taking another swallow, he began. "She was tall, and smart, smarter than anyone I'd ever known. She understood things on levels I didn't know existed. She asked questions I never thought to ask. She made me believe in life again. I was darker then, much meaner." He laughed. "Can you believe it? Meaner?" Laughing, he continued talking for some time and saw his glass was now empty. Bexx hadn't touched her wine as she listened. He poured another full glass for himself.

"In the end, she was just like every other woman I've known: attracted to the rage, wants to get close to the fire, but can't stand the heat when they get to the kitchen. Each for their own reasons, most made the mistake she made, thinking they could fix you, make you into something else. Finally, she grew tired of me and sought out other men. In the end, she tried to kill me. Funny how that is. I have a weird knack for survival. Should have been dead many times over, but here I am. Takes an ass kicking and keeps on ticking. What else do you wanna know, Mz. Bexx?"

"What happened at the gas station?"

"What do you think happened?" he roared. "They fucked up, that's what happened. They got used to being the big shark in a small pond, I guess, and had no idea who they were speaking to. Bitches better recognize!" Nick was loosening up with the alcohol. She had no idea of some of the slang references he was making but got the gist of what he said.

"Why did that make you so angry? What they did?"

"Angry? You thought that was anger?" He laughed and laughed. "That wasn't anger. That was a tune up. Me angry? That's…" He was silent. Finally, taking another drink of the wine he said, "You've seen me angry. That's me angry."

Bexx raised her eyebrows and nodded slightly. She realized she had indeed.

He continued. "The whole angry thing, it's weird. It's like I'm a spectator watching my own movie, riding this train called Nick and someone else is in the engine compartment. I'm just another passenger. Anyway, the wife, she was a lot like you in some ways, strong, physically and mentally. I just needed her to be something she could never be."

"What was that?" Bexx said, surprised.

"Strong, but not an abusive, self-centered bitch. I need a strong woman, not some candy ass teacup poodle with a bow in its hair and clicky little nails painted pink scratching on the floor. I need a woman who's formidable, a wolf, an alpha wolf. I've spent my whole damn life searching pet stores for an alpha wolf but always came away with teacup poodles or a yappy Chihuahua. Ya know?"

She did. More than Nick realized, Bexx understood this.

She took a drink from her glass finally.

"My turn. What the hell is it with you, Nõn and wolves? She had some weird ass dream about a wolf and followed me halfway around the planet. Got her ass killed following that wolf," he said as he beat on his chest, "and then you tell this story about some wolf dying to protect you. Seriously, do you both have some kind of wolf fetish or something? You like watching him lick his nuts or something"

Nick was trying to provoker her, she understood that and she ignored his comments. "I cannot speak for Nõn's dream of the wolf. She told us about her dream when she was in Ukraine, and then she had another. Her guide told her she needed to come and sit beside her. Perhaps she is now; I don't know. Maybe that was exactly what was supposed to be and how she was supposed to die. I don't know. As for me, the story was real. It happened, and for some reason it made you angry. Why?"

Nick laughed and laughed. "Angry? No, not angry. Just frustrated that you didn't get it."

"Get what?"

"Why the wolf did what he did. He didn't die to protect you. At least not completely. I swear, that's all every little girl thinks: everything, every animal out there is just begging to martyr themselves and die for the princess. Sorry, Hell no!"

"Why, then?"

"Imagine, for the first time in your life someone shows you kindness. You know, the warmth of a fire, food, rest, real rest. Not always being on guard. Then you reach out and run your fingers through his coat. Feeling his muscle, and sinew and scars. You said he growled. No shit, Bexx; to allow this kind of kindness in his world would be fatal. He can't allow it, but he wants it badly. He didn't fight to protect you; he fought because that's all he knows, and there's no way this campfire, Jack London, Call of the Wild horse shit could ever last. Better to die fighting and never see you harmed than risk his own survival and have to go back to that world again. It was a choice he made. Not to protect you, but to protect himself. No way he could live in this comfort for long. It never lasts."

"Like your wife? You felt protected?"

"Exactly! No! Yes! I guess so, and you see how that ended. She set me up to die! You can't kill shit, though; homeboy is still here." Nick stood up, drunk and weaving, and started singing a slurred song. "I can walk under water and not get wet. It's raining bullets, and I'm still here, I'm still here."

He sat back down hard, his mind wandering. "Really, what the hell did you expect me to do? Let those redneck dildos rape you? Like, seriously? I'm just gonna sit back and watch the show? Hell no! You don't get it. I'm not wired that way. When you're with me, you're under the umbrella of Nick. Punk ass, doo dah, shit kicking rednecks never had a clue. They crossed the line."

Nõn was right: nothing about Nick was what she thought.

"Is that why you are pushing us away? The team? You want us to leave because you cannot protect us. Like the wolf in my story, this is too much. You are in the same fight you have always been, and this time it is to the death."

"Duh, big red truck! Do you dye that hair? Do you know what it's like to sit in the 'Yota with you for 20 hours? Walk in on you in the shower? I don't need this shit! Wake up! Get you and your group of Victoria's Secret wannabes on down the damn road. I have a date with The Director, and I intend to keep it. Then this can end, finally."

Nick got up and said, "I'm going to sleep. 'Night, Mz. Bexx. I'm done with this episode of Doctor Phil. Tune in next week for The Asgarda, with knives and synced menstrual cycles. That'll be a nightmare I want no part of. Jesus! Shit is about to get real here in Green Acres." He stumbled off to sleep.

Bexx sat by the fire for several hours, thinking, putting every comment Nick had said into context. It all came to one single conclusion in her mind. Eventually the fire burned down, and she too went into the house and prepared herself for what tomorrow would bring.

CHAPTER TWENTY-NINE

Nick woke up the next morning hungover and irritable. He stumbled downstairs and went to the farmhouse kitchen. Bexx was already up and waiting.

"Jesus! You're still here? What does it take for you to get the hint, pack your shit and get on down the road? Hasta luego!"

She ignored him. "We have to come to an understanding, you and I. First, I do what I want to do, period. I am here because I chose to come here. I will leave when I choose to leave."

"OK, Helen Reddy, I am woman, hear me roar! Got it. Go roar somewhere else." He waved her off.

She stood up and closed the gap between them. "I will leave when I choose to."

Nick was uncomfortably aware of how close she was to him. "You might want to back the hell up before you start something you can't finish. Trust me, you don't want to go there. I'm in no mood for your Asgarda, Xena Princess Warrior bullshit this morning."

She closed the distance further, standing immediately behind him. "Does my being this close bother you, Nick?"

Nick clenched his jaw, the muscles on the side of his face rolling up and down as he tried to control his emotions.

He turned around and said, "Get up out of my face," and shoved Bexx back. She blocked his arms and redirected them to the side. She said, "Do I make you uncomfortable, Nick?"

He lunged at her, and the fight was on. They pushed back and forth at first, neither gaining the advantage, then he picked her up and slammed her on the kitchen table.

"Bitch, I will pick you up like a six pack and fold your ass up like a lawn chair if you touch me again."

She was up and driving a fist into his mouth before he could finish the rest of the threat. The punch knocked him back against the counter.

"Fold that," she said.

They rolled around on the floor and destroyed the kitchen. Moving into the living room, they punched and scratched, kicked and bit. The bandage on his head came off, and still they continued fighting.

Nick was talking trash the entire time. He stood up and flipped her over his waist, then said, "Did I mention I was a brown belt in judo? Candy ass, Ukraine communist, wannabe Russian bride. Some mercenary you are." She slammed a well-timed heel strike into his groin. Nick dropped.

"How's your brown belt feel now?" she quipped.

He started to crawl away on the floor, Bexx walking up beside him. She kicked him in the ribs repeatedly. "You will do what I tell you to. You will submit to me, Nick, or we will fight all damn day."

He laughed. "Submit to you? That's rich." She kicked him in the ribs again, but this time he caught her foot and held it. He then did a foot sweep move that took the remaining foot out from under her. She dropped hard to the floor, the wind knocked out of her. "If that's the best you got, you better go back to Ukraine. Time to bring your 'A' game, Bexx. It's all hands on deck, Princess, let's see it! Show me what you got."

He climbed on top of her and slammed her head onto the floor two or three times before she was able to swing a leg up high enough to wrap it around his shoulders and knock him off.

"Submit!" she said over and over as she grabbed his throat with both hands and began choking him.

He managed to say, "No" as he tried to shove her off.

She wasn't going anywhere. Knees spread wide as she straddled him, choking harder, she finally had the advantage. "Submit, or I will kill you," she growled.

Nick's face was turning purple. He relaxed and mouthed, "Do it, do it, end this shit!" He quit fighting and lay there, his arms at his side as he looked up at her.

Bexx eased off and said, "Say, 'I submit.' Say it!"

"No."

Bexx was furious; the stubborn ass would rather die than submit to her. She then remembered Nõn telling her, "Just when you think you understand him, you will realize you don't."

She stopped and sat back on his waist. Looking at him, she said, "You are mine now. I defeated you. Admit it, I defeated you."

"You did. You beat me. I'm willing to die. Finish this."

"No, your life is mine now. You are my property. I could have taken your life; I chose not to. Now you are mine, you belong to me."

Nick looked up at her. "You don't know what the hell you're saying."

"Yes, I do. Say it. Say, 'I am your property.'"

He shook his head no.

She came close to his face, both breathing heavily, she stared long and hard into his eyes. She then whispered fiercely, "Say it. I want to hear you say it. 'I am your property.' Say it!"

The text came later that day to The Driver. "Bring the team back tonight."

When the team arrived at the farmhouse, there was broken glass and furniture strewn about the house. There would be several hours of cleaning before the house would be clear of the shattered furniture and shards of glass. The team was quietly whispering to each other while they cleaned up the mess. Nick's truck was gone when they arrived, and they assumed Bexx had made him leave. One of them checked in his room, and all of his belongings were also gone. The whispers continued...what had happened?

A couple hours later, Nick pulled up, much to the surprise of the Asgarda. He got out of the 'Yota and walked to the house. Entering, he said nothing. He made eye contact with no one. He grabbed a drink and went to the barn. Buffy went up to Bexx's room to tell her Nick was headed to the barn. She opened the door and found Bexx nursing some scratches and a deep cut on her thigh. She was beat up and bruised, dark purple and green bruises covering her body. Buffy was angry. "He beat you up?" she said. "That son of a bitch beat you up?" Bexx told her to close the door.

Buffy left the room a few minutes later and went to the Bat Cave to tell The Driver what she'd seen in Bexx's room. The Driver was angry at her description of the bruises and cuts covering Bexx.

"I'm going to go talk to him right now! Where is he?"

Buffy said he was in the barn.

The Driver walked angrily to the barn and walked into the stall that had been Nick's. Nick was there, gingerly trying to take off his shirt. He too was covered with cuts and bruises, bite marks covered his shoulders, and deep scratches crisscrossed his back. The Driver stopped cold in his tracks. "Dude, what happened to you? You look like the main event at a porn convention in Vegas."

Nick grimaced. "Help me take off my shirt, man. I went to the gym to try to work out some of the soreness, but I think that was a mistake. I feel worse."

"You look like death warmed over, my friend. What happened?"

"Don't ask, never mind. Just let it go, OK? Don't say anything to anyone."

"Sure, man, no problem." The Driver helped Nick put on a new sweatshirt, then went straight to Buffy and told her Nick was beat up, and beat up bad. They then told the rest of the Asgarda what they'd both seen, whispering to each other, trying to imagine what had happened.

That night at the fire, they all gathered around; there was an unspoken tension in the air. The Asgarda had no idea what to expect. The Driver and Buffy explained there was nothing in all of the documents and computer hard drives that led them anywhere near The Director. He'd carefully covered his tracks so nothing led back to him. The Driver apologized to the group, explaining that in all the years he'd been a hacker, he'd never met anyone so careful. There was always something you could exploit and use; however, he was at a loss as to what they would do now. To Nick, it all felt so familiar. The Director had been a whisper in the wind for so long now, he seemed supernatural. Like a ghost or a demon. The group was quietly thinking about what The Driver had said. Bexx asked Special K to bring Lennie from the barn. When she arrived at the fire, Bexx asked her to recount for all of them as best she could remember everything about her meeting with The Director.

Nick stared quietly into the fire as he listened again to Lennie talk about her interview with The Director.

"Well, he was a well-dressed man, and I remember he wore a purple tie. I liked that. Purple is my favorite color, you know. Oh, and he had a beautiful purple rug that just so made the room glow." She droned on and on about various meaningless details, the fabric of the chairs, his expensive suit, etc. Nick said nothing; just listened. He'd heard all of this before. He thought silently, *I should have killed her when I had the chance. This shit is so tedious; purple this, attractive that. Jesus. She mentioned his name again, Firestone.* His attention snapped back to when she mentioned being cut by one of the sharp whiskey glasses. She hadn't mentioned it when he spoke to her in the barn.

Nick looked at Bexx urgently but didn't say a word. She looked back, then turned to Lennie. "What was that about the glasses? Say that again."

"Oh, I said he told me he had them made. They were custom glasses. They'd been cut, but not polished, so they were dangerous to drink from if you didn't use a cloth to hold them."

Nick turned to the fire and cleared his throat. "May I speak?"

Eyebrows rose around the fire. Did Nick really just ask for permission to speak? No one moved, no one breathed...surprised Asgarda exchanged curious looks. What the hell had happened while they were gone?

Bexx spoke quietly, "Please do."

Nick looked at her and no one else. "That's it. That's our in, the glasses. That's his mistake. They'll be special ordered, and if I'm right, they'll be very high end and excellent quality. He'll have made a request for them and probably had to sign a waiver agreeing not to hold the company liable should anyone be harmed by them."

He said, "May I offer a suggestion?" his eyes piercing the fire light as he looked at Bexx.

She quietly said, "Yes," knowing how difficult this was for him.

"I'd suggest The Driver and Buffy direct their hacking search towards the top ten manufacturers of these types of glasses, looking for this special order and waiver. If they find nothing, do the next ten, and so on. He'll be in there somewhere."

Bexx nodded. "Thank you," she said quietly, secretly acknowledging more than the statements he'd made. Nick's eyes returned to the fire.

Bexx turned to The Driver and Buffy and said, "What do you think? Can that be done?"

Both The Driver and Buffy were still too stunned by the exchange with Nick. The Driver stammered, "Um…yes, I think that makes sense. It's possible. I mean, yes, that makes a lot of sense the more I think about it. The Driver is on it like a porn star riding a Sybian." He nudged Buffy and said, "Let's go!"

No one said a word for several minutes after The Driver and Buffy had left the fire. Eyes looked at Nick curiously, then to Bexx. Back and forth the Asgarda glanced.

Finally, Bexx spoke to Nick. "Would you excuse us? I will be upstairs in a moment." The hidden meaning of this statement caught everyone by surprise. Now the mystery of where Nick's stuff had gone made sense. He'd moved into Bexx's room.

Nick rose, saying nothing, and walked to the house.

Bexx waited for him to enter the house, then spoke to the Asgarda in their native tongue.

"As you may have noticed, we came to an agreement. Nick will no longer be a problem for any of you. I will be talking over the hunt for The Director. Nick will be here to assist us as we continue the search. As you saw tonight, he does have a unique way of seeing things we should be able to exploit. Are there any questions?"

One of the Powerpuff Girls spoke up. "Yes, I have a question. What happened while we were gone?" The group laughed uneasily. Finally, someone had spoken what they all were thinking.

Bexx smiled and said mysteriously, "It took me a while, but I just heard what he had been saying. That is all, really. I just listened."

CHAPTER THIRTY

The next morning, the Asgarda awoke at the normal time and began their morning routine. Each day, a different team member was tasked with bringing Lennie her breakfast after the morning workout. One of the team members noticed Nick wasn't around this morning and asked where he was. Bexx said, "He is still asleep." The team snickered. "Still asleep, huh," someone muttered. Bexx, smiling, replied, "Yes, I don't think he has slept more than an hour or two a day for quite some time. I would be surprised if he is up before noon." More laughter. Special K asked, "So what is the story behind all the scratches and bruises? The house looked like a nasty brawl occurred while we were gone." Bexx replied, "You don't honestly think he would just submit to me just because I asked him to, do you?" Special K replied, "Yes, I did, after seeing the way he looks at you when your back is turned. I think he would do anything you asked, if you only would." Bexx was surprised. "What do you mean, the way he looks at me when my back is turned?" She looked around the group as they all smiled sheepishly. "You mean all of you knew this, and no one said a thing to me?" She searched their laughing eyes. They all smiled. "How come no one told me?" "You are our leader," Special K said, "but in some aspects, you and Nick are very much alike. What do you imagine your response would have been had we told you Nick's eyes follow you everywhere you go, like a little boy looks at his first crush? Neither one of you would have admitted anything. You are both too damn stubborn."

Nick finally did wake up and came downstairs to the farmhouse kitchen. The Asgarda met him with knowing smirks and giggles as he made himself lunch. Embarrassed and somewhat angry, his face turned a burning red and his ears tingled, but he said nothing. The day wore on, he went to the gym, came back to the farmhouse, and sat by the fire at night. For several days, there was no progress in the search for The Director. The Driver and Buffy were hard at it in the Bat Cave. They'd hacked the first top ten sellers of crystal whiskey glasses and found nothing in their sales records, so they went on to the next 10. Nick felt a calmness he hadn't felt in some time. He was nearly positive the hackers would find The Director. His focus now was what to do when they did. At night lying in Bexx's bed, he would stare at the ceiling after she fell asleep. He ran through scenario after scenario of how they could exploit the crystal glasses to their benefit. He knew this was the way in; he just had no idea how to exploit it…not yet.

Finally, one night Bexx called a meeting at the nighttime fire. The Driver and Buffy had finally found the purchase order and the signed waiver of liability. They explained the order had been placed with Cash Crystal. When they found the order, it had a name associated with it. They cross-referenced it on the Web.

Bexx nodded to The Driver and Buffy to begin.

"We found The Director," The Driver began. "It took a while, but Nick was spot on. The crystal whiskey glasses were a special order from Cash Crystal. It's a small company in Ireland that produces high end crystal and is sold exclusively through Crystal Classics in the United States. It took a while, but we have his name and information. He's spent considerable effort concealing his identity. First, the purchase was made by an Arthur Look. I did a search on Mr. Look and found he was in fact an administrative assistant employed by the government. He's The Director's administrative assistant and has worked exclusively for The Director for several years."

Bexx asked, "And The Director is?"

"His name is Oelsen Hauer. The other name, Firestone, is one of many dead-end names associated with Hauer. Anyway, the point is, we know who he is. He's the Chief of Staff to the Director of Homeland Security."

Buffy looked at Bexx, making eye contact with her and nodding in Nick's direction.

Bexx had been absorbed in the conversation with The Driver and had been unaware of the Asgarda backing away from Nick, carefully and slowly creating a safe distance around him. Bexx looked at Nick, aware now that he'd wrapped his arms around his legs. He sat rocking, breathing heavily, barely able to contain his rage. He sat there rocking, unaware Bexx had been speaking to him. Finally he heard her. "Nick, are you OK?" He nodded but couldn't speak. He rocked for several minutes and finally with great effort spoke in a shaking voice, "I'm sorry. I can barely contain this. I don't want you to be afraid of me, but you're probably wise to do so. This anger has always been here, deep inside. I keep it locked down. But knowing who he is now, hearing his name, I want to rip him apart. I want to hear his screams and smell his blood. This has been a part of me for as long as I can remember. I've kept it under control until…until Nõn died. Now it's awake again, and it wants to be set free. It's a struggle to keep contained. Just give me a minute, and I'll be OK." Slowly, his breathing normalized and the rocking slowed. Nick smiled at Bexx. "It's OK. It's passed."

Bexx nodded and returned to the conversation with The Driver. "Do you have any ideas of how to exploit this information?"

"No, not yet."

Bexx turned to the group and said, "I want all of you to think of a plan. No matter how ridiculous, I want to discuss it. We'll meet again tomorrow night here at the fire and discuss them."

The group understood they were dismissed and gradually left the fire in ones and twos. The Driver and Buffy were about to peel off as well, and Nick spoke up.

"Please let them stay," he said to Bexx.

"Stay," she said.

Nick got up and walked to The Driver. "Thanks, man. You found him. Outstanding!

"Told you, brother. The Driver was on it like a porn star riding a Sybian. I'm not letting go till we get this fascist bastard."

Nick nodded to Buffy as well and said, "Thank you."

He then sat down. "So,The Director is housed in a government building?"

Nick smiled. "This is ironic. My wife, the one that tried to kill me, she worked for a contractor. This particular contractor worked a contract for the GSA. Do any of you know what the GSA does?" No one did. "General Services Administration. They're the government agency that supplies all the equipment and office supplies for the rest of the government agencies. Paper clips to computers, you name it, they supply it. Another role they have is landlord. They're the landlord for every government building out there. They have a listing of every building custodian and responsible party for the entire federal government. Do you see where this is going?"

The Driver smiled. "Yes, I do. Through the GSA we can gain access to the building."

"Exactly. You don't go at Homeland Security using Homeland. You use the GSA. My deadly, scheming wife used to remark how the GSA was particularly lax in their security. They used Google a lot for online meetings, and email. Amazon for their cloud services. If I remember correctly from our recent election, a certain Russian hacker was able to access John Podesta's Gmail account quite easily and spread all of Hillary's dirty little secrets all over the Web. Imagine if that same hacker could get into the GSA and snoop around." Nick smiled at The Driver.

The Driver smiled back. "Yes, imagine what that same Russian hacker could do."

"Still doesn't answer how we get to the bastard, but we're closing in on him." Nick smiled.

The Driver and Buffy left the fire, leaving Nick and Bexx alone as the fire continued to burn down.

Bexx was deep in thought and finally spoke. "I want you to come up with a method of getting to The Director that does not require you to self-destruct. I know you have envisioned this as a final desperate suicidal act, but that is no longer an option. You no longer have the right to make that decision. Are we clear?" She looked at him.

Nick took a deep breath, then slowly letting it out, he nodded.

After the fire burned out, they went up to her room. Nick stared at the ceiling for hours. They were so close, but they needed a plan, an epic, kick-ass, Ocean's 13 kind of plan that would catch the master of puppets himself off guard. The Director had been paying the piper and choosing the tune long enough; the time had come to change the song.

CHAPTER THIRTY-ONE

The next morning, Nick woke up early and headed to the single bathroom for the old farmhouse. He planned on hitting the gym this morning but always made sure he brushed his teeth before working out; bad breath in Ali's gym was strictly forbidden. He'd watched her throw a guy out last week after ridiculing him relentlessly for spouting toxic waste and polluting her pure gym air, as she called it, with his bad breath. The bathroom was occupied. Nick waited. Several minutes later, Special K exited the bathroom and smiled an embarrassed smile. "You may want to wait a minute or two until it airs out in there. Sorry! My apologies. Chinese food is new to me. I love it, but my stomach disagrees."

Nick thought, *Yeah. how bad can it be, really?* Special K was an Asgarda, but the smallest of the group, a tiny, petite badass.

Nick went into the bathroom and tested the proverbial waters. "OH MY GOD!" he cried out, horrified as he ran out of the bathroom. As he sat in the hallway recovering, he seriously wondered how Chinese food could produce anything that disgusting. If the farm had a fire alarm, he would have pulled the red handle. Stunned, an idea came to him like a brick thrown through a plate glass window. It was like a puzzle he'd been trying to solve showed its secret answer and all the pieces fell into place. He knew exactly how to get to The Director.

Nick went to the gym after the toxicity of Special K had finally vacated the bathroom. His eyes watered as he brushed his teeth and tried not to breathe. *Jesus*, he thought, *imagine if I was with her instead of Bexx.* He gagged and spit out the toothpaste in his mouth. Best not to go down that road.

Nick went to the gym and went through his workout. He'd picked up the latest installment of black market pharmaceuticals and left the gym, headed for the farmhouse. He was pretty sure the plan would work, but it all hinged on one thing. They needed someone to get them inside the building, unnoticed and disguised, as part of the normal routine of the building.

The Driver met with him and Bexx and explained he'd been able to hack the GSA database and found the custodian for the building. He asked Nick, "What now, sport? Make a midnight trip to his house and pry off his toenails? Force him to watch Three's Company reruns? Or better yet, Dancing with the Stars until he breaks out in a pool of sweat?"

Nick thought for a moment. "We need to visit him in person and size him up. Government employees aren't like the rest of us. I worked in the government most of my life, and no one is more paranoid than federal employees. They're encouraged to report anything and everything remotely suspicious. They're constantly briefed about any attempt to breach security in their building. It breeds a culture of fear and suspicion. I was amazed at how ridiculous all the people I worked with became. Everything was a spy attempting to gain information and had to be reported and investigated."

Nick turned to The Driver and said, "Can you book us a couple of round trip tickets to D.C.?"

"Us? You mean you and I?"

"Sure, I need someone that can think on their feet. We'll be an investigative team checking the security of the building. If the guy bites, we set the plan in motion. If he shuts us down, we'll have to find another way."

Two days later, Nick and The Driver were on their way to D.C., flying first class on Delta Airlines Flight 1484. They laid over in Minneapolis, then traveled on to the Baltimore International Thurgood Marshall Airport.

The Driver had a detailed folder on all the GSA employees' information that had been listed as the building custodian. He'd been a 25-year employee for the GSA and was nearing retirement. The Driver had set up an appointment with him to meet at the Southwest neighborhood library at 900 Welsley Place, at 1300 hours. Twenty minutes into the interview, Nick ended it abruptly.

"Well, Bill," Nick said, turning to The Driver, "I'm satisfied, are you?" The Driver had no idea what Nick was talking about but went along with his line. "I sure am, Bob." Nick turned to the suspicious custodian and said, "Sir, congratulations, you passed our security check. We've attempted this same scam on every government building in the area, and you're the first custodian that wouldn't take the bait. I feel much better now knowing that at least one of our GSA employees is up to the task of maintaining our government's security measures. We'll be contacting your supervisor and passing along the good news. I would expect an excellent work award in your near future. It's been a pleasure, sir!" Nick extended his hand and vigorously shook the man's hand. "An absolute pleasure!"

The formerly suspicious man was now beaming. Twenty-five years of government service, and no one had ever appreciated the importance of his job in the huge, slowly grinding machine that's the federal system. He always felt his job was underappreciated, and most definitely undercompensated. Finally, he would receive the recognition he so richly deserved.

Nick and The Driver left the library. Nick said, "No way that guy was going to play. He's about as structured and set in his routine as he can be. He's exactly what I was afraid he would be. No wiggle room there; we need someone that has issues we can leverage." They were quiet for most of the trip back to Spokane. Somewhere over Idaho, just before they landed, Nick turned to The Driver and said, "What about Arthur? What do we know about him?"

The Driver replied, "Not a lot. I never thought to look there. Our focus has been on GSA employees. I'll begin a search. What do you want me to look for?"

"Anything that can be exploited. Affairs, addictions, debts, secrets, anything at all. Didn't Morticia say she'd met him as well?"

"You mean Doctor Warsaw?"

"Yes, Morticia, the Bene Gesserit, goth chick, forensic proctologist. She mentioned she'd met Arthur."

The Driver stared at Nick. His hatred for the psychologist knew no bounds; he really hated her. "Glad we're friends now, man. You just never let it go, do you?"

"Let what go? What do you mean?"

"Never mind."

Once they were back at Moses Lake, they briefed Bexx and the Asgarda of their failure. They had to find another way into the building. The plan was solid; the way in was not.

While they sat and talked about various aspects of the plan, Nick said to Bexx, "I think it may be a good idea for me to talk to Morticia again. She may have insight into The Director that we've missed."

Bexx smiled. "I think not. If you speak to her at all, it will be with me present. I don't need her damaged any more than you already have. She is our only link to The Director that has survived your communication efforts. Let's keep her that way. She is no good to us dead."

Nick sulked, staring into the fire. He had to admit, he liked the idea of taking an ear, or maybe a nose. Yes, that was it: the nose; much harder to hide. People would stare at her in horror for the rest of her life. He smiled.

Looking up, he saw Bexx watching him with a disapproving look. "What?"

"You know what."

He sighed and looked back at the fire, another smile growing on his face.

Bexx looked on skeptically. He needed to be constantly watched. Nõn was right: he was annoyingly juvenile. She thought about what he'd said and saw there was some merit in it. She asked Special K to bring Lennie to the fire to speak with them.

Lennie arrived a short time later, and Bexx asked her if she had much contact with The Director's secretary.

"You mean that lovely man, Arthur? Yes, some."

"What can you tell us about him, and maybe his relationship with The Director?"

"Well, of course. I am a forensic psychologist."

Nick rolled his eyes in disgust.

Lennie continued. "I should be able to give you some insight into their relationship, specifically Arthur."

"Excellent! How long would that take?" Bexx replied.

"A day or two, I should think."

As Lennie compiled her profile, The Driver was diving deep into Arthur's life, and the lives of those in his immediate family. He was searching through health insurance enrollment files after bypassing the GSA's insurance enrollment software and finally started to get some traction, cross-referencing the information there with another list of patients needing bone marrow transplants. He then looked again at Arthur's financial records and GSA pay scales. The Driver had finally found an in, a definite avenue they could exploit.

Meanwhile, Lennie had finished her profile. Both finished within an hour of the other.

Bexx canceled the Asgarda afternoon sparring session, and everyone met in the kitchen, Special K bringing Lennie into the farm house for the first time. Lennie sat at the kitchen table and began her report. It started with her usual self-important detailing of her training and experience in the field as a forensic psychologist and how she normally was paid "X" amount of dollars for completing a profile like this one. She looked around the room to make sure everyone understood she was doing them a favor, then began to detail how she'd been recognized by the Turkish government as an ambassador after a terrible earthquake. When her eyes fell on Nick's, and the murderously hateful glare that looked back at her as he thumbed the edge of a knife he'd stealthy removed from his boot, she thought better of continuing down that road.

"Perhaps I should move on," she said, "and paraphrase my findings." Her voice was wavering nervously, now looking to Bexx for protection.

"Yes, I think that might be a wise thing to do, Lennie," Bexx replied, smiling thinly.

"Well, let's see then. To paraphrase…um…yes, well, it is my opinion that given The Director's position and his complete trust in Arthur with intimate details of his, shall we say, professional endeavors "

"Like Cachibaché," Nick interrupted loudly.

"Yes, exactly," she continued, "that kind of trust implies to me that

The Director – Oelsen, I mean – has some leverage over Arthur that's so complete, so all-encompassing that Arthur would never consider challenging it. He has Arthur between a rock and a hard place and has made sure Arthur knows it. If Arthur breaks confidence with him, the consequences would be dire for him and those he loves."

"So kind of like you, in your current position," Nick said, smiling darkly.

Bexx interrupted, "Yes, thank you, Lennie," and she nodded to Special K to take her back to the barn.

Bexx looked sternly at Nick as they waited for Special K to return.

"What?" Nick said innocently. "I just wanted to make sure I understood exactly what she meant, that's all. You know all that psychological terminology is so above my tiny head, as damaged as it is. You do realize what she just did, right? She used The Director's real name. Oelsen. Who told her that name? Up until today, it's always been Firestone. Think about that." He smiled.

Bexx nodded, her eyes widened and suddenly murderously cold. The man could be so incredibly tiresome, but he did notice the details.

Special K returned, and Bexx nodded to The Driver to begin.

"I think I know exactly what leverage The Director has over Arthur. First, Arthur has a wife. They've been married for 25 years. They met in high school and have been married ever since. Five years ago, she was diagnosed with stage 3 symptomatic myeloma. She needs a bone marrow transplant and is about to age out for the marrow list. Transplants are normally sought out for patients 18-44 years of age. In a few months, she'll be too old to stay on the list, and she'll drop off and will most certainly die." The Driver let that news sink in.

"Second, The Director pays Arthur twice the amount he should be receiving for his pay grade at the GSA. He's heavily compensated, which allows him to be able to pay the minimum payments on his wife's skyrocketing medical bills."

The Driver paused, then said, "There you go: a rock and a hard place, just like the doctor said."

Nick stared, his eyes not seeing the room as he processed the information Morticia and The Driver had found.

Finally, he snapped out of it, blinked a couple of times, and said to Bexx, "We won't have any better leverage than this. I need to be on a plane to D.C. as soon as possible. I need to speak with Arthur alone."

Bexx replied, "You will be on a plane as soon as The Driver can secure a flight, but you will not be going alone. I will go with you."

"No! The rules of interviewing require a one-on-one meeting with the subject in a nondescript room with little distraction, if any. You'll be a distraction."

"I don't care. You will do fine. You are not going alone."

Nick was angry and loudly demanded, "WHY?"

Bexx said nothing for some time; she just met his gaze calmly.

They sat eye locked for a long minute. Finally, Nick looked away and mumbled quietly, "Sorry, it's just…we're close, and we get one shot at this, only one." He looked down at the floor, feeling the weight of her gaze still on him.

Bexx turned to The Driver and said, "As soon as we can leave, please secure two round trip tickets. We will need lodging and a car as well."

In less than 24 hours, Nick and Bexx were on Delta Flight 1484, headed back to Washington, D.C.

CHAPTER THIRTY-TWO

Nick was studying every detail of the brief Lennie had prepared, and all of the documents that The Driver had as well. He had to be able to use everything there to try to convince Arthur it was in his best interest to work with them. Bexx being present ensured he couldn't use more "direct" means of ensuring Arthur's compliance. As he studied, Bexx began to doze off. Sitting next to him, she reached out and laid her hand on his thigh, it being more a statement of their relationship roles than an act of affection. He looked at her hand curiously. Never had he imagined a touch could communicate so much without a word being said. He watched her fall asleep, then immersed himself back in the paperwork.

Arthur was sitting in his chair in his office, the fate of his wife weighing heavily on his mind. He felt trapped and felt he had no way out of his current predicament. He felt completely powerless. The Director had him by the balls, literally. His wife would die if he couldn't find her a bone marrow donor. She was nearing an expiration date he couldn't imagine was legal, moral or just. What human being could just remove another from the donor list based on age? How was this possible? Who made these inhuman rules? His mind raced, trying to find a solution. The clock was ticking, time pressed on, and in a few short months his wife would be given a death sentence. Not by a court of law for some egregious crime she'd committed, but by an insurance company whose only concern was cost cutting and getting the most for their buck, making the most of their bottom line so their shareholders could maintain their own standard of living. They didn't give a damn about his wife.

Arthur was vaguely aware of Hector Berlioz: Symphonie Fantastique — Dream Of A Witches Sabbath, being played in The Director's office. "NO, not again," he whispered to himself. Arthur's life had become hell.

"Arthur, would you come in here," The Director called out over the interoffice communications system. Arthur clenched his teeth. "Not again… please, not again." But he already knew what the classical piece meant.

"Yes, sir. Gladly, sir," Arthur replied falsely.

Arthur got up and walked reluctantly to the double doors of The Director's office, then turned and closed them, resigned to the fact that he'd have to satisfy The Director's needs once again.

Several minutes later, The Director looked down at Arthur and said,

"Arthur, forgive me, but you seem less enthusiastic about the task than you have been in the past. Is something wrong?

Arthur stopped and wiped the spit running down his chin. "No, sir. I'll try to do better, sir." Arthur continued, more enthusiastically than before.

"That's it…excellent job, Arthur…excellent job."

Later, Arthur went into the men's room and forced himself to vomit. He had to swallow, The Director demanded it, but he didn't have to keep it down. He would fight back as best he could until another option presented itself. Little did Arthur know, the option he'd so desperately looked for was rapidly approaching, at eight miles a minute.

The Driver had been able to locate the direct line to Arthur's desk and added it to the file. Nick dialed the number and waited.

Arthur returned to his desk after rinsing his mouth with a small travel sized bottle of mouth wash in the bathroom. The phone was ringing as he sat down. He picked it up and spoke.

"Arthur Look, how may I help you?"

"Arthur, I need you to listen carefully. Can you do that? Can you give me your full attention?"

"Who is this?"

"You may not have known me, but a while back I was known to your boss as the Wild Card. Does that help?"

It did sound vaguely familiar, but Arthur couldn't remember from where. "It sounds familiar. Do I know you?"

"How about Baroota? Does that ring a bell?"

Arthur spoke quietly, "Yes, it does."

"And Cachibaché? Ring another bell?"

"Yes."

"I would like to meet, Arthur; just you and I, face to face. It's taken me some time to locate your boss, and I have a proposition for you. However, one word to your boss, and it all fades away. Like a fart in the wind, I'll be gone. And the next time we meet, it'll be too late for your sweet wife, too late for you, and too late for The Director. Are you familiar with Shakespeare, Arthur?"

"I am."

"In his play Julius Caesar, Act 3, Scene 1, Marcus Antonius says the famous quote, 'Cry havoc and let slip the dogs of war.' I am the dogs of war, Arthur. I am coming, and I will not stop until I see your boss dead. You don't have to be collateral damage in this fight. The choice is yours. I'll be at Masala Art, at 1101 4th Street, at 1800 hrs. You'll easily find me, trust me. I and my companion will stand out. I look forward to meeting you, Arthur.

Please listen carefully. I can make the countdown issue meaningless, Arthur: one word to Oelsen Hauer, and the deal is off and your wife will clock out and die in front of you. Do you understand me?"

"Yes, I believe so."

"1800 hours then, Arthur."

"I'll be there. Thank you."

Arthur hung up and closed his eyes. The Wild Card, still alive! And he was behind the demise of Baroota and Cachibaché? Arthur smiled. If it was the Wild Card and he'd survived, The Director had no idea. Perhaps it was time for karma to come calling at The Director's door and bite him square in the ass.

Arthur had never heard of Masala Art, so he Googled it and found out it was a restaurant only 3 minutes from The Department of Homeland Security that specialized in Indian food. He was also surprised to learn it was one of the highest rated restaurants in the area. He wondered why The Wild Card had chosen it.

Arthur arrived just before 1800 hours and looked around the restaurant. He saw no one who stood out. The Wild Card said he would be easy to spot, and yet here Arthur stood, unable to tell who he was supposed to meet. Panic set in...had The Director set him up? If he had, Arthur knew his life was over. It had been 7 minutes now, and still nothing. As he was just about to turn and leave, a woman stood up and walked toward him. She was exceptionally tall and athletic. "Hello, Arthur, come and sit with me," she said.

He sat with her, then she smiled and said, "Would you like to order some food, or a drink perhaps?"

Arthur replied, "Where's the Wild Card? You aren't the Wild Card. He told me he'd be here."

"You mean Nick? Oh, he is here. He is just making sure that no one has followed you. You see, your boss has been extremely resourceful and cautious, and Nick trusts no one. He will be here when he is reasonably sure that I am safe."

"Who are you?"

"I am Nick's...let's just say Nick and I have an arrangement, and leave it at that."

Arthur's brows furrowed. What did that mean? Anyway, he sat for a minute, then said, "Are you going to order food as well?"

"No, we have been here for some time. Nick insisted we sit and get the feel of the place; that way, when you arrived we would know if something was wrong immediately. We have eaten already. You may order anything you like, it is on us."

Arthur ordered the Mutton ki Nizami Pudina Seekh, paired with a 2013 Pinot Grigio from Valcantara, Granacha, Spain, for the first course.

When the food arrived, Nick came into the restaurant quietly and sat next to Bexx.

"Arthur, you made it! Glad to see you still have the stones to step out on that walking human dildo you work for."

Arthur said nothing. He just looked at Nick. "You're the Wild Card?"

"Yep, that was the line of shit your boy Jay sold me. Guess he had no idea, really. Funny when you think about it in retrospect; wasn't funny at the time, though. I promise you that."

Nick stared at him intensely. Arthur had feared The Director for years, looking for a way out of his nightmare. Now looking across the table at Nick, he shivered and thought, *If you're going to kill the devil, you bring someone insane enough to do it.*

"Are you alright, Arthur? Having second thoughts?"

"No, I'm not having second thoughts."

"Good. So, let's begin. I'll speak, you'll listen. If you have any questions, you can ask them after I'm done. Deal?"

"Yes."

Nick began to detail what they knew about Arthur's situation, his wife's illness, the fact that she was about to drop off the donor list and had been nowhere near the top of the list to begin with.

"Do you know why that is, Arthur? Do you know why she's never reached the top of the list?"

"No, I don't."

"The Director has kept her where she is. He doesn't want her to get better, or to even have the chance to get better. Do you know why?"

Arthur was suddenly sick. "No."

"Because he doesn't want to lose the control and leverage her sickness gives him over you. You're in a position of tremendous power; I know it doesn't feel like it, but you are. You know all his deepest secrets, and he trusts you to keep them as long as your wife is ill. Has the thought ever occurred to you what'll happen when she drops off the donor list?"

Arthur sat, eyes widening. He'd never thought about what would happen if his wife dropped off the donor list. He'd been so focused on her survival; the what ifs had never occurred to him. Now that they did, he realized his wife wasn't the only one with a death sentence hanging over her head.

"Making sense, Arthur?"

Arthur nodded.

"Then this is what I propose. First, in a show of good faith, your wife is now at the top of the donor list. You can verify this, but for now just listen. She won't receive confirmation of a donor match until you send me proof The Director is dead. Second, you don't need to do a thing until I contact you. When I do, I'll have instructions that must be followed to the letter. When I do call, you'll arrange for a pass to be issued that allows entrance into your building. One pass, that's it. You'll escort this person to your floor. She'll be bringing one box. It'll contain exact replicas of The Director's Cash Crystal whiskey glasses, minus the deadly edges. When the time comes, you'll switch them out. You'll keep the originals in your desk or locker, wherever is convenient, then she'll leave the building escorted by you. You wait until I call. When it's over, you'll replace the new glasses with the old ones. Simple as that. Basically, it's a variation of the old amusement park game of the ball and cups. Simple and elegant. No evidence, nothing comes back to you, your problems are over. Make sense?"

Arthur nodded. "But how do you know about the glasses?"

Nick smiled an evil smile. "Best for you not to know, Arthur. Just trust me, I'm knee deep in The Director's ass; he just can't feel me squirming yet. Can you do this simple switch to be free from his weekly sessions? To have your wife go to the top of the donor list?"

Arthur's face was instantly burning hot. His faced flushed. "How did you know about the sessions?" he whispered.

Nick smiled and raised an eyebrow but said nothing.

"Is it a deal?"

"Yes," Arthur whispered, now deeply embarrassed by the secrets the Wild Card knew. "Yes, I'll do it."

"Excellent." Nick handed him a cell phone. "This is a burner phone. This will be the only way we communicate. It'll take me about 10 days to get everything lined up. Remember, your wife is at the top of the donor list, but no match will occur until I have proof of The Director's death."

"How will I provide the proof to you that he's dead?"

"You'll take a picture of The Director's death with the phone and send it to the only number saved in the phone's memory. When I've received it, I'll confirm it by sending a text back. Your wife will magically have a donor, and it'll all be over. Then throw the phone away. Simple."

Arthur stared at him quietly and said nothing.

"How's the food, Arthur? Eat up, man. Your troubles are over."

Arthur picked at his food and looked at Bexx. "What's your part in this?"

Nick spoke up, "She's your insurance policy, Arthur."

"Insurance for what?"

"If you said no to my offer, she knew I'd kill you rather than risk The

Director knowing how close I am. She's here to make sure I don't do just that." Nick smiled.

Arthur looked at Bexx. She smiled back. "It's true, Arthur," she said.

Arthur left the rest of the food on the table and drank the wine. They concluded their discussion. "Top of the list, Arthur. Check it. I'll be in touch; until then, life goes on as normal…well, as normal as it can be in the stain of The Director's dark shadow."

Nick and Bexx walked away.

Later that night as they lay in the hotel room, Bexx said, "How did you know The Director prevented Arthur's wife from being at the top of the donor list?"

"I didn't. I lied. I lied about most of that. The Driver has put her at the top of the list, and we can make sure she gets a donor that matches. The rest was a guess. Part of interviewing is following the logical progression of events. I have no idea what the sessions are between Arthur and The Director. I just guessed that if he had that much power over Arthur, he'd abuse it somehow. Apparently, he is, but I have no idea what he's doing. That's why I used a very ambiguous word like 'session.'"

"It could mean anything, and only Arthur could assign a specific meaning to it. Make sense? In interviewing, you weave lies with truth. That's all I did. Arthur filled in the rest on his own, with assumptions he now thinks I know."

Bexx smiled. Nick was full of surprises. She turned off the light and pulled him close. "Now what mystery, man?" she said.

"Now we go back to where it all began," he replied.

CHAPTER THIRTY-THREE

Nick had some details to take care of when they arrived back in Moses Lake. He decided to send Nõn's article about The Asgarda on to Carrie at NPR. He didn't tell her Nõn was dead; the questions that would lead to could possibly derail the plan he'd devised. Once that was done, he asked The Driver for a round trip ticket to Panama. He'd planned on going alone, but Bexx, ever watchful, put the nix on that immediately and made sure they'd go together.

Nick and Bexx took off from Spokane, then had a short layover in Denver. From there they traveled on to the George Bush International Airport in Houston. After a three-hour layover, they went on to Panama City, Panama. Nick's plan was to locate the woman who had been the interpreter between he and Nõn and the Woonaan people.

Nick explained to Bexx this was a very hostile area and there were no guarantees of what the outcome of this trip would be. The Darien Gap was one of the most remote and hostile areas in the world. He explained further The Wounann hadn't warmed to him in their last meeting. Bexx smiled at this comment and remarked, "Really? Imagine!"

When they arrived at Sambu Airfield, they began to make it known they were there to contact the Wounaan. Part of Nick's plan was sending out feelers, trying to locate the interpreter they'd spoken with during the incidents at Baroota. He was hoping the Wounaan had spies at the airfield and the word would be passed along; however, two days had passed, and no one had bit on the feelers Nick had put out. One day, however, a woman approached him as he sat outside the roughed out shack they'd rented at the airfield.

"You have sent word you wanted to speak with the Wounaan?"

"I have, yes!" Nick said excitedly.

"I am the woman you spoke with on your last trip. Where is the black woman, the woman with the spirit guide?"

Nick said, "She's dead."

Bexx heard Nick talking to the woman and came out of the shack to listen.

"And how did she die?"

"The Director, he killed her. I found another camp, and we attacked it. One of The Director's men shot her."

"And yet you live?"

"Yes."

"Why are you here?"

"I need a favor only the Wounaan people can provide. I had hoped that with our shared experience with The Director, the tribal elders would hear my request for help."

"Why would the tribal elders hear your pleas for help?"

"I don't have a reason to expect their help."

"No, you do not. They will not help you."

The woman turned and walked away. Nick was speechless. The Wounaan were critical for the plan to succeed. This couldn't be the end of it.

Bexx let the woman walk a distance away, then stepped out from the shed. "Stay here," she said to Nick and walked out towards the woman. When she was far enough away that Nick couldn't hear what she said, she called out to the woman to stop.

Bexx walked up to the woman and stood in front of her. At 6'3" and nearly 190 pounds, she was a formidable sight. The woman had never seen another woman of her height and size. Bexx began to speak, and the Wounaan's interpreter listened.

An hour later, they were still speaking. Finally, Bexx turned and came back.

"What happened?" Nick said.

"She will deliver our request to the tribal elders. That is all she would agree to do, and getting that concession wasn't easy."

"Now what?"

Bexx said, "I guess we wait and see what happens."

"What did you say to her?"

"I thought I would try a page from your book. Nõn had told me of her latest dream when we were on the plane from Ukraine. I told the Wounaan's interpreter about that dream and added that Nõn had also dreamt they would help you finish this. I guess I wasn't very convincing."

The next day was uneventful. No one came, and it appeared the trip was a bust. Nick said, "I don't know of another way to make this happen. Without their help, it gets more complicated, and traceable."

The next day, the small plane that had taken them to Sambu Field was scheduled to return and take them back to Panama City, Panama. From there they would head home, apparently empty-handed.

The Wounaan's interpreter had delivered the message to the tribal elders, and their decision was made: they would not help Nick with his request. It wouldn't be difficult to supply him with what he needed, but no one liked the idea of working with the outsiders again. The decision was final. In the shadows of the forest, another set of eyes watched as the elders, old and set in their ways, made the decision.

The day had come for Nick and Bexx to leave. The plane was sup-posed to arrive at 1300 hours local. They were packed and ready to go. The trip had been a bust. They had to find some other way to make the plan work. It was that simple. Nick was down and admitted he was depressed. The idea of this battle coming back full circle to Baroota just made sense to him. It was hard to accept that this wasn't the right path to bring The Direc-tor's reign to an end.

Nick waited, watching the forest around the airfield for any sign of the Wounaan. There was none. Finally, they loaded their single bag of luggage onto the small plane. Bexx got on first, then Nick carrying the box of Cash Crystal whiskey glasses they'd brought. The pilot wound up the motor's RPMs to take off speed and began to taxi. As the plane picked up speed, Nick looked out the window and thought back to the last time he'd been to Panama. It seemed like a lifetime ago. Bexx tapped him on the shoulder and pointed out her window. There in the grassy field surrounding the airstrip, a small boy was running, waving his arms. Nick looked out; it was a small boy, a Wounaan. Nick unbuckled his seat belt and looked again. No doubt it was a Wounaan. He went up front and told the pilot to turn around and land.

The boy was waiting for them when the plane landed. He ran to the plane, carrying a medium sized woven basket. The Wounaan were famous for the craftsmanship of their woven baskets. This one was about the size of a large dinner plate and had a tightly woven, well-fitting lid. Nick unlocked the door to the plane and dropped the small stairway. He climbed out, hop-ing the basket held what he'd asked for.

Nick walked to the boy and knelt down. Looking at the boy's eyes and face, he thought, *He can't be more than 12 or 13...why would the Wou-naan send him to complete the task?* It was a hard day and night travel on foot, through the jungle.

The boy hugged him and motioned back and forth from Nick to himself, over and over. It took Nick several moments to realize what he was saying. He was the same boy the Demon and Kerry had been preparing to torture back in Baroota. The ballsy little bastard had made the trip on his own. Nick picked him up and hugged him back. The boy opened the basket. Inside, Nick saw the yellow striped bodies of several Kokoe poison frogs, one of the most poisonous frogs on the planet, and native to Panama. Nick smiled and thanked the boy again and again. He walked back to the plane and grabbed the whiskey glasses. When he returned to the boy, he took one glass at a time and carefully rolled the lip of each glass against each of the frog's backs until all four glasses had a small amount of their poison sur-rounding the lip of the glass. He carefully put the glasses back into the box upside down. When Nick was done, he put the box back on the plane, then came back to the boy. "I wish you could understand what you've done for me," Nick said. "Thank you." Nick waved goodbye and walked back to the plane. The pilot began to taxi, and the boy watched until the plane took off and disappeared into the northern sky.

Bexx asked, "Who was that?"

Nick said, "The ballsy little man Nõn and I saved from her Demon and some other sick bastard the last time we were here."

The glasses cleared U.S. customs with very little inspection. They weren't remarkable, and not contraband. No one had any idea of the pow-erful steroidal alkaloid toxin surrounding the lip of each expensive crystal glass.

Once they arrived back in Moses Lake, Nick went back over the plan with Bexx, The Driver and Special K. Nick insisted the plan be as sim-ple as possible, with as few moving parts as required. They examined and reexamined every aspect of the plan until they were satisfied it was done, then Nick made the call to Arthur.

"Hello, Arthur. Have you checked to see if I kept my word concern-ing your wife now being at the top of the donor list?"

"Hello, yes, I did. You were right, she's there. Thank you for that."

"Are you still on board, still ready to play your part?"

"Yes. I am."

"You'll need to secure a visitor's pass for a young woman to enter the Department of Homeland Security Building, exactly two days from to-day. She'll arrive with a box of Cash Crystal whiskey glasses, wrapped as a gift. Of course, they'll be inspected by security and X-rayed. They'll pass through security, but keep in mind you must not touch the lip of any of the glasses. To do so would be instantly fatal."

"I understand."

"Good. Once you've obtained the glasses, you'll text me and we'll remotely activate the building's fire alarm. Everyone will be required to leave the building until it's declared all clear. Standard government regu-lations require it. When The Director has left the floor, you'll exchange his glasses with the new ones. Put the old glasses in the box and put it back in your desk. If all goes well, your wife will be scheduled for the bone marrow transplant by week's end. The guest will leave the building, and the rest is up to you."

"What do I do after he's gone? The Director, I mean. What do I do after he's dead?"

"You replace the new glasses with the old. Make sure you touch an old glass to his lips, leaving a mark. Nothing must look amiss. When all that's done, then you call for medical. Make sure he's dead before you call."

"Two days, Arthur. Two days, and you'll be free from The Director and your wife gets her bone marrow transplant. Any questions?"

"No, I have none."

"Excellent. Keep the phone charged and nearby in case things change. We have to be able to adapt at the last minute if needed."

"Understood."

CHAPTER THIRTY-FOUR

T hat night the Asgarda, Nick, Bexx and The Driver all sat around the fire. They talked over the plan as a group, Bexx asking each of them for their input and opinions of every aspect of the plan. One of the Powerpuff Girls spoke up and said, "So Nick, what was it that gave you the idea for this plan?"

Nick laughed and looked at Special K, smiling. "It doesn't matter, really."

But the team now all spoke, saying they wanted to know. Special K cringed and shook her head no.

Nick said, "One morning, I got up early to go to the gym. I went to the bathroom to brush my teeth, and someone was already up and in the bathroom. When that someone finished, she warned me to let the room air out before I went in. She apparently has discovered that she loves Chinese food, but it doesn't love her back. Anyway, I waited and then thought, *How bad can it be? I mean, she's a tiny little thing!* I was shocked after I went in. Keep in mind, I'd let it clear out for several minutes. I gagged and left the room, and I thought at the time if the house had fire alarms, I would have set them off. Then the idea came to me: poison, fire alarms and The Director. I knew where I could get a poison that would make it look like The Director had a heart attack. We just had to find a way into the building. The first plans were too elaborate and had way too many points of failure. As we went down this road, I refined it and cleaned up the plan until you see what we have now."

The girls were laughing at Nick's story about the bathroom. One of them said, "What's really funny is, all this time we thought it was you that was leaving the bathroom in that state. Now we know the real story! It was Special K!" They all laughed.

In the morning, Special K left for Washington, D.C. The original plan had them shipping the glasses, but they squashed that idea. If something happened during shipping and the glasses had been broken, there wouldn't be another chance to obtain the poison. The glasses had to be hand carried to the building. Special K arrived in D.C. with no issues. The flight went smoothly, and her room was booked in advance. Once she arrived in D.C., the plan required her to go in the morning to the Department of Homeland security and announce at the security desk she had an appointment with Arthur Look. After they'd made it back to his desk, she would then give him the glasses and return to the airport. Her return flight would leave that day; the rest was up to Arthur.

Special K sat in her room and channel surfed the television there, finding nothing on television to watch. She realized she was hungry and started thinking about ordering room service, when there was a knock at the door. She looked out the peep hole and saw a young man carrying two sacks of small white square containers. She opened the door.

"Hi, I have your takeout Chinese. One order of Moo goo Gaipan, and one order of pork chop suey with crunchy noodles."

She said, "I didn't order any food."

He replied, "It was ordered by phone, and this room number was given. The man who ordered was very specific that it was to be delivered here."

"What was the man's name?"

"Hold on, let me check the receipt. I'm sorry, am I wrong? This is the right room. I checked." He looked at the receipt, and the name on the bill was Nick. He said, "It was ordered by Nick, see" and he showed her the receipt. She smiled. "Oh yes, of course. Thank you."

The next day went according to plan. Everything went smoothly. The glasses went through security, and Special K made her flight with no problems. It was now up to Arthur.

Arthur had waited all morning for The Director to show up to work. Finally, he'd texted Nick and said, *The Director isn't here yet. I'm going to replace the glasses now instead of waiting for him to get here and then leave after you trigger the fire alarm.*

The reply came immediately. *Your call, Arthur, just don't get caught.*

Arthur thought it over, then called down to security and asked them to call when The Director signed in.

Arthur picked up the box of glasses and opened the double doors to The Director's office. He went to the bar and took a picture of the bar, as Nick had instructed. That way, he would have a reference to make sure everything went back in its original place. Arthur removed the original glasses, then replaced them with the toxic ones. He checked the picture to make sure everything was exactly the same. When he was sure everything was in place, he turned around, and there standing in the doorway was The Director, watching him.

"Arthur, what exactly are you doing?"

"Oh, good morning, sir. I was just cleaning up around the bar and making sure everything was ready for you when you arrived today. How are you feeling?"

The Director stood silently watching Arthur. "And the box? It looks like a gift."

"Oh yes, sir. I wanted to thank you, for all you've done for me. I bought another set of the glasses you had me order, but I made a mistake. I forgot about how you liked them to have the sharp edges, not the polished ones. I just realized that, so I put them back in the box. I was planning on returning them."

The Director replied, "I see," and walked into his office.

Arthur walked out of the office and closed the double doors.

The phone rang at Arthur's desk, and he picked it up. "Sir, this is security. I just realized after you called, Mr. Hauer is already in the building. I thought I'd let you know. Would you like me to page him?"

"No, that's fine. He's here now, thank you." Arthur closed his eyes and took a deep breath. That had been close.

The day went on, and nothing happened out of the ordinary. The Director called Arthur into the office several times, requesting files on this project or telling Arthur to set up an appointment with that person. Each time Arthur entered the office, he cast a glance at the crystal glasses. They hadn't moved. Arthur swore The Director knew something was wrong; he felt The Director's eyes on him every time he entered the room, watching his every move suspiciously.

Arthur was correct, The Director was watching him, but for another reason: at 3 o'clock, he cued Hector Berlioz: Symphonie Fantastique — Dream Of A Witches Sabbath.

Arthur heard the piece begin and sat straight up in his chair. He'd learned to hate Berlioz. He felt sick, as he knew it would be moments before the demand was made again for him to service The Director. Arthur wanted to scream.

"Arthur, would you come in here, please," The Director called out over the intercom.

Arthur cleared his throat and said, "Yes, sir. Right away."

Arthur opened the double doors, then turned to close them. His eyes clenched shut, he thought to himself, *Just one more day, and it'll be over. I just have to get through this day!*

He turned to walk to The Director's desk and begin the disgusting task. As he walked past the desk, he cast a glance at the bar. It couldn't be! A glass had been removed. The whiskey bottle had been opened, and the lid remained on the counter.

For Arthur, everything felt like it was in slow motion. He glanced at The Director and saw the crystal glass in his hand, held by the dried blood red colored cloth he preferred the most. Arthur wondered, *Has he already tasted the poison? Is it going to work? Or has Nick set me up?*

Arthur stopped and waited, watching The Director. There was no sign of anything happening. He hadn't drank from the cup yet.

The Director was staring out the window of his office, lost deep in thought. He was thinking about the description the spotter had given him of the team of women at Cachibaché. The man was avid they'd taken two of the team out with the first shot, one shot and two kills. He must have been mistaken. No one gets up after being shot in the head. The Director realized Arthur hadn't begun yet, and his attention snapped back to the room.

"Arthur? What are you doing?"

Arthur replied, "I was waiting, sir, for you to take a drink from the glass you hold. I hoped it would relax you so you might better enjoy this."

"Nonsense, Arthur. Get to it."

"Yes, sir." Arthur realized there was no way out of performing one last service for The Director, and he kneeled down and reached to unzip The Director's pants – but just as he did, The Director brought the glass to his lips and took a long, deep draw of the whiskey.

Arthur froze. He held his breath. If Nick had been right, the reaction would be immediate. The Director took the glass from his lips and started to speak

"Arthur, what is your problem today? Let's get on with –"

He dropped the glass. The toxin first affected the victim's peripheral nervous system, hands, feet, and then arms and legs.

Arthur spoke, "Oh, sir, you've dropped your glass. Let me get you another," as he carefully picked up the glass.

"Arthur, be careful. The crystal will cut you, and you will bleed all over my beautiful rug."

Arthur stood. "No, it won't, sir. You see, I've replaced your sharp glasses with glasses of my own. I will be quite all right, so will your beautiful rug."

The Director had broken into a sweat. He felt funny now and tried to get up, but his legs and arms wouldn't cooperate. He found he couldn't move as he watched Arthur return the glass to the bar.

"Arthur, what are you talking about? Replacing my glasses? Why?"

Arthur smiled. "Sir, I replaced them so I could put new ones in their place. The new ones have been treated with poison, which you're starting to feel the impact of now." Arthur returned to The Director's desk and took out the phone. He prepared to take the picture Nick had requested, then thought it over. He selected the video option instead.

Ten minutes later, 2592 miles away, Nick received a text from Arthur. He was supposed to check in with a picture of The Director's dead body when it was finished; instead, Arthur sent a video of the man dying.

Nick watched with grim satisfaction as The Director died a painful death from cardiac arrest, the inevitable result of the frog's toxin. It was done. Nick sat the phone down and closed his eyes for a moment. "Got you, you bastard!" he whispered with a smile on his face. "I got you!"

An hour had passed since the video had been sent. Arthur took the toxic glasses out of the room and replaced them with the originals. He made sure he held a glass to The Director's lips, checking to make sure they left a mark on the glass. When the office had been reset, Arthur left the office, closing the double doors. He sat at his desk for a moment and gathered himself, then finally called Nick.

"Hello, Nick, did you get the video I sent?"

"Yes, I did, Arthur. How are you doing, my friend?"

"I'm well. The best I've been in a long time. Will my wife now get her donor?"

"Of course. The release has already been made. You'll be notified as soon as they make a match. When will you call the security staff, Arthur?"

"I don't know. I know you wanted me to wait until he was dead, but I kind of like the idea of leaving him where he is for a while longer, perhaps letting the nighttime custodial staff find him. That would have horrified him, you know; he always felt they were beneath him and should never be in his office when he was present. It was a standing order of his: no cleaning staff allowed when he was present."

"Enjoy the moment, my friend. You've earned it. Just get rid of the glasses as quickly and cleanly as possible."

"Understood, Nick. Thank you for allowing me to be a part of this."

The call ended. Arthur was supposed to get rid of the glasses and phone immediately, but he waited.

Another week had passed. Buffy and The Driver were in The Bat Cave working on trying to hack the 2017 potential release of the classified investigation of JFK's assassination. If they could release it before the current president made his decision on the matter, it would be a tremendous embarrassment. The burner phone Nick had used on The Director mission was in the Bat Cave as well. It buzzed loudly.

Buffy picked up the phone and read the text, then showed it to The Driver. They looked at each other in silence for several minutes. "Bexx needs to see this," Buffy said. The Driver nodded, then they went to find her.

They found Bexx in the kitchen, sitting and talking to Nick. He was laughing and jovial. Since The Director's death, the change in him had been dramatic. A huge weight had been taken off his shoulders. They entered the room and waited quietly. Bexx could tell they had something to talk to her about, but they were waiting until she was alone. She nodded, quietly acknowledging them.

"Nick, would you give us a moment? I need to speak privately to The Driver."

"Sure, I'm going to the gym. I'll be back in a while. Enjoy!" Nick left the kitchen, patting The Driver on the shoulder as he walked past. "Why so serious?" he said with a gravelly voice. "Cheer up, man!" Nick grabbed his gym bag, heading out the door.

When they heard the 'Yota fire up and back out of the driveway, Bexx said, "What is it?"

The Driver brought up the text message and handed it to Bexx. She started to read:

Nick, I got rid of the phone and glasses like you said. I wrote down your number in case I needed it. My wife just had her bone marrow transplant. I just wanted to tell you thank you. We have hope for the first time in a long time. I had thought about not sending you this picture. I took it in The Director's office when I replaced the glasses. As you can see, the glasses are there, his favorite brand of whiskey, and to the left on a shelf there are 6 bottles of wine. Look closely at the bottles. You will see one named Baroota, one named Cachibaché, each camp had been named for a wine The Director liked to drink. Nick, there are 4 more bottles.

I'm still working in the office. The Director's replacement is moving into the office tomorrow and has asked me to stay on. Good luck to you. A.L.

Bexx looked at the picture of the wine bottles, then up at The Driver and Buffy. The room was silent for a long time as they exchanged glances, then finally she handed them the phone and said, "let's sit on this for a while. Keep it just between us."